IF ANYONE ASKS, TELL THEM "IT'S COMPLICATED"

BY COMPLICATED CHRISSY

Complicated ♥ Chrissy
LIFE IN PROGRESS

www.ComplicatedChrissy.com

Book design by Brittany Myers (Artwork provided by Canva)

For my mom...
I promise to always make you proud.

"Through my writings, I found appreciation in learning how to counterbalance my on-going battles with depression. *Complicated Chrissy*, as a platform and alter ego, provides an outlet for creativity, expression, and truths. Within a humanity full of contentment, of those aggressively and eagerly desiring conformation, I felt most majestic when I resisted."

-Brittany Myers,
Creator of Complicated Chrissy

I am not a hoe; I just happen to be intensely and immeasurably in love with a man that I've known for over 15 years, 7 months, 3 weeks, and 2 days....and by unfortunate circumstances, he happens to be married. 1 day. 1 day and 7 hours until I walk down the aisle to marry "the guy". Not the married guy, no, this is another guy. The guy who I am marrying is perfect. He accepted me despite my many flaws, my $137,562.84 worth of student loans, my lower than average credit score, and still manages to love me more than life itself, and here I am...stuck in a dilemma on whether he's the one for me. Now anyone with any ounce of common sense would consider this to be an easy fix. Undoubtedly, the married guy shouldn't even be an option, especially considering the circumstances at hand. Never in a million years could I have ever imagined that at 33 I'd be in this predicament.

Sitting alone, sipping from my Olivia Pope sized glass of Moscato, my glass table in the dining room is full monogrammed "H" wedding favors. And while I should be in complete bliss right now anticipating becoming Mrs. Harrigan within the upcoming hours, I find myself thinking about my other "him".

Now the other him, the married him, he's been around since the beginning of time, freshmen year of undergrad, 15 years ago to be exact. Oh, we really had some good times. I smile erratically just reminiscing about our memories. Back in those days, I would've done anything for him and he would've done the same, but somehow our "us" got lost in the transition of growing. I was the fun party girl, down for sporadic trips and impromptu events, him, not so much. He was more structured and focused, things needed to be planned and itineraries needed to be put in place. But I was the ying to his yang and as complete opposite as we were, we uncannily completed each other. I kept him on his toes and added that spice in his life that he wasn't used to, that's what made us "us". If, for some reason something occurred resulting in us being apart and loosing contact for some duration of time, something, some random event would always lead us back to one another and we'd pick back up right where we left off.

The emotions and love that we had for one another were like Teflon, they could never disintegrate. The sex.... oh chile...amazing!!! One could compare our relationship to that of a drug addict; it was just something about him that kept me weak. The craziest confession surrounding our entire situation was that we were never officially an item; we never had a relationship title of any sort. We'd date and fuck, date a little more, followed by more fucking. We'd take a trip here and there, had a few pregnancy scares, did some more fucking, randomly have jealousy spurs, and interacted with each other's families, but there were never any titles involved. It was understood, he was my boo. When you saw him, you knew that was me and vice versa.

This will be easier to comprehend if "my boo" had a name. We'll call him Kris. A few years back, the word on the street, or better yet via social media, was that Kris was getting married. At first, I wasn't necessarily hurt, but more so confused. After all the years we spent together, who was this bitch and where did she come from? I use the word "bitch" in the nicest, most respectable way possible. I'm sure she was a lovely woman but what did she have that I didn't? What the hell made her so damn special? I had a lot of questions and I didn't enjoy interrogating my own self. I was never really bothered by the fact that what we had wasn't your typical standardized defined and refined relationship; we were constantly around each other and engaged in activities that normal nuclear couples did. We would check in with each other all day long, have lunch together, email back and forth while at work and grocery shop together, I mean we carried on like this for years!!! What part of the game was this? I mean, I hadn't been completely faithful to him the entire time; there was this guy from back home, a guy from my African Diaspora class, the party promoter, oh and I can't forget about the one night stand while I was on spring break out in Cancun (which seemed to continue once I returned back home), but I didn't necessarily need to be. What was understood never had to be said. But this unexpected information that I stumbled upon online, threw me for a loop.

Matter of fact, he had just come to visit me when I first moved back home to Philly, prior to me finding out about his situation. I remember we drank until we both were way too intoxicated to drive. We grabbed a slice of pizza, caught a cab over to the art museum and proceeded to do some thangs by the water that I'm positive I could've received at least a citation for. Sexual acts that would make my mother's head pop off if she ever found out. We concluded the night by checking into a boutique hotel in downtown Old City, and progressively ended up having some of the best drunken sex that I would ever experience to this day. My pussy pulsates just thinking of the ways he ate the shit out of Miss Kitty that night. Almost an entire hour, with my head hanging off the bed; so long that in another 45 seconds, I was for sure going to pass out. Way too good to stop, I fought to keep coherent, focusing my sight on the brightly lit alarm clock, occasionally lifting my head to restore blood flow. That night, set the record for the most orgasms that I've ever achieved in one session. As I mentioned before, there were so many unforgettable moments, followed by an early-staged abortion (that he has no idea about and that I vowed to take to my grave) that bonded us. The fact of the matter is, we still had been in contact with each other, although it wasn't as frequent as it had once been, he never cared to mention this girl before, let alone an engagement. WTF? When I would boldly muster up the courage to confront him with my newly acquired information, he'd brushed it off, said it was nothing serious, that she was just some girl and he was just buying time. Nevertheless, I still had my life and he had his, we just had a little piece of "us" that remained intact.

After Kris's marriage secretly took place in a destination ceremony, our interactions became few and far between, only communicating on birthdays, homecomings and major holidays. I didn't like what happened but eventually and foolishly, I became content. Since learning of his marriage, I had been in 2 serious relationships, one being my current fiancé, Brandon, and the other being this jerk,

Reece, from my old neighborhood. Brandon was a pleasingly genuine good guy. Not like anyone that I would've normally been interested in or would've typically given the time of day to, but he had the most perfect chocolate skin tone with an amazing smile and greenish-brown eyes. A little bit too... ummm, for the lack of better words, "un-urban", than I particularly liked. I don't essentially like them "hood-hood", with their pants sagging off their behinds and I didn't like the boys that stood out on the block, but I did enjoy a man who could talk politics, let's say, at a company outing, but could still argue which battle rapper was better when the time was right. Brandon is the type of guy that your parents dreamed for you and prayed for you to be with. With an Ivy League education, he graduated third of his class in law school. He came from a good environment with his parents being married for 41 years, they were so sweet and gentle you would think they slept on clouds instead of mattresses at night.

I mean, don't get me wrong, I'm definitely something to write home about too. I may not have had everything that he had, but at 28 I had become the National Leader for Social Science Research at the USDA, easily raking in over 130k a year. But anyways, I met him at a Firm softball game, though my best friend Sabrina. Poor girl, I'm sure I stress her out more than her 3 children and the husband she goes home to every night. She is always pleading and insisting for me to find a nice guy and finally settle down. She believes I am falling behind in the family prepping curve and encourages, better yet, nags me to leave Kris alone for good. At my age, she thinks that I am in desperate need of more structure in my life. To be honest, I think she envies my freedom and bachelorette lifestyle. Like who really settles down at 24, gets married and has kids? She and the others around me that built long standing friendships with in college, ruined my 20's.

I envisioned myself with an early adult life of traveling, seeing the world, parties & hangovers, living la Vida loca! After she learned of Kris's marriage she felt that I continued to torture myself by allowing him to occupy space in my heart. She doesn't know the full extent of things between us, however she feels that even the slightest bit of conversation is too much. "It's disrespectful to his wife and to you" she claims, but she just doesn't understand, nor can she relate to the chemistry we share. Honestly speaking, no one really does. Shit, at this point I'm not sure if I even still know, but one thing is for sure, I can always depend on my other best friend Jasmine to justify all my wrongdoings.

Jas has always had my back, right, wrong or indifferent. A real go getter, she lets nothing stand in the way of her goals. She is my down bitch, ride or die. She keeps it 100 and lacks concern to whomever she may offend. She'll make you cry then stays around to help wipe away the tears and coddle you. Sabrina is more conservative; more reserved and thinks logically, she's the un-elected maternal figure in our trio. She mentally matured at an earlier age than Jas and me. While we were still planning our annual thot trips to Miami, Sabrina was becoming the youngest partner at one of the most prestigious law firms in Washington, DC. Sabrina and Jas are more than my best friends, they are my sisters; they're all I ever need. With Jas being the CEO of the largest Property Management Company nationwide and me completing my 5th year here at the USDA, we all had created one heck of a lifestyle for ourselves.

Growing up poor, I knew that I was destined to be better than the environment I was cultivated in. Although, today I do very much enjoy brushing shoulders with the elites, I seldomly appreciate a ratchet "turn up" every now and then at a neighborhood lounge in attempts to preserve my youth. Besides, popping a bottle here and there, making it rain in the strip clubs of Atlanta and Miami never hurt anyone, right? Which further goes to explain why initially Brandon wasn't really my type. But those eyes, my Lord...and did I mention that smile? It makes me melt like a popsicle on a 90-degree day.

Getting back on topic, Brandon and I at the softball game...I wasn't particularly interested in the game itself, it was just a gorgeous day and I didn't feel like going straight home. Having left work early, I needed to go home and pack for a business trip, but the warm weather often distracts me, that and my self-diagnosed Attention Deficit Disorder. Anyways, I go by Sabrina's office to harass her with my daily dose of drama caused by Reece and his bullshit. As my self-appointed therapist, she was the closest person to me geographically since Jas decided that she was relocating to LA about 6 months earlier. When I arrived at Sabrina's spacious corner office with the most amazing view of Chocolate City, she informs me that she too planned on leaving the office earlier than she normally did to attend her Firm's softball game. Their office team had advanced to the finals and she was going to go out to the field to show support for her colleagues. I wasn't really into sports and neither was she but who turns down free victory food and beer? Not I.

Pushing my responsibilities to the side, I decide to tag along. On the way there I continue to talk her head off about Reece. I had been dealing with him on and off, and again, I knew better. He hustled for a living but also had a job on paper; therefore, I would selectively pick and choose what I wanted or needed to know. He showered me with materialistic things; bags, sneakers, shoes, etc. No matter where he was going or what he was doing, he was always draped in designer labels and he made sure that I was too. Reese bought me things that he thought I deserved and I appreciated it. He also knew that I would and could return the courtesy when I decided to splurge on shopping sprees. He's one of those guys that your daddy hated and forbade you to date, but you do it anyways because you think that your parents are old, don't know anything, and don't understand. I knew right from wrong and had my heart broken by some lames before, but I was casually writing this off as fun. Although we had fun and took lots of trips, Reece was the one who stressed me out the most with unnecessary drama and bullshit. When things were good, they were good, but when things got bad it was like World War III, and things right now for us were bad. Girls calling my phone, lies upon more lies, STD's and irregular pap smears, it was always an excuse for everything and I was at my breaking point with him.

So, there I am, sitting in the grass on a fleece company blanket. I'm making small talk and cheering while sipping my libations. Mid-sentence of a conversation, I catch a glimpse of this guy constantly making eye contact with me. I've never been one to assume things, so naturally I didn't think he was checking for the kid, but I do know that my Indian Remy was laid to the Gods, so yeah, it was possible. By drink 2 of liquid courage, I had engaged in the exchange of flashing pearly whites and eye-fucking. As the game concluded, I started heading out; I had a long night ahead of me, so I responsibly decided not to stay and indulge in the after-game celebrations at the nearby bar after all.

Plus, Kris would eventually be at my condo soon and I didn't want to keep him waiting too long. Just as we'd done in the past, we'd meet up the night before every business trip I took. I would receive my dosage of what I'd like to call "Vitamin D" and he would give me spending money for my trips to treat myself to something nice while I was away suffering from withdraw of him, or at least that's what he thought. Now, don't get me wrong, I do truly believe in the sanctity of marriage and at no point had I had any intention or goal to becoming his side piece, but things just happened to turn out that way. I mean, as my friend Jas would tell me, "I technically had him first. I didn't take any vows, those were his commitments. I was single and doing what single people did, they have sex with whomever they want and don't feel the need to be judged." You have got to love her. It sounded good and I often repeated it to justify and rationalize every time I would let him slide his dick up inside of me. I'm really not a bad person though, I swear! And I've tried to cut this off a million times before but when we see each other the feelings become too strong to overpower and we both end up cumming, I mean succumbing. Instead of resisting our urges, now we just give in facing the consequences as they may come.

So, leaving the field, I purposely found a way to walk pass Brandon while he was in a huddle with his constituents. Softly I congratulated him, "good game number 5", I said with a sensual smile. Returning the gesture, he thanked me and that was that. Heading home I couldn't help but to think about him. In my mind I fascinated about what type of person he was, how he acted, and what he probably did for fun. I imagined how he dressed outside of his uniform and if he was the stuck up and snooty type, like most of the attorneys at Sabrina's Firm. I wondered what his version of fun looked like or if he even dated black girls. My mind wandered with silly adolescent thoughts.

Pulling up to my condo, I took notice to an unfamiliar and unattended SUV parked in one of my reserved spots. "I'm really getting sick of this shit", I thought to myself. "These rude ass neighbors of mine and their guests think they the run shit, huh? They're starting to take my kindness for granted." "Fuck them, I'm tired of being so nice all the damn time. If that car is still here by the time Kris comes, Imma have that bitch towed. My man aint gonna be parking in the visitors spot down the street, that's where the hell their asses need to be parked." Parking and fussing, I glanced at the time and realized that it was much later than I thought. Where the hell was Kris at anyway? I didn't see his car in any of the guest parking spaces, did he get caught up doing something or is he running late, why isn't he here yet? That's really unlike him. I scrambled through my Marc Jacobs bag to find my phone to check and see if I had any missed texts, calls or voicemails from him.

Nope. I had nothing from him, but what I did have was a text from a random number reading, "Has anyone ever told you how attractive you are? What does a man need to do to request you as their personal cheerleader?" followed by a smiley face. My mind perceptually flashed back to the man I had been flirting with back at the field, but it couldn't be him, I hadn't had the opportunity to give him my number yet. Distracted, yet intrigued, before deciding to get out of my car, I called Sabrina. Starting the conversation off complaining about my asshole neighbors and them parking in my space, I mentioned the mysterious text message that I received from a random Virginia number. "Wow that was fast" she replied. "People don't waste any time nowadays." Still confused but I now have a better inclination of what was going on. She continues "after you left, as normal, the team went out to celebrate and I decided to go since my husband had already agreed to pick up the kids. While out, one of my colleagues went out of his way to converse with me. Mind you, I thought it was extremely awkward because he only says hi & bye when I see him around the office. After making small talk for a few minutes, he starts asking about you, which makes things more understandable." Feeling like a teenage girl, I begin smiling from ear to ear. "He's asking how I know you, if we're related, things of that nature. He goes on to talk about how cute you are blah, blah, blah. In my head, I'm thinking you are so not her type, but then I thought to myself that I would desperately do anything to get from wasting anymore time dealing with Reese, so when he asked me to relay the message, that he was feeling you, I jumped at the opportunity and offered him your number. I hoped to have had a chance to tell you before he reached out to you, damn." At that moment, I was totally geeking. Forgetting about the fact that Kris still wasn't here, I mentally visualized how the conversation between Brandon and Sabrina went. "By the way, his name is Brandon. He's 31 from Silver Spring, Maryland. No kids, no girlfriend, no baby momma drama. He works at the Firm as an Attorney and does some volunteering in his spare time for numerous organizations. So what do you think?" I kept it calm; I didn't want to seem too excited. "I'll see."

Putting back my pocketbook contents that I pulled out of my bag when I was searching for my phone, I headed to the door of my residence as she continues to vouch for Brandon's character. "I asked around and from what I've been told, he seems like a good guy, maybe you should just step out of your box and try something new. He's not hard on the eyes either, he's actually really cute. He's a little young, but he's legal." She keeps going on and on about how I sell myself short by continuing to deal with these losers, and so on and so forth.

As I approach my door and turn the key, I notice that the door has already been unlocked. "Sabrina, I'll call you back" as I press the end call button. Opening the door, Kris is standing by the window overlooking my car. "What took you so long to get out of the car? Were you talking to your little boyfriend or something?" he asks as I laughed it off. "No, I was talking to Sabrina." Leaning in for a kiss, I ask about his car. "Well, where did you park? Is that your new car parked out there in my spot? If not, I was about to call and get it towed." Not being totally observant of my surroundings, he leans in and pulls me extremely close shadowed by a tight hug. Out of the corner of my eye, I catch a glimpse of a large bottle of Moet accompanied by 2 champagne glasses on the counter. "What's going on?" I asked. "We're celebrating! We closed a major deal today at the office; I wanted to come celebrate with you. What took you so long to get home?" Evading an answer, I inquired more details of the business deal. "This company has been interested in merging with us for a while now, this time offering a deal that I absolutely could not refuse. Not wanting to seem too anxious, I told them that this was something that I would need to sleep on and get back to them. But babe! I am so happy right now. Things are really looking up for me. We're about to be good." He was ecstatic, and I was elated for him. It's nothing like the feeling you get from watching the people whom you deeply love and care about, succeed in this crazy game of life. Working long thankless hours, busting his ass, going above and beyond, taking major bullshit from clients and colleagues, it all finally payed off. Besides that, when he's happy, he tends to make me happy, so it's basically a win-win situation.

In the back of my mind, realistically speaking and harsh to acknowledge, I know that his wife is the ultimate winner in all of this, but he almost never neglects me. I mean, for one, he does pay my mortgage each month along with my costly association fees. Secondly, he handles my most expensive college loan payment and my parking garage fee for work so that I am not forced to take that God-awful metro. In addition to everything, the random shopping binges and generous allowance became the icing on the cake. It's not that I don't make enough money to do for myself, it's just that he's always been the provider type. Even back when we were in college, he'd always made sure that I was taken care of, even offering me a bi-weekly allowance when he would get paid. Most people's college experiences are stories of them struggling to survive, meals of peanut butter and jelly or Ramen noodles, ordering from the dollar menu at McDonalds, calling home begging for money, and get rich quick pyramid schemes. At that time, he was the only person I knew as a full-time student, banking over 50 grand a year. Books, groceries, and often, even rent, he had me covered without me even asking. It was definitely a blessing then just as it serves to be now.

Don't get me wrong, I've never been a gold digger or interested in seeking out someone who I could profit from or live off, and no, my parents have never made me feel like money was ever an immense issue. Actually, I grew up watching my mother work 2 and sometimes 3 jobs to ensure that my siblings and I always had what we needed. I wore hand-me-downs from both of my sisters until at least the 10th grade. I was raised to be strong and free, able to survive independently in the event that I would need to. Learning that nothing in life comes easy, I started my first job at 15 in a sneaker store, and I've been working ever since, learning the culture of appreciating the ethics and values of hard work. I've worked damn hard for everything that I got thus far and I am determined to make my momma proud. Having Kris around has been a pleasure and his generosity has objectively been an added benefit, especially since it freed up a lot of my money to do other things for my family.

"Congratulations!!! That's incredibly awesome babe, I am so proud of you. I don't know of anyone else who deserves this more than you do." Grinning and pulling him in closer to me, I placed my arms around his neck, and softly caressed the waves in his jet-black hair. Giving him a celebratory kiss, followed by another, then another, we were interrupted by the notification of a text message from my phone. I drop my arms in an attempt to retrieve it when he interrupts. "What are you doing? This is my time." He says as he grabs me by the waist, eliminating the idea of gaining too much distance in between our bodies. His demand almost immediately sent a chill running up my back. Pulsating vibrations traveled through my vaginal region, giving my arms and legs uncontrollable goosebumps. After all these years, my body still reacts as if he's touching me for the very first time. I smile overwhelmingly. I sometimes secretly like it when he mandates my attention; it does something to me that I can't explain. Gazing into his beautiful brown eyes he sits on the couch in front of me, still holding my hands, while he begins to thank me. His knee stance resembles the beginning to an engagement proposal, except I know that it isn't at all feasible. He thanks me for my abundance of patience that came along with dealing with him throughout this entire process and he goes into detail of how he could never have done this without me. It was because of me that all of this had been possible. My constant encouragement, my networking talents, resources and connections, it was me that made this dream come true for him.

I don't hesitate in assisting when I can. Over the years, I've made a lot of strong connections and established plenty of professional relationships. I've come to know a lot of people and people owe me a lot of favors, so I don't mind utilizing my assets. Like I stated before, I want all of my friends to be in successful positions within their careers. We work hard so we can play hard. Plus, it's nothing for me to support him after he has been my saving grace for so long.

In the midst of his thank you speech, my mind drifts off and I somehow lose focus. I began thinking of all I need to do in preparation of tomorrow's departure. I still needed to pack, call to check-in on my mom and make sure she had enough food and that her medication was refilled before I left. Even though I have siblings, out of her 5 children, no one seems to be capable of doing a damn thing that benefits anyone other than themselves. I needed to check the weather and prepare the documents that I needed for my flight. Lastly, I needed to locate my passport, where the hell did I last put that? My mind ran about 100 miles per hour, regaining consciousness when I heard him mention that he was filing for divorce. Divorce? Wait what did I miss? I soon realized that I had missed the entire gist of his conversation while I was daydreaming. It caught me off guard because this was the first time that I ever heard him mention it.

Kris had only been married for 4 years. Although, I often envisioned that we could've been married instead, I've never once expected him to leave her. Over the years, I had come to terms with the unfortunate situation and was content with how things were between us. In my experiences from stories I had heard, married men almost never leave their wives and if they did, they were never in a rush to remarry again and I knew that I eventually wanted to be married. Early on, I identified the dynamics of this mess that I had gotten myself into, but I never desired to be the foundation of anyone's failing relationship. I had succeeded in shying away from guys that had cohabiting situations and drawn-out baby-momma stories. I understood karma was real. I once had my heart broken before and I would never wish that pain on any other woman, let alone be the cause of it. People may view me as being cold and heartless to be consistently engaged in having a relationship and sexual interactions with a married man; however, I do have a heart, somewhere. If they were to divorce because of irreconcilable differences, that's beyond my control. I just don't want to be the source of the shit. But then again, maybe it would be nice to have him all to myself again, then I could finally leave Reece's ass alone for good. A vast array of emotions clutters my heart, I'm not sure what to say or do. Should I pretend to be sad, do I speak words of positivity and encourage him into working things out with her as I did in the past when they got into minor altercations or do I reassure and incite his thoughts?

"Yes, a divorce. Things just aren't the same; she doesn't make me happy. It's like the spark in our relationship is gone, her main concern has always been her career but it's much more evident now. I mean, take today for example. When I called her to tell her about the good news; she acted as if she was too busy to talk. Her job isn't really that demanding. Every night I sit home and listen to all her bullshit ass stories about the stupid hoes at her job and about her dumb ass friends and their fucked up relationships, but yet and still, she's too senseless to realize that our relationship is fucked up. She hasn't given me no ass lately, no head, no nothing! Actually, she can keep that raggedy-ass head to herself, don't nobody want that whack shit. Most nights we don't even sleep together, like not even in the same bed. I'll fall asleep on the couch and she won't even wake me up, she leaves my black ass lying right there like I'm her fucking roommate or some shit. Like what the fuck? She gets home from work every day before me and still manages to have the nerve to ask me what's for dinner. Bitch dinner should be fixed already! I should be asking her that shit. I was so pissed off earlier; after hanging up with her, I figured that I'd make my way down to see you. I realized that I was a little early, so I stopped pass the car dealership to waste a little time. I ended up picking you up a little something. On some real shit, you're the one who deserves it. You're the one that's there for me when it should be her. I spoil her all the time with shit, she doesn't appreciate any of it. She lives bill free, so she doesn't have any worries. She's got thousand-dollar bags and shoes just thrown and left all around the house. All she wants to do is brag to her friends, she doesn't really appreciate shit. It's all for show and social media. Man, fuck her."

The mood in the room unexpectedly changed. The loving and jovial atmosphere that was once filled with excitement less than 15 minutes ago, was now gone. I was at a loss for words, but also intrigued at what he was communicating to me. His concerns reiterated that he really was a piece of shit, but his words stung because I knew that I was one too. The difference is I owned my shit. I knew that my shit was fucked up. How couldn't he see his role of wrongdoings and shortcomings in their relationship? How did he feel like she was the only one to blame? The bitter truth in all of this was whatever he was doing for her, he was doing for me. For some reckless reason, at this very moment, that didn't sit well with me. I didn't feel bad for him during his time of venting; I was now more excited with the idea that I got a gift. That is what he said, right?

During his emotional expression session? Lord knows, I'm not trying to make it all about me, but now I was eager in wanting to know what my special gift was. I looked down at him, still sitting on my imported white Italian leather sofa; I grabbed his chin and gently lifted his head up towards me. I felt like I needed to say something, I just didn't know what. "Babe, look at me, calm down" I said to lighten the atmosphere and put us both in a better mood. "Let's not do this now. We've got some celebrating to do. Let's pop this bottle open and let's toast. Let's toast to the business deal of a lifetime, to success, and to your undeniable dedication which led to incredible rewards. Let's toast to the better days ahead." He stood up and smiled. "You know what? You're right, that's why I love you and that's exactly why I'm leaving her". Geez, this is way too much to handle at one time. My buzz from the beers I had earlier at the game is definitely gone now and I can't seem to get my head straight. Shit, I need a drink now, even if he doesn't. I'm tempted to take this bottle straight to the head, freshman year, club style. But being subtle and modest I reply, "Whoa buddy, take it easy boyfriend. Let's not get carried away, let's take it one day at a time."

Walking away from him to go get the champagne, I felt myself trying to keep a straight face, my facial expressions always gave away my true feelings, and at this point, I was slightly irritated. I didn't know what to say or what else to do. The one thing that I knew for sure was that I was starving, and I wasn't even about to ask him what was for dinner in fear that it would trigger a memory from his wife and I'd have to listen to more of his rants. Normally I'd suggest going out to celebrate but I had a rack load of shit that needed to be done before I left for this business trip. I assumed that tonight would be our normal encounter filled with evening passion and financial compensation, not his marital woes. As he turned on the TV, it solidified the idea that we weren't going anywhere; I better throw something together if I had any intentions on catering to the gremlin in my growling stomach.

"So, are you not even going to ask what I got you from the dealership? Aint this some shit? These hoes nowadays are so unappreciative." He says under his breath. "Excuse me?" I asked with a serious face, I was technically not in the mood for his jokes. His wife may go for that shit, but I'm not. "I was waiting for you to elaborate on it. You sounded like you were going through a little something a few minutes ago, I thought you were about to cry so I just let you vent homeboy." As I walked over to where he was standing, I snuggle up to him, "so what is it? Huh? Huh?" I ask in my most innocent childlike voice. "You already saw it outside anyways, that's yours." he responded. "You mean that car that I was about to get towed?" totally forgetting the fact that I was supposed to be calling property management to get the unidentified car removed from my spot. "The Land Rover", I said with a repulsed facial expression. "That's what you got me? Do I look like a land rover type of girl? After all I've done for you, that's all you think I'm worth?" A look of disgust shot from the corner of his eye. "I love it! I love it!" I scream running to the window eagerly trying to catch another glimpse of it. Trying hard to maintain his composure and not show any emotion, I created a small scene. Jumping up and down mimicking the actions of a small child, I leap into his arms, placing small pecks of kisses all over his face, forcing him to engage in my excitement. "Now you can finally give up that old ass Lexus you got" he says sarcastically. First things first, my car is not old, it's paid for, that's what it is. I don't feel like I need to go out every 3 to 4 years and cop a new vehicle.

What do I need to prove to anyone? I mean, honestly who am I out here trying to impress? I'm content with what I have. It's not busted and raggedy, it has a few interior blemishes from Sabrina's bad ass kids, but they're my god babies so it's ok. I take good care of it, get her washed every 2 weeks, detailed once every 2 months, oil changes, tune ups, you know, the works. "By the way, who's paying for this gift?" I asked with one eyebrow raised, using my fingers as quotation marks. See cuz what I don't have time for is a $900/$1100 dollar liability.

I got plans; I'm trying out this debt diet thing that Dave Ramsey always talks about. I'm trying to save some money and eventually treat myself to something really special. "Really? No, like really Brooke? You just want to add to my stress today huh? You tryna be funny or something because you're going to piss me off? Do I ever make you pay?" He was serious, but so was I. "I should make you pay, but do I? What the hell do you spend your money on anyways? I pay for basically everything in this bitch." With one eyebrow raised, "Who the hell are you talking to?" I responded. "I never asked you to pay for anything! Take your gifts back, take your car. What you won't do is give me stuff and do nice gestures, just to throw it back up in my face later. I'm good". I said it and I meant it. I read a post once that said, "Never eat with people, who brag about feeding you" and I felt that shit. "See why you gotta do this? I came over here to come see your face because I've been missing you. I wanted to share my news with you and I came bearing gifts, brought you something special as a token of my appreciation. I wanted to hug you, kiss on you, and do some other things to you" he said with a devilish smirk. "Didn't you miss me?" Of course I missed him; actually, we could've done without all these extra bells and whistles and cut straight to the fucking part. I was going through withdraw and with all this liquor in my system, I'm in the mood. "I, more than usual, have missed the hell out of you sir" I said in a seductive tone "come here". As he comes closer to me, I can feel my body starting to get warm. I bite my bottom lip as I anticipate his body soon touching mine. His soft hands make contact with my skin that peaks through from my elevated shirt, and just like that, the flood gates open.

I can feel the secretion slowly moistening the inner canal of my pussy lips. She's ready, he's ready, and so am I. As I start to place my gentle kisses upon his lips, taking my time, I want to make sure that I have his total undivided attention. Using my tongue, I outline the shape of his lips, giving him a teaser of what I have in store for his dick momentarily. The unintentional gentle moan that escapes his mouth lets me know that he's aroused. His erect penis creates a bulge underneath the front of his navy-blue trousers. With my nipples now standing at attention, they make their presence known through my white buttoned-down shirt. Hearing his second moan of excitement intensifies my emotional situation. It feels good watching him starting to relax and enjoy himself. Slowly my lips make their way over to this left ear lobe. Leading my hands down in the direction of his private areas and stroking the imprint of his larger than average dick, I single handedly undo the clasp of his belt buckle, gradually unbuttoning the single inner button and unzipping his pants. I gently began to caress the tip of my tongue around the structure of his ear. Very softly and seductively, I whisper the things I'd plan to do to and for him as an expression of my gratitude. "Babe, do you know how proud I am of you? You know I love it when you take charge, but this time, I plan on taking control. What I need is for you to sit back and enjoy the ride, and when I mean ride, I definitely mean the ride that I'm about give this dick."

Dropping to my knees and bringing his boxer briefs and pants down to his ankles, I direct his body into having a seat. I was ready to unleash this inner prostitute-like alter ego that only Kris could gain access to. He was more introverted when it came to sex and I fed off his innocence. Kris and I have had some of the best sexual experiences but he damn sure wasn't the best partner that I'd encountered. Hands down, if I had to rate it, I'd have to give it to Reece. When I met him, he taught me things about myself that I hadn't yet discovered. He taught me how to incorporate toys, fuck on camera, talk dirty in the bedroom, and not to mention have memorable sex in public places. And not to brag, he made me a proud VIP member of the mile-high club. Nervous, shy, and timid at first, he was very patient with me. Reece brought out the side of me that I never knew existed. What he taught me, I would, in turn, use it to blow Kris' mind. Honestly, even though Kris would never admit it, I think the fact that our sexual encounters were so unpredictable is probably what kept him around for so long.

I've always been somewhat of a mystery to him, never being able to figure out my next move, his curiosity kept him intrigued. I was the epitome of the commonly used phrase, "a lady in the streets, but a freak in the sheets." My good girl image would never depict any classlessness and I would never casually flaunt my sexual talents for just anyone. I could trust him though. He never ran his mouth or was sloppy with our business. Hell, we were 15 years in and neither of our friends knew what we had been carrying on thus far. As far as anyone was concerned, he was just an old college friend that I sparingly kept in contact with.

"And you know what I like and how I like it. I want you to grab all this when I sit this wet pussy on that dick. When I speed it up, grab harder. I've been waiting for this all day, I'm gonna show you just how much I've missed and appreciate you." Spreading his knees apart, he starts to unbutton my already half open shirt. Guiding his hands to each of the sofa's cushions. "I got this, just relax." Undoing the remaining buttons of my work shirt, now exposing my favorite black laced bra. As I carefully slid each of my arms from the crisp sleeves, I tossed the shirt to the floor. With my face to his penis, I lick my lips further enticing him. I began sensually kissing on his chest, making sure that I paid great attention to each one of his nipples as I made a saliva guided path heading down toward his abdomen. I can sense his eager tension for wanting to participate as his dick jumped with every swipe of my tongue across the head of it. I want to tease him a little more, I wanted him to practically beg me for it. Plead for me to let him put all 8 inches of hard milk-chocolate dick in this slippery situation that was occurring in my panties. I want him to be so excited with pleasure so that the very moment that I give in, allowing him inside of me, the warmth of my body's secretions and the friction from the head slowly maneuvering and scaling my walls, makes him cum almost immediately and uncontrollably.

Look ma, no hands! I visualize his dick to be my favorite frozen fudge bar snack. I treat it is as if it's melting and I'm working hard to prevent the sweet dessert from dripping. As my mouth salivates, I force the accrual of more spit in my mouth. My journey starts at the shaft, bobbing my head with slow upward strokes, bringing my mouth to the tip. Outlining the circumference of the penis head, while receiving a small dosage of sweet tasting precum that somehow has managed to escape, he is undeniably aroused. Slurping his dick like one of those tricolored popsicles while watching his eyes lose the fight of trying to remain focused, passionately stimulates my body, creating a sensation which causes me to utter various moans as my body excretes even more lubrication onto my very sexy thongs.

Without breaking focus or causing interruption, I single-handedly unhooked the metal clasp of my form fitting charcoal grey work pants and slowly disengage the zipper. Almost activating the reaction of my gag reflex by going in for another mouthful, I nearly manage to maneuver my pants off when I hear a customized vibrating tone of a cell phone coming from his pants. Don't judge me, but I find it somewhat exciting and enticing in stimulating him while he is trying to focus while taking a call. Trying to manage to keep his composure and carry on a conversation deviously turns me on. I look up to see if he is interested in reaching for his phone, he doesn't budge and neither do I. Reaching for his hands, I slowly guide him into placing them on my head for the purposes of heightening the mood and elevating the experience. We both find great pleasure in him running his fingers through my hair, gripping it tightly and directing my head where he ultimately wants it to go. Once again, his phone goes off, followed by the indication that a voice mail has now been received. Repeatedly now, the phone consistently rings. I can tell by his reaction that he has an idea who might be calling and now is debating on whether he should answer it. Releasing his grasps, he allows my hair to fall onto my face as he tries to reach down to the floor for his pants. Breaking my concentration, I assist him with the retrieving of his property. Viewing the contents of the phone, I'm left to assume that he is viewing a compiled list of the approximately 14 missed calls and several combined text messages and voicemails. Using this time to give my jaw a break and fully remove my pants, I wipe my saliva messed face and glimpse over at him in hopes of measuring his reaction to what he was reading. His stare is blank. Still navigating and manipulating thru his phone, a woman's voice comes through the speaker. "Yo, where are you? Call..." he quickly shuts off the recorded message. "Is everything ok?" I ask.

Without speaking a word and without removing his eyes from the screen, he sucks his teeth and lets out a sigh of frustration. "Shall I take that as a no?" I question again. "She's blowing my phone up" I assume that he is referring to his wife, as the vibrating phone continues to ring in his hand. He turns the phone around towards me exposing the background picture of them blissfully kissing while dressed in their wedding attire, with the title "wife" scrolling across the top of the phone. "She's looking for me. I got a text from Drew saying that she gathered some of my friends and family at the house as a surprise to commemorate my business deal. He's asking me where I am. He said that she's pretty pissed off. I got missed calls from my mom and sister too. What the fuck man?!" he yelled. Grabbing the throw blanket from the back of the couch, I cover my now fully naked body as I walk towards the bedroom. Pretending to be concerned and empathetic, I suggest for him to answer and at least provide her with the peace of mind that he was at least alive. "Say that you went somewhere, make up something, I'll turn off the tv. I'll be quiet." He looks as if he is having some inner struggles as he decides what the best course of action is. "See, and you thought that she didn't care talking all that divorce shit." I added as I let out a small giggle. Frustrated and ready for him to go, "it's ok if you need to leave, I get it. You probably should head home before she really gets upset, packs your shit and turns the table by asking you for a divorce." He sits there in silence just staring into the corner of the room. "She won't leave me. There's too much involved. She couldn't survive without me" he says cockily as he reaches for his clothing. It was then, at that moment, I realized that the statements made earlier surrounding me being the one that has always been there for him and him finally realizing it, and not to mention, his thoughts of possibly leaving, was just him talking out of his ass. I knew better, I'm not even sure why I mentally entertained those thoughts either. He wasn't going anywhere, they never do.

Loudly speaking from my bedroom and overcome by my defensive attitude "Well whatever you decide to do is up to you. I can't be playing with you all night anyway; I still got work to do and still gotta pack." I can hear the wresting around of him getting dressed. He makes a phone call to let whoever know that he's on his way and will be there shortly. As I look at myself in the dresser mirror, I roll my eyes and shake my head in irritation. I'm in my feelings yet again and he knows it. Normally, he attentively caters to me when I start having a bitch fit, but he's trying to get out fast. Within the last couple years all the materialistic items that he tries to compensate with, means nothing. The bags, shoes, and cars appear worthless when I'm home consoling my own feelings. It's unfortunate that I repetitively put myself through this. I will face yet another night consisting of disappointed emotions, trying to convince myself that I don't care while reminding myself that this is the life in which I created and continue to settle for. I generate excuses for my own self as to why I've become so comfortable with my position in his life, but deep inside it still hurts.

Originally, that's how Reece entered the picture. When Kris would leave me and go home to his wife, I'd call Reece up. He didn't need much notice. He liked the fact that that he could tell his friends that he was fucking with a boss bitch. I'd go scoop him up off the block late in the evenings and he'd come chill with me providing affection and most of all GD...good dick. He was fond of my condo and its picturesque views of DC, plus every now and then I'd let him leave some of his shit, so he felt like he was doing a little something. I even let him hold my key every now and then, you know, keep him interested, to make him feel important. As of lately, it seems like every 3 weeks or so, I find myself asking the same questions and feeling the same way. But how much longer am I really going to put myself through this? One would think that after all this time, I might be used to it but I'm not and this doesn't get any easier.

Fully dressed in my pink satin pajama short set, and without saying a word, I grab my work computer and walk from the bedroom to the kitchen, gently tossing my laptop onto the couch next to him. Out of my peripheral vision I can feel him staring at me. I already know what he's preparing to say, but at this point it doesn't matter. He just continues to stare as if he's at a loss for words or trying to find something to say will let me down easy. Purposely avoiding eye contact, I pour a generous amount of champagne into my glass. Taking a sip, I return to the couch grabbing the remote and changing the channel to CNN. No, I'm not one of those news people but ever since the whole protests coverage in Ferguson, Missouri and the many other civil rights issues that have been broadcasted, CNN has been my go to channel. It helps me keep abreast of what's going on in the nation and helps me better understand white people's perspective regarding certain situations. "Alright, well, I guess I'll talk to you later. Have fun." I say sarcastically, still avoiding eye contact with him. I am so ready for him to go. Like just leave already, it's no point of us engaging in this conversation for the 1,000th time. All we're doing is wasting more time. As long as he remembers to leave my new car keys, I'll temporarily be ok.

As predicted, he makes his way towards me. I pretend not to notice as I find a reason to walk away in the opposite direction of him. He stops walking and stands in place. Shutting down is a normal behavior of mine especially when I'm highly irritated. Call it spoiled, call it whatever you want. It works for me and it eliminates me saying something out of anger that I may regret later. To avoid giving him eye contact and exposing my emotions (which are probably written all over my face already), I grabbed my glass and had a seat on the sofa. Opening my laptop and preparing to begin my work, he approaches me from behind, gently placing his arms around me and softly speaking in my ear. "I don't want to go. I'm right where I want and feel like I need to be. Don't worry babe, I promise you it won't be like this forever. I love you so much. It's just that I..." I stop him mid-sentence, focusing on the computer screen, "Its ok, I said I understand. Go ahead, you're already late, everyone is waiting on you." "I love you B, like really really love you. I honestly don't think that you know how much I deeply care for and about you. You are so smart. I don't know what I would do without you. You are always so understanding, and you get me. Not a lot of people do, she doesn't even get me all the time. You're there when I need you, always without any hesitation. You deserve it all. I can't wait to share the rest of my life with you and have that little baby girl that we've talked about for years." He leans over and kisses the top of my head. In my mind, I'm just thinking how pathetic and outlandish these departure statements have become as of lately. Share the rest of my life with you? Kids? Come on buddy, who are you fooling? Those lines may have worked years ago, I'm not buying it now.

I'm 33 vastly approaching 34, I know bull shit when I hear it. Plus, him reminding me of all the wonderful things that I do for him, is a constant reminder of how senseless I am to keep investing the majority of my time and energy into him for so many years. "I put a little extra in your allowance this month for your trip'" as he points to the money he left on the coffee table. Grabbing the SUV keys, "And I know how you like your windows tinted so I'll have this all finished for you by the time you get back. 20% tint, right? Or do you just want to keep it and I can give you the money to get it done yourself?" "No, you can do it, its fine. It would just be sitting here anyway until I got back, and how the hell would you get back home? I'm really not in the mood to make that trip right now" I replied. "Ok bet, no doubt. I got you babe. Give me a kiss so I can go and pretend to be happy for this lame get-together". In my mind, I wanted to say how I really felt but I knew the trouble and aggravation that it would cause, not mention the conversation that would have ultimately followed, so I digressed. I just tilted my head upwards and poked out my lips. We exchanged a sultry kiss followed by a quick peck. "I'll miss u", he says, "I'll miss you too. I'll call you when I get to my destination" I replied. In less than 30 seconds he was out of the door.

There I was, sitting alone, legs folded Indian style, laptop on my thighs and television on. I no longer had the attention to focus on anything work related and I was uninterested in whatever was being shown on tv. After about 5 mins of replaying the past hour over in my head, I reached for my phone to see what was going on in the wonderful world of social media. I needed me a pick me up, something to lift my spirits. I thought about calling Reece over to slide through quick and finish up what I had started with Kris, but I really didn't feel like being bothered with him either. I felt like I needed to be alone, but I didn't want to be. I hated the fact that Kris's actions always had the power to alter my mood. Nobody ever quite got up under my skin the way that he could. As I unlocked my phone, my message application was still opened showing a response message from Brandon that I must have overlooked. Rereading this message thread made me smirk. Although I wasn't in the best of moods, I felt like I should respond, but what would I say? Was it too late to write something back?

Typing a few words and deleting them, followed by a few more, just to delete those too, I've never been good at this type of stuff. Easily distracted, I will do almost anything other than doing what I'm supposed to be doing. After 7 whole minutes of trying to figure out what to say, I simply responded "Hey", that was the best thing that I could come up with. If he were to respond, then of course, my thinking process would need to be activated all over again on what or what not to say, but then again, I wasn't sure if 10:18pm was an inappropriate time to text. I stared at the phone trying to see if my iPhone would indicate whether the text was delivered and read. I waited for the typing bubble to appear, but it didn't. He was probably sleep or home with his wife and kids, on a date with some lovely lady who texted back faster than I did, or somewhere in Dupont Circle taking body shots with a trio of young horny snowflakes still actively celebrating their winning victory of today's game. See, how my mind wanders? After waiting a few minutes, I made an executive decision to just go to bed, I was mentally drained. Making an agenda to wake up early and accomplish my tasks seemed to be the best alternative. Although this strategy has never worked in the past, this time would be different, I didn't have that much to do. Lying down, I could feel myself overthinking and jumping to conclusions, switching back and forth between Brandon and Kris, I hated when I let myself do that. With my stomach making obscenely odd noises from the lack of food that I had given it, I turned off the television and peeled myself from the couch. I never leave for a trip with my house in a disarray, you know just in case anything happened while I was away; I couldn't have people coming into my living quarters judging me. I gulped down the remaining champagne that was in my glass and the sip that was left from Kris' glass, washed them out, and went to go lay down. I knew that I wouldn't be hearing from Kris for the rest of the night so I took my talents to sleep.

Hitting the alarm clock more times than I was supposed to, I woke up with a splitting headache and the shits. I've never really been a hard drinker and I'm assuming that the

Moet from last night didn't really agree with me. This was not one of those mornings where I had extra time to deal with these issues. I had already procrastinated from the night before. It was 7:43am and I needed to put some pep in my step to avoid missing my 10:15 flight. From the porcelain throne, I checked my phone. I have a guilty confession, I am so one of those people that check my social media outlets before getting out of bed and before brushing my teeth. It's a bad habit, but I like to see what I've missed while I was sleep. Before I had time to open my Instagram app, I noticed that I had 3 messages. I had already assumed that I would have one from Kris telling me goodnight right as he lays next to his wife, begging her for forgiveness from embarrassing her at the impromptu celebration, but maybe the other two were from Brandon?

Unlocking my phone, I wanted to know who potentially had me on their mind early this morning. Surprisingly enough, I was wrong. Two of the messages were from my mother, sending me her daily good morning text and a prayer for safe travels as she always did before a flight and the other was from Sprint advising me to pay my bill. No Kris, no Brandon, no Sabrina, not even Reece. Damn, I'm feeling neglected out here in these streets. After a quick shower, I threw on my favorite form-fitting jeans and cleavage bearing white tee. I tossed my hair into a sloppy ponytail and I proceeded to accomplish one of the fastest packing jobs that I'd done since my college days when all you needed to do was grab a pair of panties and toothbrush to stash in a creep bag. After realizing that there was no time for me to print out my work because my computer conveniently was participating in some sort of update, I called for an uber. I pray the hotel has some sort of corporate center that I have access to or I will officially be shit out of luck.

Riding in the car, listening to the driver as he attempts to make small talk, I think to make sure that I hadn't forgotten anything. Glancing at my watch to make sure I was still on schedule, I pray that this DC traffic works in my favor. This is nothing new to me, I've been late mostly all my life. My mom pokes fun at the fact that I was even born late. 11 days pass my due date; it was written in the stars that I would never be on time. And this isn't my first rodeo with this business trip travel; I've missed plenty of flights, so I am more than familiar with the protocol. I plan on checking my over-sized packed bag outside and tip the baggage handler to avoid paying the additional fee for the extra weight and check-in on my phone while I'm in route, so hopefully that will be my saving grace. Oh shit, my phone, where is it? I remembered having it in my hand when I was losing my mind over the computer not working, but did I place it down somewhere? Did I throw it in my bag? How in the hell could I forget my phone?

Rummaging through my new Bordeaux Saffron Marc Jacobs Super Trooper bag Reece brought me, I pulled out everything, exposing the contents onto the back seats. Disappointed in myself, I audibly criticized myself for being so careless and unprepared. There is no way that I would be able to exist for nearly 2 weeks without my phone, but Lord knows that I do not want to hear my boss's mouth for the 3rd time this year about missing another flight. Decisions, decisions...Fuck it, I'll take my chances. I absolutely wouldn't be able to survive without it. Not too too far from my house, but far enough, I ask the driver to take me back home. It wasn't the ideal choice, but it was necessary. Meanwhile, I'm trying to think long and hard where I could have left it.

Heading towards my spot, I had the genius idea of having the driver call it. Maybe just by some miraculous chance, in the rush of things, I possibly tossed it into my luggage or carryon bag. I humbly requested him to turn down the music so I could listen for it to ring, but I'm not even sure if it's on sound or vibrate. At this point, I'm almost positive that I have gotten on his last nerve. Hell, I barely wanted to engage in small talk with him, now I'm asking him to do a million and one favors on my behalf.

Coming to a complete stop at a red light, I faintly hear the sound, of what I thought could possibly be my ringtone, coming from the trunk. I listened as closely as I could with my ear to the back of my seat. "I think I hear it!" I say with excitement "Is it possible that you can pop the trunk so I can grab my bag out the back?" The driver shoots me a look through his rearview mirror. "I owe you" I plead. He pulls the car over and I hop out. "Can you call it again?" I ask. It rings as I let out a sigh of relief. I'm almost sure that I didn't pack my charger, but that the least of my worries right now, I could easily grab one at the airports kiosks. My luggage and I get back in the car as I scramble for my phone through the zippered compartments. Noticing that the car is stationary, I look up to see the driver giving me a look through the mirror as if he needs confirmation that I now have what I need. I give him an innocent smile and a thumb up. "We're good" I said, "we can go straight to the airport now." In my most innocent voice I ask "but do u think we can kinda.... like hurry?" he turns his head all the way around this time making full eye contact with me, we both let out a loud laugh. I was serious about my question though.

The travel gods absolutely worked in my favor because traffic was great. I made it to the airport in a record breaking time (considering the circumstances), tipped my driver a crisp $100 for his time and patience, checked-in my bag, hopped in a wheelchair which basically got me through the checkpoint security express line, and arrived just in time to board just before they were preparing to close the doors. Exhausted and running off fumes, I fell into my leather first class seat, shook my head in disappointment and let out a sigh of relief. I made it! From here on out, I vowed to myself, as I've always done, that I would NEVER wait until that last minute to prepare again. This day was one for the record books.

3 hours and 15 from Washington, DC to Dallas, Texas, and I slept the entire trip. I don't remember the flight taking off or the flight attendant offering beverage or food services. The only thing I remembered was the pilot coming over the intercom to make weather and landing announcements and still then, I couldn't manage to open my eyes. I was exhausted. I'm not sure how much work is going to get accomplished today but I feel as if it is almost impossible to be productive at this point. On our arrival to the Dallas-Fort Worth airport, regaining consciousness, I removed the airplane mode setting from my phone to check the time and weather, I had several messages notifications being delivered to my phone. With no energy to even care about who needed to get in contact with me, I rapidly placed the phone on vibrate to avoid drawing any more attention my way. Gathering my belongings and retrieving my overhead bag, an older lady that had been sitting two rows behind me on my right, comes up behind me as she tries to get my attention. "Excuse me", she says in a soft tone. I kindly ignore her. She will not rush me; she'll get off this damn plane as soon as I get off. "Excuse me" this time tenderly tapping me on the shoulder. If looks could kill, she would be a goner. I turned around with one eyebrow raised and

my Philly attitude on fleek to see what she wanted. "When you get inside the airport you might want to go to the bathroom" she said. "There is something on the back of your pants that you may want to give some attention to." Embarrassed and very meekly, I whispered thank you and immediately tied my blazer around my waist. At a faster pace and now on a mission, I began to exit the plane in search of how to get to baggage claim so I can get the fuck outta here. With the luck I'd been having, I wouldn't be surprised if my luggage never made it onto the flight.

Staying optimistic, I asked the first airport personnel I saw, where the closest bathroom was. I had been on that flight for hours, too lazy to get up from my peaceful sleep to take a pee break; my kidneys are going to kill me later in life, plus I'm nervous on what the hell is on the back of my white pants. Pointing me in the right direction, I walked swiftly in hopes that there wouldn't be a line, I really needed to go. Well, what do you know? There's a damn line, not too long, but longer than I needed it to be. With about 6 people ahead of me and with a little two step, I managed to calm my bladder down to prevent me from making a mess here on this floor. Entering the bathroom, behind me was the cutest little girl accompanied by a lady I assumed to be her mom. The little girl is doing the pee-pee dance and I was almost tempted to join her. "I can't hold it" she says as she clenches he private areas. Her mother insists that she needs to hold it for little bit longer. Being the person that I am, I insist that they go ahead of me. But, just as I give them the green light to go, I feel a gush of secreted liquids fall. The feeling sends a chill throughout my entire body causing chill bumps on my arms. Great, now I know for a fact that I didn't pack any tampons or pads with me. Why did I think that I had a least another week before Mother Nature was expected to pay me a visit? This day, I swear. Going into the next available stall, I observed what I had feared ever since the lady from the plane placed me on high alert. She was here, my monthly gift was here. What the fuck!?!? A bitch cannot catch a break.

Having been on plenty of trips, I've learned the hard way to always be prepared with an extra change of clothes in a carryon bag. One time the airlines misplaced my luggage for 3 days, and when I said I had nothing, I mean I had nothing, so I've learned to prepare for the worst but to hope for the best. Changing out of my soiled items, I rolled up a handful of tissue, creating a makeshift sanitary napkin. All I wanted to do was get to my room, take a shower, and take it down. Once again, tying the blazer around my waist, I exited the bathroom making a b-line straight towards baggage claim. I began to think my bag never made it onto the flight as I stood for 20 minutes watching the same unclaimed forest green luggage circulate the turnstile. Mentally drained, I was preparing to make my way to customer service when I saw my bag coming down the slide. Thank you Jesus, I said aloud. The gentleman standing next to me let out a small laugh.

"Can you ask Jesus if my bag is coming next?" he said. Not trying to be rude, I really didn't feel like engaging in a full-blown conversation, so I just smirked and remained silent. "Let me help you with that", he says as he reaches in to grab my overweight suitcase. "Damn girl, I'm glad this thing has wheels, its heavy as fuck" he says. I roll my eyes as I thought to myself; nobody asked for your help anyways, I could've gotten it myself. As he turns around to hand me my bag, I look him in his face as I politely say thank you. The Mr. is fine. Honey, he is drop dead gorgeous. I'm feeling like I'm a little star struck. His smile, his skin, his eyes, his haircut... good Lord have mercy. Effortlessly, I do an immediate attitude adjustment. Now flashing him a smile, I struggle to find a way to engage him in small talk. Grabbing onto the handle of my luggage, "I'm sorry, I've never been a good packer. A girl needs to have shoes, right?" I say jokingly. "Yeah, I guess" he responds. Now at a loss for words and both of us standing there looking stupid, I pretend to look through my pocketbook for my phone. "Now all I have to do is find the car rental place and I'll be ok" I mention. "Oh ok", he responds "I'm still waiting for this bag to come out. I was running late earlier and I'm not really sure if it made in on the flight or not. I'm starting to think not though". At this point, the belt has stopped and no more bags are coming out. That same green bag is still lying on its side, still unclaimed.

"That's not your bag is it?" I ask. "No ma'am, but I wonder if they wear my size though. I got a banquet to attend this evening, and I'm not sure that what I have on is considered proper attire" as he looks down at the wrinkled tee shirt and ripped jeans he has on. "Well, now you'll have a reason for an impromptu shopping trip" I suggest. "You probably want to go to customer service to see what's going on. They'd know for sure" I recommend. "Thanks, I am going to head over there now" he responds. He was oh so fine. I had totally forgotten about the desperate need for me to hurry up out of there, I was just enjoying the time I was spending looking at him. I wanted to acquire more information about him, but I didn't want to be too forthcoming. At a loss for words and small talk, "Good Luck" I tell him as I reposition my pocket book and carryon bag, making it more manageable to navigate through the airport. Maybe this will be like the movies, when I walk away, he'll stop me and ask for my name and number and ask when he can take me out. Ha! Wishful thinking. I walked away with a little switch in my hips hoping to grab his attention, I listened hard to see if he would try to stop me, but he didn't. I purposely stopped and slightly turned to see if I could catch another glimpse of him but he was nowhere in sight. Oh well, you win some, you lose some.

Stepping outside to catch the shuttle to the car rentals, the humidity nearly made me light headed and nauseous. How do people exist here? It was too damn hot, this was some bullshiggity. Already feeling sticky, I waited for what seemed to be another 30 minutes before the shuttle arrived. As I sat down, I couldn't help but think about the guy that I just met. Maybe I should have pursued him and asked for his number or showed a little more interest, so he would've tried to bag me. Did I curve him and not even realize? I've been told in the past that I have a tendency of inadvertently doing so. Maybe I wasn't his type or he just might not have been attracted to me. Was my breath not as fresh from the nap on the plane? Oh my God, was he around when the nice lady told me about the marking on my pants, had he seen it? Maybe it was for the best that we didn't get a chance to exchange conversation. Maybe it wasn't me at all. Maybe he was here in Texas seeing his girlfriend, or wife even, and she, the kids and the dog were in the car patiently awaiting his arrival, but then again, he said that he had a business banquet to go to tonight, didn't he?

Here I go again with these crazy thoughts. With my mind all over the place, I am the absolute worse when it comes to overthinking; yup I'm guilty on all charges. Before I know it, I arrive at the car rental place, and once again I am gathering my weighty belongings. The man from the airport was right, this bag is indeed heavy. With 3 people ahead of me, I rummage through my pocketbook looking for my identification, credit card, and insurance information. Being the clumsy person that I am, I manage to drop the entire bag causing it to fall on the floor, creating a small deterrence. Bending over as I drop down and get my eagle on, I overhear the customer service representative mention that the system just went down and that it will be a few minutes before she will be able to proceed in processing any reservation. She then makes the announcement to the rest of us who are patiently waiting in line. Plagued with one thing after another, I cannot even describe how much I need to get to this room. We were given the option to have a seat if we'd like or we could continue standing. I chose to stand. I thought that in my decision to remain standing, the universe might have some pity on me and make the machine come back up faster. Almost the same concept that people have when they're waiting for the bus in the middle of the street, wishfully hoping and thinking that the bus will come faster if they are actually looking for it. Shit, with the way I'm feeling, they could keep all my info, just toss me the keys and I could come back later to tie up loose ends. They could give me a Geo Metro for all I cared at this point. As the system comes back up, I was feeling optimistically hopeful that I was one step closer to showering and crawling in the bed; I could finally see the light at the end of the tunnel. Approaching the desk, the reservation process ran smoothly as the short Latina lady briefly and wholeheartedly apologized for the inconvenience, offering me a Buick Enclave as a free upgrade. Transaction completed!

The thought of being in the shower in less than an hour and being comfortably snuggled up in a king size deluxe suite hotel room, watching whatever happened to be on tv at this time of day, or better yet, having the tv watching me, brings my soul great excitement. Heading outside to locate my rental car, who do I see getting off the shuttle but Mr. Baggage claim? Pondering my next move, I must think quickly. Do I make myself be seen or just pretend as if I didn't see him at all? Before I even had a chance to come up with an action plan, he spotted me and we locked eyes. Loudly speaking, "So what happened? Did they have your bags or nah?" (I learned that slang from my niece, that's what the young kids are saying now.) Pitifully laughing he starts to explain the situation and how pissed off he is that his bag wouldn't be ready for pick up until later today or tomorrow morning at the latest. Cutting him off, to lighten the mood and ease his frustration, I knew the situation all too well. I had been in that position more times than I would like at admit to. "You'll be alright for a day. You could always just buy something, leave the tags on it and take it back tomorrow." The look he gave me made me burst out laughing. It was almost as if he was questioning my integrity and my lifestyle.

"It was a joke" I said as I removed my hand from my mouth in attempts to discretely try to conceal my laughter. "I see how you roll Ms." He said cutting his eyes "It would be cool, if I was just relaxing for the rest of the day, but I have work to do." he sighs, "I need to find a suit, something to wear for tonight. I have a meet and greet banquet that I must attend. There's going to be at least 150 to 200 associates from my corporation from all over the country. I most definitely can't show up dressed like this", as he looks down at his clothes. Me, being a frequent visitor to the area and a compulsive shopper, "there's a mall not too far from here. I'm not sure what you're looking for, but you definitely should be able to find something there. It's probably only about 26 miles from here, like 30 minutes tops if you're driving. It called the North Park Mall, I believe. They have Nordstrom and Neiman Marcus, Versace, Gucci.... I mean they have lower-budget friendly stores too like H&M and Gap too. It's all what you're into." I said empathetically. "I'm not sure what time your event starts but if you don't have time to go to the mall, I'm sure there's a Target or Walmart close, your good looking enough to pull it off." "Oh, you got jokes huh?" He responds as he looks at his gold watch to check the time. "Fortunately, I do have a few hours; I may take your advice and go check it out. You seem to know a little bit about everything, I'm assuming that you travel often. I should keep you around while I'm here. First you knew where to send me to find my bag, now you're coming through in the clutch for me again by telling me where I can go to find clothes. How about you come with me to the mall, I'm sure that you could probably tell me exactly which stores to go to, which racks to look on, which cashier to go to. You got all the answers. You the real MVP." He says jokingly. Keeping a straight face, I held in my smile. He was too good-looking not to smile at and then with his little sarcastic comments, his attractiveness increased.

So those that know me know that I, Brooke Imani Harrigan, do not turn down a shopping experience, especially when I'm away from home. It's nothing like traveling and finding little signature pieces from some small boutique, then later having someone back at home asking you where you got it from. I like that exclusive feeling, that "nobody else has it" feeling. The only problem was, number one, I'm not sure if that was an official invite or if he was just talking, and second, I am not about to go anywhere without getting my ass in somebody's tub first. "I mean... I'm not sure who usually dresses you" that was my way of fishing for information "but I'm sure I can help you out a little. I came down a day early for my business trip, so I do have some extra time to spare." I'm not a forward person, so this was as direct as it was going to get from me. A part of me, sometimes, would like to step out of my shell but I stay reserved for the most part, unless I have a drink of course. "Aww, you would do that for me, maybe I can treat you to something to show my appreciation if you do a good job? On second thought, I don't know, you up here talking about some Gucci and Versace, you might try to kill a brother's pockets out here. I'm not sure if I have that much available funds on my credit card. I left the black card at home this time, I didn't think I'd be needing it. I can feed you. Do you like pretzels or Cinnamon buns?" "Ok, so good luck, I'm going to go take a nap" I said as I turned to walk away. Gently grabbing my arm, "That was a joke, that was a joke. Don't be like that, I'm sorry, I joke a lot, that's just what I do. I mean I wasn't joking about the Versace and Gucci part though." He says with a serious face. "But if your down to ride out with me, I would really enjoy having you as my company. Come on, once I grab this car, we can be out." Thinking to myself if I would be willing to go with this stranger that I met less than an hour ago, I'm indecisive.

I watch the ID channel all day every day, it's hard for me to trust people. People are crazy, and I most definitely did not feel like dying today. They won't be telling my story on there. "I would go with you, but I really need to stop at my room first. If you could give me a few minutes to drop off my car, put my bags in the room, and freshen up a little bit, I'll go with you." In my mind, I'm thinking that will give me enough time to charge up my stun gun too, just in case this dude does turn out to be crazy, I can zap his ass and get away. "I'm not staying far from here, so by the time that you wait in that line inside of there" pointing to the lobby area of the car rental place, "I'll be ready."

That was totally a lie and his facial expression expressed that he knew it too. "I know how ya'll women are, and ya'll talking bout it will only take 10 minutes", as he mimics a female voice "and ya'll know damn well that really means 45 minutes to an hour. Now listen woman, I'm on a time constraint, don't have me waiting forever" as he raised one eyebrow. "I don't know who you're used to dealing with, but when I say that I won't be long, it won't take me long" that was more than likely a lie, "but, you know what, I have a car so feel free to go without me, I can always just meet you there. I mean, you did ask me for my help, I didn't ask you, humph, don't get all demanding with me" I said slightly irritated. I don't like being rushed or talked to like I'm a child, I do what I want, when I want and that's how I like it. Plus, I'm damn sure not going to be bossed around by someone that I don't even know; he got this sister here fucked all the way up.

"Just make sure that while you're getting yourself together that you let your man know first, don't be having him rolling up on us, asking me who I am. You cute and all but I aint with the shits...you know." he said. Touché! I'm sure that was his way of trying to pry into my business. But just as he conveniently disregarded my attempts of inquiry, I was going to curve his ass too. Smirking and rolling my eyes I gave the address of my hotel and my phone number to call me when he was outside. "I'll see u in a few" I said walking away. "Aight" he replied "15 minutes, right?" I just kept walking, If I had to have another conversation about this, I was not going to partake in this mall excursion.

There was no doubt about it; I was most definitely going to need a shower. Catching a glimpse of my reflection in the window of the SUV that I had rented, I could see that my African American heritage was starting to show. Just from standing outside talking to him for that short period of time, I've done already sweated out my edges. After gaining access to the trunk, I put my belongings in there, delicately sitting in the car not wanting to shift my improvised sanitary napkin too much while trying to avoid soiling the tan colored seats of the car. Isn't it something about that smell of a new car that gives you the urge to want to go out and cop up. Speaking of new cars, where did I put my phone? More than likely I have a few missed calls from Kris and/or my momma, but I'll call them when I get to the room and wait for this guy to come get me. I laughed out loud to myself. Within both encounters with this dude, I don't ever remember asking him for his name, or did he tell me and I was too enchanted by his smile to listen? Come to think of it, I don't really remember him asking me about mine either. This will be interesting trip to say the least. Maybe when he calls me, I'll jokingly ask, "who's this" and see how that goes, otherwise, I'll just have to come out and bluntly ask him what it is. I need to give a heads up to my home girl and my momma that I plan on venturing out with this person that I just met too, just in case anything happens to me or I do go missing. I customarily attach a picture of the persons license plates to the text, so they know how to track the person down, but since it's not his car per say, I'm not sure how that works. I'll still do it anyways, safety before sorry, got to take all precautions nowadays. I've learned that the cutest ones are typically the craziest ones.

Entering the address of the Grand Hyatt hotel into my GPS, I suddenly realized that dude was right, there was no way that I was going to be ready by the time he picked up the rental and arrived here to pick me up. My estimated time of arrival to the hotel was less than 7 minutes. **inserts the emoji crying face**

Following the voice guided directions to my destination and thinking out loud, I still needed to get checked in, showered, and hopefully find some kind of clothing items that complement each other in my luggage, and are not too wrinkled. I'm seriously debating if I should even go. Feeling overwhelmed by what I still needed to do, I'm suddenly not feeling it anymore. I mean, I don't even know this guy, why do I feel obligated to help him? I don't owe him anything. I probably should just call him now and tell him so he won't even waste his time circling the airport to come here. I guess it would've been helpful if I had taken his number when I gave him mine. Sitting in the car mentally preparing myself as I arrange to let valet take the car, great, now I don't know his name or his number, criticizing myself while placing my hand upon my forehead, I am officially the smartest person I know. Exiting the car, I had never been so happy to see the bellhop in my life. I had grown tired of lugging these bags around, I was mentally and physically drained.

Allowing valet and the bellhop to take my belongings, I entered the beautifully designed hotel, and checked in. Still carrying my handheld tote that I used as my carryon bag. I navigated my way towards my hotel room still debating this master plan. So far, I hadn't heard from the guy and it's been over 15 mins. Maybe he changed his mind, maybe I was free and clear of having to tag along with him and didn't even know it. But on second thought who the hell was he to stand me up, who did he think he was? I mean he was cute and all, but he wasn't all that. Just as I held my key up to gain entry into the room, I felt my phone vibrate. Letting out a chuckle, I proceeded in the room to put down my bags and completely dumping out my bag to find my phone. Laying my pocket book down on the bed, I grabbed my phone just in time to see it still ringing, but I wasn't sure if I wanted to answer just yet though. I could buy myself a little time by getting in the shower, then telling him I missed the call because I was in the shower or I could use the missed call as an excuse to find out his name when I called the number back. I figured that I would keep it funky with him, inform him that I just got to my room and see what he says. "Hello" "Hey, this is Carter" "Oh hey, Carter" I said laughing as I looked over a receipt that was in the clutter of my pocketbook contents now scattered on the bed. Also finding an emergency stashed tampon. "What's so funny?" he asks. "Oh nothing" I answer while smiling extremely hard. "Is your hotel actually located in the airport? When I entered it in the GPS, it's telling me that I'm less than 4 minutes away, but the directions have me circling the airport. I wasn't sure if you messed up the address or not." "The funny thing is that it is at the airport. I didn't realize it until I was attempting to find my way here." "Ok well, in that case, I will be there momentarily, so I'll see you in a second." "Ok." I said. Hanging up the phone, I fell on the bed backwards and burst out laughing. Why didn't I just say something while I had him on the phone? I should've told him that I needed a few extra minutes to freshen up. Oh well, I can be ready in 6.5minutes, I'm sure he won't mind.

21 minutes, a knock on the door, 13 text messages, and 5 missed calls later, I'm still not dressed nor, can I find my other sandal. The bellhop had already dropped off my bags while I was in the shower and Carter had called to make sure that I was ok about 5 minutes ago. At that time, I told him that I was on my way down. I found it! I grabbed the shoe and my bag as I darted out of the room. Fresh out of the shower I knew the elevator would take some time; I could put my other shoe on then and fix my pony tail on

the ride down. I had sunglasses to hide my bare makeup-free eyes, so I could be presentable. I was effortlessly cute. Thank God for the good genes that my momma passed down to me. My skin is practically flawless and with the help of edge control my edges were laid. And I wasn't one of those girls that felt the need to wear a full face of makeup or beat my face on a daily basis. On special occasions, I may show off, but for the most part, I kept it cute and simple. Of course, now that I'm on the elevator, it is going to stop at every floor since I'm in a hurry. At this point I wouldn't be surprised if he had left and gone without me. Regretfully, I had been left before for taking too long getting ready. That was one of Kris' biggest pet peeves. He definitely was not one of those men that had a lot of patience when it came down to time.

Finally making it to the lobby and out to the main entrance, not knowing what kind of car I'm looking for, I just stand there looking at the line of cars sitting on the side of the valet parked. Hoping that he would recognize my presence and beep the horn, rev the engine, or something, the 45 seconds of me standing in this Godforsaken heat, helped convince me that he had left. Turning around to walk back inside to the air-conditioned building to call him, I hear a horn beep. Quickly turning back around I see him. Unlike the last time, he isn't smiling. "Where were you?" I asked "I've been standing out in this heat for like 10 minutes already. Don't you see this sweat beading up on my forehead?" He was not here for my humor and I was not here for this heat. How is it that I was fresh out the shower, had only been outside for all of 2 minutes max, and I feel like I need another shower? Forming my face to make the most innocent expression I could think of, I turned towards him to see if he would have any sympathy for me and my tardiness. He didn't even look my way, he just asked for the name of the mall so he could put it into the GPS. Usually I would try to make small talk to slowly dig myself out of the dog house, this time I didn't really feel the need to. I was just trying to gauge a feel for him and his reactions. After about 5 miles of driving with the faint sound of the radio in the background, he looks at me and says, "You look nice". That's all he says. "Thank you", I respond. "You smell nice too" he adds. "Thank you" I respond again. "I'm assuming that's what took you so long?" Not sure if he was trying to lure me into his convo, so he could go off on me or not, so I didn't say a word. Now looking in his direction, pretending to be checking out the scenery and avoiding eye contact with him, in a baby talk tone he says "Aww, I feel special. You wanted to get cute for little ol' me?" We both just laugh.

Engaging in small talk, I learned a few interesting things about Mr. Carter Alex Grant. He is 37, a father of two little girls, 7 & 10 which he showed me pictures in his phone, originally from Durham, NC now staying in Redwood Shore, CA, working as a Business Intelligence Designer, meaning that he is responsible for the delivery of operational reporting and performance metrics to various business domains including Sales and Sales Operations, Marketing, Finance, and Employee Success, simply speaking, he is important. Now usually I do not entertain a man who has kids, especially not two of them, but what was I going to do, catch an Uber home? After all, he didn't ask me to marry him, he asked me to chaperone him to the mall. As we arrive at the North Park Center, he pulls up to have the car valeted. Pretending to be accustomed to valet parking at the mall, I didn't say anything; I just went with the flow. I grabbed my bag, braced myself for this heat that was about to pistol whip me and exited the car. "Let's try to make this quick and painless, please?" he said as he looked at his wristwatch. I pulled out my phone took at the time, 3 missed calls. It was 4:18pm. He never said what time the event started, but I assumed that it was around 7/8 ish we should have enough time to find him something and possibly find myself something while I'm here.

"Where do you usually shop?" trying to decide which store I should take him to first. "Take me to the store that you would like to see me in if I was your man" he replied. Aww shit, I thought to myself. It was a little corny, but I'll give him an "A" for effort. If we were home, I may have taken him to Zara for a quick fix, they are my absolute fave. "Do you trust me?" I asked serious-faced as I looked into his beautiful brown eyes. "I trusted that it would only take you 10 minutes to get dressed and look where that got me?" he says jokingly. "I guess I need to earn your trust back again then, huh?" I add. "Let's try J. Crew, they have nice suits. I think that you might be able to pull it off." To me, J. Crew was safe. Not too much, but just enough. I had been getting Kris stuff from there for as long as I could remember, but then again, Kris had swag, I'm not sure what this guy Carter is capable of. Entering the store, we are greeted by the sales woman who asks if we are looking for anything.

Taking charge, "My boyfriend and I have a very important dinner that we were attending this evening. He is being honored with a prestigious award and the airline lost our luggage. Our driver is outside waiting and we need a suit that when he walks into the room, everyone will know that he is the man of the year." now touching his chest, "Now he has a Ludlow suit in Italian cashmere from here at home, so let's try something a little different this time. I was thinking more like the Ludlow suit in Italian cotton piqué this time. What you think babe?" turning to look at him. The expression on

his face looks like I was just speaking in Arabic, but I can tell that he was impressed. All I know is whatever comes out of his mouth better not sound retarded and embarrass me. "Good choice babe. Either that one or the Ludlow suit in herringbone Italian linen-silk. I looked at that one last week, but I wanted to wait and get your opinion on it before I purchased it." WELL DAMN! That caught me off guard, I was impressed and from the look on the sales lady's face she was impressed too, maybe a little too impressed, because she took him by the arm and led him to the back of the store very eager to get him suited. He turned and looked at me winking his right eye and I just stood there smiling. I could feel it, if our relationship grew, we'd make one hell of a team. Feeling my phone vibrate in my back pocket, I reach for it and look at the screen, it's Kris. If I answer, he's going to expect the details of my whereabouts for the past 3 or so hours since my plane touched down and I don't know how long he's going to want to carry on a conversation. But then again, he could just be simply making sure that I had arrived safely. If I chose to answer, this would be the perfect time since Carter is in the back. There would be no way I'm going to be able to pull off talking to him with the new guy hanging around.

"Hey" "Hey, my ass", he rebuttals, "It's nice to see that you made it safely." Stopping for a brief pause, "I know you saw my calls and texts." Sensing attitude in his tone, "babe, I'm sorry. I have had one of the most hectic days. It was like Murphy's Law. Any and everything that could go wrong, did. Then I thought that I left my phone, but really it ended up being in my bag, then I was late for my flight and almost missed it, then my period came on and I had on my favorite white pants. It's just been a catastrophe. But, I made it. How are you? What's been going on over there on that end? I haven't talked to you since you left last night, how was the party?" I reply as I try to gain control of the conversation and lighten the mood. I couldn't have cared less how the party was or even if there really was a party. When he would pick fights and arguments, or wanted to question me, I would always want to remind him to that I was not his wife. I am not required, nor did I take any vows to have to put up with his shit, but I always refrained from saying such, just to avoid whatever heated dialogue was to come after that. Sometimes I would just be so over him.

"The reason you haven't heard from me is because you decided not to answer my phone calls." There was complete silence. I didn't want to engage in this topic he was luring me into, so I just stayed quiet. "And it wasn't a party, she just invited a few people over. Once I got there all she wanted to do was give me the silent treatment anyways and act like the bitch she is. I could have just stayed with you for all of that". I don't know what the fuck that was supposed to mean, but whatever. "Well, to say the least, it was a nice gesture, you have to admit, she tried to please your miserable ass. If you would have been home like a good little husband, everything would've went as planned, but nooooo, you want to be out buying cars for your mistress, who is super supportive, who helps put you in the position to maximize your potential, and not to mention, who also has the best pussy you've ever had. Hell, she should've been throwing us both a party, for all of the work that I put in." "Who said you were the best pussy that I ever had? There was this one hoe...", cutting him off mid-sentence, "Boy please, you tried it. You and I both know I'm the best that you've had. Your selection has always been weak. You've always gone for the prissy type. The ones with their little pearl necklaces and bracelets that complement their Anne Klein watches, that are scared to get a little dirty, too timid to deep throat that dick, too concerned about their esophagus and gag reflexes, complaining about their jaw getting tired, too shy to fuck outside or in plain eye view, the "don't get it in my hair" type. They never tell you how they want you to fuck them, they never tell you to choke them or pull their hair. I know they're not letting you put your finger in their ass, incorporate toys in to foreplay, shit they probably don't even let you smack their ass, and if they did, they'd probably want you to do it gently so it doesn't leave a mark. Don't even let me bring up the girl I let you bring home with us from the club back in college, trying to turn you on to something new. She was the most untalented female I ever met." Letting out a sarcastic laugh, "plus every time I let you slide in, you make sure to let me know how good it is." "Damn girl, come home. I miss you" he says in agreement. "Now tell me you love me" I command of him. "I love you babe."

Continuing to make small talk for the next 11 minutes, I turned back around to see if any progress was being made with Carter's situation, I could see that they were ready for my opinion of his outfit. "Ok luv, I need to call you back in a few." Rushing to get him off the phone, he informs me that he will be out with his wife this evening. Something about an event that is work related. Unbothered, and unfocused, he says that he will call me later. It all made sense on why he was calling me so much earlier. He doesn't think that I pick up on his trends and how he chooses to handle certain situations. I am constantly accused of always making something out of nothing and overthinking things, but it's just how he operates when he knows that he won't be available to talk when I try to call him later. Whatever.

Stepping out of the fitting area, Carter is looking very dapper. He has on the suit, the one which I suggested, and if I may say, he looks better than before. I felt like I was in a movie, I could hear the choir of angels harmonizing in my head. He and the sales woman had paired the French navy-blue suit with a white Ludlow spread-collar shirt with convertible cuffs and a striped tie. If the sales lady wasn't there, I could envision myself escorting him back into the dressing area and helping him remove his clothing, but I had to come back to reality. "What do you think?" Carter asks as he looks in the mirror. "I think it fits you very well and you look very dignified. I might want to change the tie though." Walking over to him adjusting the accurateness and precision of the tie, "what do you think?" I asked him. It was in that moment in which we locked eyes. He stared for a second as if he was thinking about saying something. "So, what do you think?" I asked, reiterating my question as I brushed off the small dust particles on his suit jacket. "I like it, it'll work" he answered in a calm nonchalant tone. "So now", the sales lady asks, "What about you?" "I'm ok, I'm good."

Shrugging off the fact that I hadn't seen anything that caught my eye which I wanted him to purchase for me "so what are you going to wear tonight? he asks. Starring at him, I'm confused. I'm wearing my pajamas fool, I don't have anywhere to go, and he's starting to take this role-playing thing too far. "You need something to wear to the affair also." Ok now I'm totally confused and I'm sure that my face is showing it. Did I somehow ignore him when he asked me to accompany him? Did I agree already? Jesus, I need a nap. He grabs my hand and leans in towards my face. "I'll give you two a minute to decide", the saleswoman says as she excuses herself from the area. "You expect me to go alone as good as I look?" I laugh it off, "something is wrong with you." "But seriously, do you have plans for tonight, if not, I would like for you to come with me."

Why would I want to go to the dinner? It's not like I would know anyone there. I was good at freestyling, but I'm not sure if I could pull this one off. I was so used to playing things pretty safe for the most part, and I had already stepped out of my comfort zone by traveling to the mall with this stranger, how far was I going to push the envelope? With the day that I had been having, I don't know if I was capable of being the bubbly, jovial spirited person that I usual am at these types of events, especially without getting a nap. I'm tired. I didn't get much rest the previous night, I'm cramping, and I had work to do. "You do look nice, if I must say so myself, but you wouldn't want me to go with you. It would be awkward, wouldn't it?" I asked. "Listen, it will be people from all over, they don't personally know me, and I don't know them. You were fast on your feet when you were talking to that lady. I'll make sure you're comfortable and I'll make sure that I take care of you for the night." With one eyebrow raised, he asks, "Besides what else were you going to do?" "You do know that I came to Texas on work also? I'm important too you know. Maybe not as important as you, but I consider myself to be a big deal. I work hard. It's not all parties and fun for me. Some of us actually do hard labor for a couple dollars." I responded with my black girl neck roll. "Oh please, you work for the government. Everyone knows that they do the least work, but they do make some good money, and from the sounds of it, you might be pretty high up there. I don't want you to think that I'm counting your coins or anything…. but even so, everyone deserves a little break sometimes. If you really can't come or don't want to come, I understand, but I would truly be honored if you decided to be my date for the evening. I'm not going to beg you though, just know, I think that you would have a good time and I think that you would look nice in that dress" as he points to the picture on the wall.

Slowly turning my head around to be able to view the picture that he is referencing, I spot it. It's a cute little champagne one shouldered dress, maybe not something that I would have picked out, but it was alright. It was definitely a no go with this whole "mother nature" situation I got going on over here. That's the last thing I needed to do was embarrassed myself and him. "Oh, that's nice" I responded. "So, am I going alone tonight or what?" he asked. I can feel my mind slowly starting to over analyze the situation. Without thinking everything through, I agreed to go. "And I promise not to have you out too late Cinderella", he offered to go to any store that I wanted to in efforts to find me a dress. After approximately 4 stores, and 2 hours and 27 mins later, we both settled on a dress that appropriated the both of us. I got shoes and accessories as so did he. His card had to be on fire because we swiped the hell out of that thing. I did my very best to be modestly fiscal, but I still managed to do some financial damage. Carting our bags to the valet desk awaiting the vehicle, he turns to me and questions, "Should I even want to know how long it's going to take you to get ready?" Looking at my phone for the time, I realized that I had one more stop to make. I needed to hit up some kind of store that sold toiletries. I felt a little uncomfortable asking him to take me, but if I didn't, it would to take me longer to get ready. "Ummm, it shouldn't take me that long, I know what I'm wearing already" I say making a very innocent childlike facial expression. He flashes his smile. That damn thing is going to be the death of me.

"Ok, so here's the deal" as he ran down the itinerary. "I need to be there by 9pm at the absolute latest. Meaning we need to be there by 9" emphasizing on the word we. "I'd prefer to be earlier, but I don't want to put too much pressure on you. I have to get changed, come back and get you, and still drive there. We might have actually spent a little longer in the mall than I would have expected to but do you think that this is feasible?" he asks with a serious face as he glances at his watch. In my mind, I'm thinking to myself, if I can make it to a CVS, things could be a lot simpler. All of a sudden he blurts out, "Shit!" "What's wrong?" I ask. "I still need to make another stop to get some lotion and deodorant. This lost bag thing is really fucking me up." He looks pissed off. Campaigning for the stop at the store, "we could just stop somewhere like a CVS or Rite Aid really quick, just run in and run out. If you know what brand you want, I'll even go in and grab it for you." This last-minute discovery of his was genius. Thank you airline gods! I couldn't have planned it to work out this way if I tried. Now I could easily go in the store, get both his and my items, slide the tampons in my bag without him noticing a thing, but I'm nervous. I don't know why but I was undeniably reluctant when it came to buying feminine items, I always have been. "Ok, we can do that" he says, still irritated. I was jumping for joy on the inside.

Riding in the car his phone, which has been paired with the Bluetooth sync system in the car, starts ringing in the tune of something that sounds like a children's lullaby. Not wanting to be all in his business, I find myself discreetly glancing at the car's screen now displaying the title "my love" and a phone number with the area code 650. Curious as to if he was going to answer or not, I sat in silence and continued to glance out of the window. My side chick tendencies got the best of me at times and old habits are hard to break. I wonder if it was his girlfriend from back home, I was not 100% convinced that he was single, not as fine as he was. The odds of finding someone that is totally single, I mean like they're not talking or involved with anyone at all, is completely slim. "This is my baby girl calling. She calls to check on me, she thinks she is the boss." He says as he shows the picture that popped up on his phone. Smiling, "aww. That's so cute. She is undeniably adorable" I comment. He answers the phone via Bluetooth and proceeds to have a conversation. The small child is asking him about his trip so far and giving him the details of her day. She mentions how the airline called the house in regard to his misplaced luggage. He was right she was a little bossy. She was fussing with him and questioning him on how he could lose his bag and what was he going to wear. He kindly laughs it off and assures her that he will be fine. The little girl goes on to express how much she misses him already and wants him to come back and how she wishes that she and her sister could have come along on the trip. He eases the girls mind, calming her concerns about him. They carry on a conversation long enough for us to reach our destination of the Target store. Illegally parking, I whisper to him to ask the brand of deodorant and lotion that he wants, he forms his lips to tell me what he prefers and hand me a $50.00 bill. Leaving his money in his hand, I slowly get out the car, trying to prevent that uncomfortable gush of blood that comes down once you've been sitting for a while, making sure to grab my bag and my wallet to conceal my hidden supplies upon completing my purchase. The relationship between Target and I is dangerous. Our love-hate relationship allows me to go in for one item and end up leaving with curtains, washcloths, and a picture frame that was marked down on the clearance rack by only 10 percent. But since this time, I was on a mission, I was determined to stay focused. Walking over to the health and beauty department, I grabbed Carter's items first and made a b-line straight to the sanitary products. While standing there deciding on which brand to get and which sales was the better deal, guess who pops up?? If the floor could've opened and I could've fell through, I would've gladly went with no fuss. Like a deer in headlights, I couldn't move. I felt like a kid that gets caught doing something they know they're not supposed to be doing. I just stood there in shock. Still talking on the phone via headset now, he whispers, "I forgot that I needed a razor too." Helping me to free up my arms, he takes the items that I have wedged between my arm and the side of my ribcage. He continues his conversation while walking over to the next aisle. I'm not even sure if he took any notice to the aisle I was in or if he noticed the items that I was standing there pondering on. He might have been playing it cool or he truly might have been distracted and not have took notice, either way I was grateful for the lack of embarrassment. As I mentioned before I had been extremely particular about certain things since I was adolescence, and this was one of the major ones. Grabbing a bag of pads and a small box of tampons, I headed towards the cashier. Finalizing my purchase, I immediately stuffed my product into my tote, and headed towards the exit to wait for Carter, who was finishing up his sale a few lines over. Now off the phone with his earbuds still in his ear, "Did you get anything?" he asked. Walking out of the store he asks again. Still not realizing that he is speaking to me, I continue to walk through the automatic door approaching the outside. I turn around to see which direction he is walking since I was unaware of where the car was parked. Giving me a confused look, "what's wrong?" I ask, "What's wrong. Is everything ok?" He says, "I was talking to you and you were ignoring me." "Oh, I wasn't ignoring you. I thought you were still on the phone. What did you say?" I asked. "I asked if you got something. I would have paid for it." "It's not a big deal, it was something small." In my mind I'm praying that he doesn't ask what it was, hopefully he just drops it. The car ride back to the hotel was spent in conversation of him bragging on his children. Arriving at my hotel, "its show time!" he said. Here goes nothing.

"Hey, I have an idea." I say as I have a lightbulb moment. "I'm not sure how you feel about it, but for the sake of saving time, since you have all your stuff with you, if you wanted to, you could get ready in my room. That would save you from running back and forth from my hotel to yours and then back again. It's just a suggestion." I honestly should've thought the entire idea through before proposing the idea; it's possible that my room could look like a hurricane hit it from the rush earlier. "That doesn't sound like a bad idea. I have a car coming though." He adds. "Oh excuse me. Oh whatever was I thinking? A man of such excellence and stature driving himself? How foolish of me" I add in a sarcastic tone. "Girl please. It sounds like a good idea, but I think it could get a little crowded and I don't want to jeopardize anything that may hinder your process of preparation. Plus, I'm not sure who I would contact to change the reservation for the pick-up location or anything. Although I'm sure that I could make some calls and figure it out, but then that would mean that I would need to either take my belongings with me or come back and get them. I'll just let you off, that way you can get a head start, and then I will have my driver come and get you. Is that ok?" It was fine with me; I'm glad that he didn't take me up on my offer. "That's fine" I said, "I was just putting it out there." The clock in the car reads 7:13pm as I exit. "I'll call you when I'm on my way back to get you. Ok?" Carter says. "Cool. I'll probably be ready by the time that you make it back to your hotel anyways" I manage to say with a straight face. "Seriously? If that's the case, you can come with me and get dressed in my suite." he says. Not even feeding into the conversation and closing the door behind me "it was a joke, see you in a few."

I'm not sure that I like the fact that he emphasized that he had a suite. I had one too; you don't see me flaunting it all around. As I waited for the elevator, I think of the things that I need to do to prepare for tonight's events, what I decide to do with my hair will be my biggest task. Walking to my room, I smile at the thoughts of today's events thus far. I have a feeling that tonight is going to be pretty interesting.

Showered and smelling like Reb'l Fleur by Rihanna, hair pressed with a part in the middle, and face beat to the Gods, I had completed mission impossible with 10 minutes to spare. I will admit, I impressed myself.

What should I do now? Grabbing my phone from the charger, I wanted to make sure that my ringer was on and I hadn't missed Carter's call. No missed calls from him. Lying across the bed in my undergarments I had time to check all my messages and missed calls. Remembering that I neglected to send a text to my girlfriends letting them know my whereabouts for the past several hours and my plans for the evening, I will do that now. As I read through my texts, I disregarded the messages from Kris, since I had already talked to him, but I decide that I would send him a risqué pic lying on the bed in my bra and panties with a caption that reads, "Missing you". Yes, I know that he is out with his wife, but that's just what we do. I can just imagine them out at dinner or wherever he is, his phone rings and he opens the message. BAM! He's grinning from ear to ear while everyone around him is trying to figure out what's making him smile so hard. I imagine him struggling to keep his composure, however succumbing to the excitement; his penis begins to get hard. Not too long thereafter, he somehow sneaks away and calls me to tell me that he misses me and how much he loves me. Actions such as these helped keep things interesting between us. No matter how many times I've done this before and the countless amounts of nudes he has stored in a private app on his phone, it never seems to get old or played out.

Taking approximately 15 pics in various positions, I narrow my choices down to one single photo and send it. The next unread text would be my momma checking on me. Responding to her message, I let her know that I had safely made it and that I was on my way to dinner. After scrolling through the other random texts from throughout the day and responding to them, I noticed a message from unknown number. Reading thru the text thread I soon realized that it was Brandon, the guy I met the day before at the softball game. He had texted me three times. Twice earlier this morning in response to the message I sent last night and one from this afternoon, I assume from when I was at the mall. Responding to his message, I begin telling him how much of a pleasant surprise it was to see that he had reached out to me, then apologizing for my lack of communication blaming my absence on the chronicles of my traveling. I follow up by asking how his day had been. Before I got a chance to hit the send button, Carter calls. He inquires about my progress and lets me know that he was downstairs waiting. "I thought you said that you were going to call me when you were on your way, like just leaving the hotel?" I asked. "I'm sorry sweetheart, I got caught up on a call, but you said that you were ready anyways right?" he says. I was ready. All I had to do was put on my dress and shoes and rinse my mouth out with a little mouthwash, I didn't tell him that though. "I'm on my way down" I responded. Popping the tags from my new dress and sliding it onto my body's curves, I made sure that I was careful not to get any deodorant or baby oil gel onto it. Sitting on the edge of the bed, I strapped my shoes for the evening, grabbed my clutch bag and room key, sprayed another mist of perfume in the air as I walked through it and gave myself one last glance in the full-length mirror before heading out the door.

The lobby appeared to be more crowded than earlier as I waked through it. Maybe the hotel was hosting an event of some sort or as I would like to imagine, they were all there to witness me looking so stunning. As I circled through the revolving door, I saw Carter standing outside of a black Yukon Denali with tinted windows. He was on the phone not even looking in my direction. From the tone of his voice, the call sounded important and I did not want to interrupt. I walked closer in his direction, he peripherally sensed my presence. Looking me from head to toe, he informed the caller on the other end of the call that he needed to go. His staring made me feel uncomfortable. I felt shy as his undivided attention was on me. "Damn girl, you look amazing. I knew you would look nice, but you are wearing the hell out of that dress" as he continues to stare. Unable to remove his eyes from my silhouette, "let me get that door for you" he insisted. As we ride to our destination we made small talk about the ceremony dinner that we are soon to arrive at, when my phone starts to ring. Like clockwork, Kris is calling me just as I presumed, the only thing that I didn't account for was for him to call me while I was out and about. The atmosphere of the car ride was way too quiet to take the call, had we already been at the dinner that would be one thing, but this absolutely wasn't the time. I declined the call, sending him straight to voicemail. Just as the call stopped ringing, my phone notified me that I had 2 texts waiting to be read from Brandon. I'll read them and text him back once I get some downtime during the affair. I'm positive that I would have some alone time while Carter was out fraternizing with his colleagues.

Carter and I continued to discuss his job, his position, and the award that he was being honored with, as I probed for more information that I could use in conversation at the gala. Arrived at our destination, the driver opens both doors and we exit the vehicle, proceeding to the hotel. Immediately I take notice of an abundance of elegantly dressed people standing around in the lobby laughing and conversing. Tuxedo wearing hosts offered hors d'oeuvres and held trays of champagne flutes, offering drinks to each person passing through the threshold of the events doors. I attend events like this annually, but from the way Carter downplayed it I guess I was taken back by the number of people present. Ok, to be honest, I wasn't expecting so many white people. From where I was standing, I didn't see anyone who looked like us. They must be already seated or running late as our culture tends to be famous for. Staying close, but not trying to smother him, I stuck near to Carter's side as he began to introduce me to his business associates. His counterparts complimented me on my dress and criticized Carter for keeping me such a secret all this time. The odd part is that every time someone did complement my beauty, they would say it to him as if he had something to do with it. I get it from my momma, thank you very much.

As the dinner begins, I have already been introduced to an estimated 20 to 25 people, not including their spouses, ranging in various positions from the president of the company to CEO to administrative personnel, and those in between. They all were very kind and personable and spoke and thought very highly of Carter. Throughout the meet and greet session, not once did he forget about or neglect my presence. He made sure that I was ok just as he said he would. Randomly asking if I was ok, needed a drink, or needed to use the bathroom, he was a true gentleman. In the past, I'm usually the one who has made sure Kris was comfortable when we would go to my work-related events, and when it came to his events, he would either go alone or he took his wife, since everyone knew he was married. He gives the excuse of it being none of his co-worker's business what he did outside of work, plus his wife had become friends with the spouses of other associates and it would just cause too much drama. In the beginning, I would feel some type of way about it, but after a while, I stopped asking and he stopped mentioning them ahead of time. He came to the realization that I needed to be occupied in order to distract me from stressing about how much I wish I was there instead of her. To prevent backlash and me giving him attitude, he would either compensate monetarily or with gifts. This felt different. To be shown off and bragged about, having my feelings taken into consideration, I liked how it felt even if it was a lie.

With 12 place settings arranged at our table, next to me sat the President's wife. She looked about 5 years younger than me, which could have been 35 years her husband's junior. On her hand sat a diamond that looked like it was weighing her wedding finger down. With blonde streaked hair and a short a fully contoured face, she wore a form fitting black dress with black strappy Stuart Weitzman shoes. I closely watched as she interacted with her husband. She appeared to be appropriately catering, patient, submissive, and entertained by all of his innuendos and jokes. My mind was preconditioned to believe she was a gold-digging woman with this older man more than likely for his money, but she pretended to really be in love with him. The way that she looked at him, the way she touched and held his hand, it was genuine. But he was far from attractive. Maybe over the years she had grown to love him? That would be my speculation. I didn't know their story, but I was curious, and I had questions. I knew not to dare ask but, in the event, that they felt the urge to share I would be here for it.

During dinner we engaged in conversation consisting of the weather here in Texas, the food and drinks of the night, fashion, rudimentary politics, her children, etc. Very pleasant and inviting, by the end of our conversation, she ended up requesting for Carter and me to meet up with them at their hotel for breakfast and mimosa's poolside on Sunday morning. Being that Sunday is 2 days away, there's no telling the status of Carter and I's relationship by then. With his arm around my chair, Carter leaned in to whisper in my ear. As he pulled himself closer to my ear, my body flinched. My body's reaction to his body heat and minted breath gave me a chill and had made my nipples hard. "If you haven't heard it enough this evening, you are very beautiful." Blushing and now kind of horny, I slightly shifted my body in his direction. I placed my hand on his thigh and smiled. Moving his chair closer, his arm was still around my shoulders as the speakers prepared to take the stage. Four speakers in and he still hadn't been honored; so much for having Cinderella home before midnight. Fighting the urge to use the bathroom, I continued to hold off from excusing myself in fear that I might miss his recognition. Had this been one of my events, Kris and I probably would have snuck off for a short "session" and would've been making our way back now, hoping that no one noticed our absence. Even if I were to suggest my rated R idea, Mother Nature was not on my side. In addition to the way I was feeling, I felt thus far, I had already made an outstanding impression on his friends and social group, I didn't want to tarnish it. Planning my escape plan, when the next speaker goes to sit down, I'll sneak out causing the least amount of disruption possible.

As I heard the award-winning recipient wrap up his speech, I excused myself letting Carter know that I was going to go to the bathroom. He offered to walk me as a gentleman would, but I declined. "I don't want you to be in the hallway when they go to present you with the award." I whispered. He didn't show the least bit of concern. "I'll be ok" I added. In between the applause and transition of speakers, he pulled out my chair and extend his hand in assistance. Grabbing my bag, I headed towards the doors which lead out to the lobby area. Stopping to ask an employee for directions to the women's lavatory, I walked with some extra pep in my step. After utilizing the facilities and freshening up, I caught a glimpse of myself in the mirror as I washed my hands. Starring at my reflection for a second, I stopped just to take in everything that was happening. I am living on the edge. Carter along with his commendable gentleman attributes along with the people I've encountered, I was feeling beautiful, worthy, and truly appreciated, all the things that I hadn't felt in a long time. I realized that for so long I had been settling for less that I deserved, I forgot how it felt to be treated so good I've ignored the idea that this feeling, that something like this, can exist. Right in that moment I realized that I needed to take charge of my dating life.

Sure, in my current relationship, I was lavished and bathed in gifts and money and I knew he loved me, but tonight, these feelings, they put a lot into perspective. My concentration was abruptly broken by the faint sound of a round of applauses. Giving myself one final look over, I headed back into the occasion, fearing I was missing something important. Back at my table, I made it just in time for the speaker to start singing all the wonderful praises in Mr. Carter Grant's honor. Taking a seat, my newly found friend and her beautifully aligned pearly white teeth, gently squeezes my arm in excitement, as she points to Carter. Signifying that it was his turn to be awarded, she appeared to be more excited than I was. In all actuality, she probably was. She at least knew the man.

Looking over at him, he's relaxed, calm and cool. My anxiety would have been on 100 right now, but he's just sitting here, arm extended across the back of my chair, gently stroking his fingers across my upper arm, I'm happy…. for him.

The older gentleman presenting him with the award was a familiar face from earlier this evening. As he spoke highly of Carter's character to me, his face lit with excitement. He assured me that Carter was a good man. I could tell that Carter was well liked and the attitudes towards him seemed to be genuine. Mostly everyone that I had the opportunity to speak with all had the same great things to say about him, and with what I had witnessed in less than 24 hours, I believed them. The grey-haired man had an incredible sense of humor and was witty. We laughed and joked for a good 10 minutes before making our rounds to the next group of people. As he began to speak, I could feel all eyes of the predominately white crowd gleaming at us, probably more so on Carter, but since I was next to him, I felt that all my moves and expressions were in jeopardy of being scrutinized. I wanted to display the most honorable image to that I could portray, so I scooted a little closer to him and placed my hand back on his leg. I could feel my table neighbor friend just staring and smiling. As the speaker raved in Carter's favor in his contributions to the company, I came to the realization that something has got to be wrong with him. Yup, he must be crazy or something. His ex-wife probably found out once it was too late and left him when she couldn't take it anymore and the reason he's allegedly single is because everyone else already knows. We'll I won't be the fool. Nope, not this girl right here. You got to wake up pretty early…My thoughts were interrupted by a standing ovation. As I stood to my feet to participate in the congratulatory cheering, he turns towards me, hugs and kisses me. Oh my gosh, I hope my expression didn't show that I was completely caught off guard. So, he's just going to ride this thing out, huh? I agreed to be his date not his fake girlfriend or nowadays is it all the same thing? I'm not good at dating, I haven't been courted in some time now. His lips were so soft though, I wonder if he uses Vaseline.

Going up the steps to receive his award on stage. He begins thanking his colleagues for the opportunities that he has had, his growth from within the company, and then he says, "last but not least, I'd like to thank my angel, Brooke." We make eye contact. Me? What the hell is going on? Am I being punked? "If it wasn't for her, I wouldn't be standing here right now. It's because of her kindness, gentle spirit and great fashion that I'm am standing before you. Without her guidance and dedication, I'm lost." Well, technically, I guess he isn't lying, but I don't trust a man who can play with his words that effortlessly. For one, I'm good at doing it, we can't be up here smooth bullshitting each other. Returning to his seat, he leans in and softly kisses my cheek. Concluding the 2-and-a-half-hour ceremony, it's time to party.

With a few more glasses of champagne and several top shelf Grey Goose and cranberry juice, I was turned up, as the young kids say. The DJ was rocking, and Carter and I dominated the dance floor. I danced with some of his associates, I cupid shuffled, did the Nae-Nae, wobbled, "ju ju'ed on the beat", hit em with a little two step, and even took it back with the electric slide. I danced until I sweated my hair out. It's been a long time since I've partied that hard. I really had a good time, I was glad that I decided to go. Waiting outside as the car arrived, the humidity wasn't as severe, but undoubtedly it was still hot, not to mention, my feet were on fire. The valet couldn't come fast enough, I needed to sit down somewhere to give these puppies a break. I have one rule and that's never to take my shoes off and go barefoot even when they hurt. I will endure the pain gracefully and slowly walk away. I refuse to look like a pigeon out in these streets. As the car arrived, I couldn't get into it fast enough. Falling into the leather seats, I let out a sigh. "So, did you have a good time or what?" Carter asked. "I did, I did, I had a blast. I haven't partied that hard in a long time. Thank you for allowing me to tag along." "Tag along?" he laughed, "I invited you, that's not what tagging along is. But I am glad that you enjoyed yourself. We actually ended up staying much longer than I had intended for us to and I do apologize for that." "Oh please, it definitely is not an issue. Like I said, I really enjoyed myself." I rebutted. Rolling down my window, "It is such a beautiful night, this air and light breeze feels amazing right now." Agreeing with my statement, "Yes, it is. It's most definitely a much-needed break from earlier today; it was hot as all hell. How u feeling now? You still got a little energy left in you? I don't want to wear you out or anything." I'm not 100% sure where he's going with this conversation, but I aint that drunk, and I haven't had that much fun. Ok, I am feeling good and I did have a nice time, but so what, he's not getting any of this kitty. And if his plans had anything to do with me walking any further than from this car to my room, he can forget about that too, my feet won't have it.

Giving him an awkward look, "I'm not sure how to answer that." I brace myself for his response. So far, he has brought me an amazing dress and has had me serve as an escort to this job event where we went through the motions of pretending to be a real couple, we're both intoxicated, and I just know he's about to be talking some slick shit. Like, what man wouldn't? I refuse to go back to his room. I mean, had this been a few years earlier, I might've been down. But I've learned the hard way from being young and reckless. I'd like to think that I've matured once I reached my 30's. I now only participate in engagements of consistent and trustworthy dick. "It's not that type of question girl" he says laughing, "I wasn't sure if you were in a rush to go back to the room or not, but it's still fairly early and the night is still young." "Well, what did you have in mind sir?" I asked. "One of my co-workers told me about a place downtown to check out while I was here in town. I was thinking that maybe you would want to actually "tag along" this time. But if you're tired, don't worry about it. I can either go alone or I can just check it out next time I happen to come out this way. No pressure and no strings attached" he said. I swear my feet cringed when he revealed his plans. If I had brought my flip flops, I would've been down, but there was no way I was going to be able to pull off not even another 5 minutes.

Regretfully, I was going to have to decline his offer. "As tempting as that sounds and don't get me wrong, I would really love to, but I have some work that I need to prepare for tomorrow morning. See, actually, I was supposed to have worked on it before I even arrived. It needs to be completed in preparation for a site that I am scheduled to visit in the morning, but how about lunch tomorrow? Maybe I wasn't paying attention if you said it or not, but how long are you even in town for? Oh, and did I happen to mention that your CEO's wife invited us both out for breakfast?" He looked and me and gave me the puppy dog sad face. "Don't do that. I don't mind coming outside to play, but shamefully, I've been procrastinating for the past few days. Had I done what I was supposed to do before I even got here, I wouldn't be in this predicament." Still maintaining his sad face now accompanied by a whimpering noise, he was really putting on an act. "But it's my day", he says. Laughing out loud, and covering my face, "Ok, ok, ok… besides the fact that I have a shitload of work to do, my feet say NO! They shall not be moved! I literally cannot feel my third toe, it is officially numb. If I go back to the hotel to change my shoes, I'll want to change clothes too, maybe into something a little bit more non-restrictive. I'll end up sitting on the edge of the bed, hopefully not lying across it, allowing my body to get comfortable. Then there will be a very good probability that I'm not going to want to come back out. If you're going to be here for a few days, we've got time. I'm not going anywhere, everything in moderation."

"For the record, I wouldn't have let you walk far. And actually, these new shoes aren't as comfortable as you think. It just sounds a little soft and insensitive for a man to complain about his feet hurting in the presence of a woman who's been wearing the hell out of 6-inch heels for the past few hours. But it's ok, like I said before, there's no pressure. It's fine really. We could do lunch or dinner tomorrow, if you and your feet feel up to it." I agree and accept his invitation yet again, "sounds like a plan." Somewhere between our agreement to meet up the next day and him telling the driver our destination, I drifted off to sleep. I was awoken 30 minutes later by his gentle caress of him smoothing my hair away from my face. "We're here" he says as I struggle to open my eyes. Picking my head up from his shoulder and adjusting my eyes from the bright lights of the hotel's valet area, I glanced at my surroundings. Oh God, I hope I wasn't snoring. I've been told that I tend to snore after I've been consuming heavy amounts of alcohol. After taking a stretch and mentally preparing to take this pilgrimage to my room, I congratulated him once again for his achievements, thanked him for the invite to the event and apologized for being such a party pooper and placed a goodnight kiss on his cheek. Once the driver opened the door and extended his hand to help me out of the car, all I longed for the feeling of getting off my feet and laying in the bed. It sucked too, because in all reality I did have work to do but I couldn't imagine tonight would be productive.

What a night, and its only Thursday, that's all I could think to myself as I managed to use the last bit of muscles in my face to form a smile. I'm ready to officially turn in as I walk painfully pass the main desk trying to be as discreet as possible. I didn't want to give off the impression that my feet were feeling as if they are bleeding and on fire.

Making my way to the elevator I noticed random people scattered in the lobby standing completely still, gazing at the large flat screen television that was positioned on the wall. I couldn't help but to have my attention diverted. CNN was on and they were reporting an incident which occurred hours prior. Unable to audibly hear clearly what was being reported, I squinted my eyes in attempts to read the captions that slowly scrolled across the screen. An African American teenage boy had been fatally shot by a Texas police officer. Under the scope of national breaking news this evening was Denton, Texas, a small town with a little over 118,000 residents, was less than 30 miles north of where I was staying. I couldn't help but overhear this middle-aged white male standing approximately 5 feet from me say to another random woman standing closer to him, "Here we go again. Now they've just given these people another excuse to just go steal, or should I say loot....no, I'm sorry I mean riot. You know you have to be politically correct these days or everyone will be all up your ass deeming you too be a racist" as he uses his fingers as quotation marks. "These people don't even wait to hear the whole story before they start destroying shit. For God's sake let the people in charge do their damn job, that's what they get paid to do. Allow justice to be served in the court of law. The truth will eventually come out. The kid was probably up to no good anyways. He was probably drinking or getting high on those pills or marijuana, as they usually are, being a damn menace to someone or their property. And where were his parents? I'll bet that they'll be coming on the screen next talking about how he so innocent and never got into any trouble. Cut the crap. Pull his school records, I bet he's been a problem ever since he was a kid. And I'm almost positive there's some sad story that they have for that too. Oh, they're poor, his dad's incarcerated for selling dope, rape, or murder, his mother was probably home watching one of those trashy black shows, or reality tv, or whatever they're called, not caring that her other 12 kids are out terrorizing other civilians and the community. Those people always have an excuse."

The lady he was speaking to remained silent, she never said a word. She just continued to stare at the television as she listened. He kept talking, "Then...then, to make matters worse, that damn Al Sharpton and Jesse Jackson gone come into town bringing all those Negro groups and church leaders protesting, pretending to call for peace, but that's really not what they want. They just want to get their little 10 minutes of fame, get everyone all rowdy, and in an uproar, then leave once those people start to burn down everything and ruin what we work so hard for. Black lives matter? Huh, don't all lives matter? This whole so-call movement is nothing but trouble if you ask me." "Too bad nobody asked you" is what I thought to myself. The man was obviously feeling some type of way about the situation, but he wasn't as half outraged as I was. My body had been running on fumes but my second wind was now being triggered by my adrenaline. I was eager to bite into his ass. Please don't get me started. In recent events, month after month, there have been more civil rights altercations and police brutality awareness conflicts, one after another. I was disgusted and irate at the man's responses to what we were all witnessing.

To say something or not to say something is the question? In past experiences, I've found it better to remain silent because of the atmosphere that I was in, i.e. work or some type of professional setting where it could negatively reflect on my character if the situation were to escalate. But here, no one knew me and none of my business partners or company personnel were here, I could go all the way on his white ass. I'm pretty sure that I could take this white bitch too if she decided she had something to say. I mean what's the worst that could happen? They call security on me? And in the event that it did get physical, I guess they could ask me to leave, or lock me up, then next thing you know, they'd find my body hanging from my cell in some Texas prison, trying to convince my family that I committed suicide. I truly understand that every action doesn't warrant a reaction, but how much is a person really supposed to take? I've sat back countless amounts of times where someone has expressed their point of views regarding racial issues without using better judgment or being mindful of those surrounding them, without saying a word because I know how passionate I am and how defensive I can get at times. I've encounter racism plenty of times and turned the other cheek.

To be young and black in my position at work, I've dealt with it more times than I'd like to count. I'm not a racist.

Do I think that all white people are bad? Hell no. In fact, I have white people that I consider to be my close friends. I have work associates that I absolutely adore, hell, I just partied and socialized with some of the whitest people ever created, a whole damn company of them. But what I can't and will not tolerate are those individuals who act as if they are entitled to everything and who refuse to recognize and acknowledge when there are racial injustices and disparities. Do I think that all police officers are bad? No. It just so happens that the negative light that is constantly illustrated and broadcasted outshines the works of those officers who wholeheartedly feel that they can make a difference. In the past year or so the racial tension has become so edgy, that everyone just looks to blaming a selected group of individuals to place blame as a quick fix to the issues that we are facing. Do I think that these issues have continued to occur and thrive since the civil rights era when our grandparents and parents fought for equal rights? Yes, but with the advancement of modern technology such as camera phones, body cameras, and those street cameras that were placed in the "higher crime areas", outlets such as your social media (your Facebook, Twitter, & Instagram, etc.) have given the people a voice and platform to express themselves whether positive, negative or stupid, allowing images and videos to circulate worldwide causing the up rise and awareness of people everywhere.

The difference is I am a part of the generation that was taught to remain humble, to use better judgment and to be non-violent and steadfast. I had to remember not to speak too loudly and appear ghetto and to let my intelligence and hard work speak for me. Unlike this newer generation who have proven to be much more forceful, but not as wise, I was raised differently. The younger "millennials" have a total disregard for authority and ignore the evidence of a system that has been designed and formulated to execute their future. Our youth have been repetitively failed by our school systems and securitized by society. But this time, with no one looking, what would I choose to do? Sit back and let it slide once again or address the sickening and disturbing statement that I had just witnessed from this ignorant man? Technically, he wasn't talking to me, I just happened to overhear his choice of words which he was expressing to someone else. Was he allowed to have such a flawed opinion? Would I be fulfilling the stereotype that obviously he already has about "my people" by intervening?

I decided against listening to the voice of the bad angel over on my left shoulder. The voice suggested that I walk up to the couple and punch them both in the face, instead I decided to take a more mature route. I walked over to where the two were standing with their eyes still focused on the TV. I made direct eye contact with both individuals, subliminally encouraging them to say something that I didn't like so I could raise all types of havoc in this lobby. As I patiently stood there letting my presence be known, I desperately wanted to see if he had the balls to continue to talk shit with me standing in visible range. Clearing my throat, I stood there as all three of us watched in unison.

Here I am, a well-dressed black woman from the hood of Philly, raised by a single mom with the help of her mother. I've attended public schools and community colleges until I saved enough money to be able to attend a prestigious HBCU. Someone, who less than 1 hour ago, just dined, partied, and brushed shoulders with some of the upper echelon Caucasians, and not once did I ever feel out of place or as if I was being judged. Maybe it was my fine hair texture, my outrageously over-priced handbag or shoes that help silence the silent stigma of my blackness. Maybe it was my fancy dress, or maybe it was because I was the guest of their token breadwinning Negro, which made them accept my presence without feeling threatened. Whatever the case was, it was all bullshit and now I am completely disgusted with the thought of having to defend my people over something as simple as the color of their skin. I find myself standing here, no longer focusing on what has captured the room's attention, but patiently waiting for an eruption of their conversation amongst each other. My eagerness to catch them amid expressing their race biased comments once again, is fueling my adrenaline.

After standing there in complete silence, for what felt like 20 minutes on my pained feet and numbed third toe, I excused myself and gracefully walked away. Walking between the small wedge that separated them both, I was literally provoking them to say something. I could feel their eyes on me as I turned my back towards them in route towards the elevators. I wanted badly to turn around to confirm my suspicions of the stares I felt coming my way, but I knew deep down inside that I was already acting out of character. With a quick turn of my head, I locked eyes with the female that the asshole was conversing with. I shot her a look which made her quickly refocus her vision towards the floor. I wouldn't usually create a scene, but I was ready for her...and him.

Returning to my room, I found myself pacing the floor, walking past the mirror acting out what I should've said. I hate when I'd found myself in this position, it happens way too often then I am willing to accept. I've grown tired of always making the decision of having to take the high road all the time. I'm convinced, it was those evil shoes!! They impaired my judgement. With my flip flops now on my feet, I can finally think straight. Now I am upset with myself. What's the worst that could've happened if I voiced my opinion? Just like he freely expressed his, I had the same right. At this point, I was way too amped to sleep, I was wide awake. I grabbed my phone to call Sabrina as I always do when I needed to vent, then I decided not to call. She was home with her family and besides there was a small time difference. I guess I'll tackle this one alone.

Maybe those individuals were still standing down there, I could go back and get this off my chest and then maybe I'd feel better. Just as soon as the thought crossed my mind, the phone vibrated. It was Mr. Grant calling to check on me and the condition of my feet, he also wanted to let me know that he had made it back safely to his room. He went on about the rants & raves that he got on his clothing choices for the night and his praises of his date for the evening. Speaking with him for a short moment seemed to calm me down and divert my attention from the incident downstairs. "Honestly, I'm surprised that you're even still up? I imagined you would already be laid across the bed by now, shoes possibly still on, but your legs hanging off the bed." He laughed, "I know you did say that you had work to do, but you were knocked out on the ride home, I figured it was a wrap for you. I can honestly see that you're a dedicated and advent worker because I more than likely would've just opted to deal with whatever I needed to do in the morning, personally." "It's funny that you say that", I replied. After debating whether or not I was going to tell him my story, I decided that someone's ear was gonna have to be the sacrificial lamb tonight, especially if I couldn't go back downstairs. I asked if he had heard of the incident in Denton as I brought him up to speed on everything that had occurred since I'd left him. I wasn't too sure where his feelings stood with the current events of the Trayvon's, the Sandra Bland's, the Renisha McBride's, the Freddie Gray's, and the many others making national news within the last year. I didn't want to come off too Black Panther-ish, but I needed an outlet for my frustration. Although I did stop to consider his outlook may have been a little different given the nature of where he lived and his non-ethnic friends that I had just been introduced to, but I decided to proceed anyway. To my surprise, he agreed with me and unknowingly encouraged my emotions. We then began exchanging stories of our corporate encounters with racism and how we tackled it.

Leaving Durham following the passing of his grandparents, he was raised by foster parents in Oakland, California. His decisions on how he chose to combat his racial motivated incidents were more recently taken with the consideration of his children in mind. He made sure that he rationalized the entire situation and the effects of the consequences that could ultimately affect not only him as an individual, but them as a family; mine were made solely on the premises of me not willing to jeopardize my good paying job and its benefits. It was relieving and comforting to realize how conscious and "woke" he was; it was a breath of fresh air.

Shortly thereafter, we both agreed to let each other off the phone since it had grown late and we both had things to do in the morning. We agreed to touch base in the afternoon in regard to scheduling a time to meet up. With what little energy I had left, I managed to crack open my laptop and attempt to do some work but honestly, that's about as far as it got. Waking up at 5:13am to a full face of makeup on, my dress tossed at the foot of the bed and the computer still on my lap with the welcome screen still glaring, I knew

I had drank too much, my head was pounding. Regaining consciousness, I had work to be done, I needed to, as the older people would say, put some pep in my step. Taking care of what I needed to for work, I showered and got dressed. Letting the local news station on the television serve as my background noise, I threw my flats in my bag and mentally convinced myself that I was ready to take on the day.

Work seemed to drag as I constantly reminisced about the night before. From one worksite to another, time felt like it was moving at turtle speed. Coffee with a double shot of expresso didn't seem to work and I was all out of the small pocket mints that I grabbed a handful of at the ceremony last night; I needed a power nap. The only thing that was keeping me energized were the small conversations and texts that I exchanged with my family and friends throughout the day. Even though I had such an amazing time with Carter last night, Kris was still on my mind. I talked to him several times throughout the day, intentionally omitting the details of the party, however I did mention the hotel incident. He knew all too well how these situations made me feel so it is easy for him to empathize. Talking to him for a good portion of the day, it was now time for Carter and me to meet up. We agreed that a late lunch/early dinner worked well for both of our schedules, as he advised me to wear some comfortable shoes, so I couldn't bail out on him again.

Completing my work day, I headed back to the room to catch some quick z's. I set an alarm on my phone which should've given me enough time to get ready before our outing, but I'm a habitual time offender. I needed to be on time today especially since I volunteered to drive since he drove yesterday. Mapping out my directions, he was only about 20 minutes away from where I was so that gave me extra time to sleep.

Staying at the Omni hotel, I arrived at the beautifully designed building of the address he provided. When I pulled up, I thought to myself, "This looks like money." Out of all the times I've been on business here, I never really cared to venture out much in the aspects of staying at a different hotel. I was satisfied and comfortable with what I knew but next time I may have to navigate away from my safety net. Curious to see what the inside looked like, I was too shy to ask to come up to his room, I'd rather check it out online later, I'm sure they had plenty of reviews and pictures. As I waited for him to come down, I started to google the best food places in Dallas just in case he hadn't already had a place in mind. Nothing is more annoying than 2 people trying to figure out what they want to eat, going back and forth with "I don't know" and "It's up to you". I wasn't going to be that girl...at least not today. "Oh, excuse me, well aren't we fancy?" He asks upon entering the car. Smelling as wonderful as last night, I wasn't sure if he was talking about me or the car, on second thought it had to be the car because I was dressed very comfortably, but who knows, maybe he was just stroking a girl's ego; either way I didn't bother to respond. "I'm hungry!" he blurted out, "how about you?" I was. Actually, I was starving and that hangover I was suffering from had me hungrier than a hostage.

"I can eat" I managed to say with my stomach loudly growling. I figured he would want to go somewhere fancy, me, I was easy to please. Chipotle and Panera were my go-to places, closely followed by my favorite fast food place Chick-fil-a; it didn't take much to make me happy. "How about BBQ, isn't that what Texas is known for?" he asked.

With one eyebrow raised, I replied, "Yeah, I guess, that and Mexican food." We both laughed. He felt as if he should eat something out of his normal everyday menu selections. So, I'm guessing that they don't do much grilling or barbequing out in Cali because that's what he decided on. After finding an undersized BBQ spot, where the food was absolutely amazing, we took a walk down by the Arts District. Talking to him felt like we had known each other for years. Our chemistry was amazing, and we meshed very well. He was down to earth, chill & relaxed, with a great sense of humor. Never once did he attempt to push up on me or come on to me, it was a refreshing feeling. We walked and talked about our families, shared and took pictures, talked politics & current events, discussed sports and made each other laugh until our stomachs hurt. As we talked and basked in each other's company, the night grew older and the scenery became more beautiful. Buildings lit up and the sound of water from the surrounding fountains, in addition to the gorgeous weather, made the scenery picture perfect. We had been out so long that we became hungry again. We stopped in a restaurant where we agreed to dine but when I got back from the restroom, I found Mr. Grant making conversation with another patron who had convinced Carter that we should try some local truck that had remarkable food. After partaking in 2 shots of Tequila at the bar with the gentleman whom made the suggestion, we began to head in that direction. Stumbling upon a plethora of parked food trucks (with all similar, if not the same, food selections) we found it hard to remember the specifics of what the man had told us.

We ended up patronizing 5 various food trucks, ordering at least 1 item off of each menu that we would share. This go-round our themed choice of food was Tex-Mex. We found seating on the steps of a museum, where we created our smorgasbord as we washed down our food with frozen margaritas. I couldn't speak for him, but I was feeling good and feeling my alcohol. In the midst of our foolishness, he had neglected to check in with his baby girls. The youngest one decided to check in on her daddy and to give him a piece of her mind via FaceTime. Too inebriated, I failed at attempting to hold in my laugher, as she questioned and probed his unaccounted for whereabouts. She loved her father and that was very evident. It was obvious that he had a great relationship with them; it almost resembled the relationship that I had growing up with my mother.

"What's that noise? Who's that laughing Daddy? Are you with someone?" she interrogated. He semi-straightened his face as he introduced me as "his friend" Ms. Brooke, via video chat. I tried my best to pull it together as I returned stares at these two stunning brown girls struggling over the phone in attempts to catch a glimpse of who I was. I made small conversation with them both as they smiled from ear to ear and bombarded me, question after question. They wanted to know where I lived and how often I got to see the President. I'll admit, they were the most well-spoken, intellectually adorable children I had ever encountered. Carter intervened and asked if they called to speak with me or him. He was getting jealous that I was getting all his attention. The youngest one apologized to him as I heard the oldest one whisper, "She's really pretty daddy. When can we meet her?" Quickly he shifted the topic of conversation off of me and continued to inquire about their day and what was going on in their lives since he had been gone. As he carried on his conversation, I lie backwards and look up in the sky at the highly visible moon and stars. On a normal circumstance, I probably wouldn't ever lie on the ground, but the effects from the drinks made my body feel hot & heavy, and I felt unable to support my head. Thinking to myself, what my life would have been like if I had decided to have kids and what our relationship would've been like. I hadn't thought about kids since I was fresh out of school and Kris and I had a miscarriage. We tried again after that for a month or two, but then I lost interest. I became more focused on my career, making money, and enjoying what was left of my 20's with my girls, that was, just until life put us all on different paths.

With his girl's time zone being two hours behind ours, he realized that it was late, even for them, and sternly suggested the idea of them settling down and getting ready for bed. After they say their "I love you' s" and "I miss you' s", the call comes to an end. "Are you ok?" he asks. "I'm fine" I reply as he leans down next to me, supporting his head with his elbow. As he stares at me as I look back at him. He looks as if he wants to say something or like he has something on his mind, but he doesn't say anything. If we were in a romantic comedy movie, this is where he would lean in and kiss me as fireworks go off in the background, but this isn't a movie, this is real life. "I don't know about you, but this ground is hard as shit! I aint sat this long on concrete since I was a kid. My ass is numb, my damn arm is stiff, and I only been laying on my elbow for less than 3 minutes. I feel like it's going to snap when I move it. And you're up here laying down like it's a damn Posturepedic mattress or something, get up girl." His accent made things that much funnier, because for some reason, probably the alcohol, I couldn't stop laughing. I literally had tears coming from my eyes. "Ok grandpa, let's go." I suggested.

Back at the car, neither of us thought it was a good idea for me to drive, so he volunteered to drive back to the hotel. My body, still overheated, hadn't given my kidneys this

kind of workout in a long time. 3 days of drinking and staying out late, who did I think I was. Still carrying on a conversation with my forearm covering my eyes, I reclined my seat. I felt my phone start to vibrate and then I quickly remembered that my phone had been paired with the rental, I could tell by the ringtone that it was Kris. I knew that the car was currently displaying his name on the digital dashboard as well as the navigation screen. I never even opened my eyes or reached in my bag to turn it off. "Do you need to get that?" he asked. "Nope", I replied as I felt for the button on the side of the phone to reject the call. He didn't mention anything about it and neither did I. Carter asked how I felt and if I was ok to drive. His hotel was not far from the area where we had been for the past several hours. He suggested that if I wanted him to, he could drop me off back at my hotel and catch a cab back or he offered to let me come to his room until I got myself together. He offered up his bed and said that he would sleep on the pull-out sofa. I knew that I would ultimately be ok driving and technically I wasn't drunk, I just don't like to take chances in areas that I wasn't extremely familiar with. I also knew that I did not want to stay the night as his hotel, and with the clock reading 1:30am already, there wasn't much more that we could do or talk about.

I explained that I was ok to drive, but he didn't believe me. He insisted that I at least come in and get a bottled water. I couldn't tell if he was genuinely concerned or plotting, but I gave him the benefit of the doubt, despite all the crazy murderous stories that I frequently watched on the ID channel. He had the car valeted as he escorted me into the lobby of his hotel. "We can either chill down here and I can grab you a water or there we can go upstairs." He must have read my facial expression and knew that I was unsure about the options presented. "I don't want to pressure you" he said, "I just want to make sure that you're ok, I wouldn't want to live with that on my conscious if something happened after you left." "No, it's fine. We can go up. I trust you. I still have my stun gun that my mother gave me, in my bag for if you try anything funny." I said jokingly. "Aren't they illegal?" he asked. "Only if you get caught with it" I said. "You are something else Ms. Philly. Or is it Ms. DC? What do you prefer? Cuz, you know, I'm Cali all day baby!" he responds. "I'm a Philly girl til I die. I'm an Eagles fan, a Phillies fan, a Flyers fan, even a Philadelphia Soul fan, no matter what, win or lose. Don't get it fucked up." I say with the most serious face I can make. A man walking by says "I'm sorry to hear that." We all burst out in laugher, creating a scene and causing other people to stare. The passerby and Carter give each other the fist bump, while I'm standing there with the "I eat ass face", as Kevin Hart would say.

On to the elevators, he held my arm as if I was some drunken hot girl he was leading to his room after a night of partying, but I wasn't even drunk. Once we entered the suite, the first thing that caught my eye was the breathtaking view he had of the city from his oversized window. The room was filled with the scent of his cologne and was exquisitely decorated. It was absolutely amazing. I stood and looked out the window in amazement as he prepared me a glass of ice water. He hands me the glass and stands next to me as I admire the view. We sit on the couch and talk a little bit more before he decides to turn on the television.

Flipping through the stations, trying to find something that could possibly hold our attention, I casted my vote for Law & Order SVU, but he shoots it down. He says that his oldest daughter watches that show day in and day out. I go on and on telling him how it is also my favorite show of all time and how I could just sit and watch it without a care in the world too. Continuing to totally disregard my request, he continues to channel surf. Getting up to fix him a drink, I gain control of the remote, now I'm in charge. I stop at the CNN channel to see what was on. It's the 2nd night in a row that they are still reporting the live coverage of what happened in Denton. They are interviewing the residents and showing live footage of what the town looks like. Tonight nothing seems to be on fire, just an elaborate presence of police officers in riot gear, residents taunting the officers with profanity and homemade posters, and although debris being randomly tossed around, for the most part, it just seems to be a large mass of individuals, both white and black, standing on the streets in these late hours.

Being that it is a Friday night (Saturday morning) and the weather was comfortable, I'm almost sure a clear majority of people didn't have to work in the morning and kids didn't have school so that gave them free range to be out all night creating all sorts of disorder and making unfavorable situations for city officials. Carter stands and looks at the report while sipping his drink. I apologized for turning the station because it awkwardly changed the energy of our atmosphere. He explained that there was no need to apologize and how he was equally tormented by the situation. He goes further into detail about his experiences growing up and how he is racially profiled, almost on a weekly basis, especially because he drives a nice car and frequently visits his old friends and foster family in the old neighborhood. Although he briefly expressed his feelings towards the incident last night, he explained his concerns for his daughters as he aimed at providing them with a very different lifestyle that he had coming up, by moving them into the suburbs, trying to protect them from the things that he had witnessed growing up. "I don't want them to be sheltered and spoiled; my goal is for them to be well-rounded, knowing the ends and outs of both sides of this world. I want them to be book smart and street smart. It's hard though. I thought by creating an environment of a loving two parent household away from the inner city, that I could make their lives easier. I could give them the things that my folks would never have been able to afford, making sure that they have what they needed, opening their eyes and minds to experiences that a majority of children where I came from will never have. I support them and encourage them in anything they have curiosity in or want to try such as sports, orchestra, cheerleading, baking, anything and everything. I'm at recitals and games, practices and parent-teacher nights. I'm basically trying to provide them with the cheat code for a head start on life, the one that I never had. I don't want them to walk around with the mentality that they're entitled to certain things, but their surrounding peers also have a major effect on how they tend to view things, so it gets hard. I need my influence on them to be bigger and stronger than the influences they have when they walk out of our home's doors. I know it sounds cliché, but I don't want them to have to deal with race issues. I know that the day will come where everything that I provide them with and instill into them won't be enough to carry them where they need to go. There will be battles that I cannot fight for them, but I don't want race to be one of them. My family criticized me for moving so far out. They say things like I'm trying to make them white or how my children won't be cultured. Honestly, I just don't think it's true. I want to protect them and shield them from the hurt and the pains of the world, but I know that I can't. Things that I've seen and done, I would try with all my power, to prevent having them go through that. I feel like it's my job to give them everything that I didn't have. A huge part of being an adult is to learn from your mistakes and learning to rectify them. My girls didn't ask to be here and I will die trying to make it my number one job to make sure that they have everything they need to survive and be successful in this world. In my life I've played on both sides of the fence. I've done the streets, because I was hard headed and I didn't have anyone who could get through to me. I got caught up in the wrong crowd trying to fit in and made mistakes and I've paid the consequences that will follow me throughout my life.

Luckily for me, I was able to make it out alive before it was too late. I had an OG take me up under his wing and show me the ropes, show me that it was more to life than my neighborhood. I'm no outstanding citizen, I had a late start in life and it took me a while to realize my actual potential. I started at the bottom and worked my ass off to be where I am today. When I met my wife, her family hated me and hated her for choosing to be with me. When she got pregnant with Kennedy, they wanted nothing to do with her, like completely cut her off, but she believed in me and she stuck by me as I worked my way up the corporate ladder. There were plenty of times when I had my back against the wall, ready to say fuck it and go back to what I knew best, but she kept me focused. She was the support system that every man needs. She encouraged me and held me down and spoke not only encouragement into me, but she spoke life into me. I am here today because of her." He bowed his head as he reminisced with the memories of his wife. He spoke with such passion and emphasis, I wasn't sure if he was going to cry or not. I needed another drink, but I wasn't going to, dammit, I just sobered up. After hearing him speak, I had a few questions, but I wasn't sure if this was the time or place.

When people felt the need to vent to me, I usually let them talk without interruption and/or questions. I just let them have their moment and then we'd move on. This time I agreed with him and his parenting methods, reassuring him that from my small interaction with his kids, I thought that he was doing a great job, but I wanted to know more about this wife character. What happened? I'm assuming that she wasn't still around because of how we had been interacting together and from how his children were so friendly and appeared eager to meet me. Plus, I'm almost sure that he told me that he was a single father during one of our first conversations and not to mention, he wasn't wearing a ring. He also said a lot of "I's" instead of "we's" during his statement. I was confused. "So, what are her opinions on the situation? What's her take on the way the girls are being nurtured?" He looked up in confusion, "Your wife?" I asked. He told me that she had passed away five years ago from breast cancer when Cuddles, his youngest daughter, was only two, ever since then he says it's been just him and the girls. He gives props to his foster sister for being a big help in the beginning, but he understood how the 6-hour commute on the weekends became a bit too much especially when she had her own family to raise. Carter did mention that his neighbors also were very sensitive and helpful when it came to the girls, and he had a good relationship with them. They often offered help whenever he needed, but he didn't want to be a burden. He said that he refrains from dating because his hands were completely full, and he didn't feel as if he had the time or capabilities to focus on anyone else, giving them the attention that they naturally deserved, plus he wasn't completely sure of how the girls would react. He claims to have avoided dating white women because he felt in the back of his mind that he wanted the girls to have a positive female role model, particularly someone who looked like them, to help boost their self-confidence and encourage them in the areas where he fell short. At the moment, Kennedy and Cuddles were staying at a family friend's house who also had children around the same age, from the neighborhood. Although I had only known Mr. Carter Grant for a couple days, I admired his character and his sacrifices.

I'm not exactly sure what happened in between our conversation and watching tv, but I remember waking up with a slight chill from the air conditioner, fully clothed with my shoes removed, and a blanket draped over me, still on the couch. The lights and television had been turned off, but the curtains were still fully drawn allowing me to see the sun coming up over the beautiful city skyline. I never intended on being in his room overnight. In a dilemma on whether I should go back to sleep and stay there until rest of the world wakes up or whether to quietly sneak out and just touch base with him in the morning. Giving it more thought than it was worth, I decided that I wanted to do something nice for him. Maybe I could go get breakfast and coffee and leave it for him for when he wakes up, I'm sure he doesn't get to be pampered as often. After that heart wrenching story that he expressed last night, he deserved it. Not wanting to cause any commotion, I put my sneakers on, got up from the couch and folded up the blanket. Using the light from my dim cell phone, I tried to look around on the table and counter for the valet ticket to retrieve my car. My idea was to go home get showered and dressed, grab some breakfast and bring it back as a surprise to him, maybe even prepay a spa session for him to relax. Maybe I was doing too much. I didn't have much planned for the day, and although I could always do some work (since it was the reason for me being out here), I was semi-interested in possibly going to a rally that was being held by the #BlackLivesMatter division here in Texas. I've watched protests and marches engaging the efforts of demanding justice, but I've always wondered what the atmosphere actually felt like. With tensions still running high here, I imagined that the first-hand eye witness accounts I would experience would honestly be something worth blogging about.

Not wanting to wake him and unable to find the valet stub, I stumbled upon a room key that was lying on the counter. Quickly grabbing it, I figured that this fancy ass hotel should at least serve breakfast. I'm sure people are paying an arm, a leg, and a nipple to stay here, so they ought to be offering something, a croissant, a bowl of cereal, a muffin something. Barely 7am, I ventured downstairs finding more people in the lobby than I expected to at this hour. Does anyone sleep around here? Grabbing a cup of coffee and a piece of fruit I sat in the lounging area scrolling through my phone. Being an hour ahead of my time, I felt comfortable in assuming that my friends and family back home should be awake by now. As I read over my missed texts, I was deeply surprised to notice the two unread messages from Brandon. I had totally forgotten about his entire existence since I had been preoccupied here in Texas. Before responding, I thought it'd be a good idea to give my momma a call first since she can be longwinded at times. There is not a day that goes by that I don't talk to her but you wouldn't be able to tell from our lengthy conversations. Out of all my siblings, I am that designated child who directly looks after my mother. Not saying that everyone else could care less, but what I am saying is that they could all stand to care a lot more. She began her rant with dramas of my sister and her kids doing this and that, followed by the neighborhood gossip and then lastly with an update on my grandma. Always keeping me updated on the family nonsense, poor lady, they keep her busy.

After talking with her until the lobby grew busier, I told her that I had work to do and that I planned on going to the rally. Only God knows why I let that slip from my mouth. She is such a worrywart. For the next 10 minutes she elaborated on what she had been watching on the news and how it wasn't safe out there. She explains her opinions of society's broken system and how the mentality of our people would need to change in order to see real results, blah, blah, blah. Bottom line was that she didn't approve and did not have good feelings towards it.

Promising her that I would be careful, I told her that I would check in with her later to let her know I was ok. Wrapping up our conversation, I proceeded to send Brandon a good morning text. It was early and a Saturday so there was a good chance that he wouldn't be awake yet. Wrong! He texted right back as if he had the phone sitting in his hand, I was not expecting that. He asked about the trip and made small talk, he probed on what I'd generally liked to do for fun and in my spare time. We exchanged several messages before he mentioned going for a morning run. Before ending the conversation, he expressed his interest in physically speaking with me on the phone, he wanted to hear my voice. I told him that he was welcome to call my phone anytime he'd like and that there was no need for him to make a formal request. Wrapping up we agree to chat later on that afternoon. Receiving a "good morning" text from Carter, prompted me to grab my half-drunken coffee and fruit. Purchasing items I could return to the room with for him, I picked out a variety of foods that I thought he would enjoy, even though I got a little carried away. Not taking into consideration that I wouldn't be able to carry it all, my hands and arms were full. An adorable young Hispanic hotel employee glanced at me as I struggled to balance coffees, orange juice, bottled water, and treats, and insisted to let him help me carry the items back up to the room. Extremely thankful for his kindness, I predetermined that I was going to give him a nice tip since the bitch that rang me and failed to let me know that they didn't have any carrying bags and couldn't have cared less about my struggle with her busted weave ass and obnoxiously long eyelashes. Riding the elevator, the young man and I would randomly and awkwardly make eye contact and he would just smile and wink. It felt a little peculiar but he was such a cutie so I didn't mind much. With my hand holding the coffee, I instructed the gentleman to retrieve the key from my back pocket, I knew that would slightly make his day. Entering unannounced, Carter was standing there shielding his private area with only a throw pillow from the couch, startled, as we entered through the door. Staggered and embarrassed, the young man and I both didn't know what to do. "Sorry, maybe I should've knocked" I apologized. Quickly tipping young Pedro as he placed the items on the counter, making sure not to look in Carter's direction, he thanked me, apologized once more and left.

Facing the door and my back towards Carter, I asked if it was safe to turn around. I could hear him rummaging around putting on some clothes as I explained to him what happened this morning and how I wanted to leave but couldn't find my parking slip and didn't want to wake him, etc. He didn't seem to care but was appreciative of the food gesture. "It's safe to turn around now" he said laughing. Being the simple person that I am, I still wouldn't turn around to face him. Instead, I covered my eyes with my hands as I walked backwards to the couch and sat down. I could hear him walk towards me but I refused to uncover my eyes. I could feel his presence as he stood over me. I thought to myself how I really hoped that he had clothes on, but sneakily I was kinda wishing that he didn't. I heard him say "Here." As I removed my hands from my eyes, he handed me the slip for my car. "Thanks" I said and then I thought about it for a second. "Oh, is this a sign letting me subliminally know it's time for me to leave? It's cool, I've been thrown out of way better places than this", I say as I grab for my bag. Intervening me from picking up my pocketbook, he asks why I have to be so dramatic.

Asking my plans for the day, he positions himself on the floor to prepare to exercise. Glaring in admiration at his perfect bodily stature to perform sit-ups and push-ups, I tell him my interest in going out to the rally in the afternoon or early evening. He hoped that I didn't have anything planned and would find pleasure in escorting him to meet up with some people he knew who were still in the area, also mentioning how he agreed to meet up with his CEO and his wife today for lunch. He forgot to tell me earlier that he confirmed our attendance for the lunch invite.

Who the hell does he think he is? I make my own plans, plus, who even said that I wanted to hang with him for a third day? The gig was up, how long would we have to keep this charade going? Not that his plans were a bad idea, it's just not what I wanted to do, and secretly I had hoped that he wanted to do what I wanted to do, so I wouldn't have to do it alone. And to be truly honest, I didn't remember all the bogus details surrounding the dynamic of our relationship that I constructed the other night, so it would be hard to keep the lie going. I felt myself slowly going into shut down mode and it must have been written all over my face because he quickly suggested rescheduling the meet up for another time. Making myself feel even worse, I didn't want him to cancel his plans with his CEO. This could be his moment for professional advancement and I didn't want to ruin that for him. Yeah, I didn't know him fo'real, fo'real, but I was all for uplifting the black man, I just didn't want to neglect my wants for his. I was so used to doing it with Kris because I felt obligated, but I wasn't about to let some stranger put me back in the same position. "You don't have to reschedule, you can go do your thing and I can do mine, and if you're not too busy later, maybe we can plan to meet up somewhere. Just tell your boss that I wasn't feeling well and had to stay back at the room" I offered. His demeanor displayed that he wasn't completely thrilled with my idea, but he verbally agreed.

Settling on the notion that I would touch base with him later, I got my stuff together and left. As I was waiting for valet to retrieve my car, who did I run into? Mr. and Mrs. Morris, the nice couple that I had sat with at the awards ceremony on Thursday night, the CEO of Carter's company. They were having breakfast in the lobby's restaurant. Only I would have the type of luck to run into them as I was taking my walk of shame with yesterday's clothes on; meanwhile Mrs. Morris was already dressed and flawlessly looking like Miss. America. Unpredictably Mrs. Morris, with her overly enthusiastic self, recognized and approached me and even remembered my name. After we greeted each other and asked about each other's itineraries since we last spoke, valet returned with my vehicle. Excusing myself to claim my car, I told them that I would see them around. Mrs. Morris, who preferred that I called her Barbie (oh, how fitting), reminded me that we were scheduled to have lunch and let me know that she would see me in a few hours. How was I going to tell her that I wasn't going to be able to go knowing that Carter had already RSVP'd for both of us, and obviously she could see that I'm not sick, so that lie probably wouldn't work. Smiling in agreeance, I nodded. Once in the car, I called Carter but he didn't answer. I sent him a text saying that I would be back after I got dressed, and that I would accompany him to attend lunch with Mr. Morris and his wife.

By the time that I had got back to my hotel, Carter had called me and questioned the foundations of my change of heart. I told him about the interaction that I had with the Morris's and told them that I unintentionally, non-verbally, semi agreed, that I would see them later. He insisted that if I did not want to go, that I didn't have to, he would let them know that I couldn't make it. He didn't want me to have to compromise my agenda for him. I convinced him and myself that it was fine that I could still possibly do both. Looking at the coordinates I packed while I was rushing, I was not about to let Barbie outdo me. I had an image to uphold. I threw on some heels and the best sexy casual outfit I could put together. I was not one to toot my own horn, but toot toot mutherfucker. I was feeling good and looking good with some time to spare. Being on time has never really been my strongest characteristic, so anytime that I happened to be on schedule, I would make a production of it. I also had a good habit of doing something meaningless thinking I had extra time and then ultimately wind up being late. I packed a bag with a more comfortable outfit that I could change into for the rally, if I had time.

Admiring myself in the full-length mirror, my flattering was interrupted by the ringing of my phone. Swiftly moving to answer it in time, I saw that it was Brandon, he must've already finished up his morning exercise routine. Fortunately for him, I had some extra time to spare, so I answered. His voice did not resemble what I remembered him to look like. It was strong and deep as he asked if this was a bad time for us to talk. He told me how he had seen me on several different occasions at the office when I would come and visit Sabrina and how he finally got enough liquid courage in his system to inquire about me through her. He mentioned that he was shocked when Sabrina communicated to him that I was single because he knew for sure if I wasn't married then I definitely was off the market in terms of dating. If he asked why I was single my first intention would be to act like I lost service and accidently hang up on him.

I hated when guys would ask me why I was single. How is someone really supposed to answer that? Am I supposed to downgrade myself in efforts to figure out why nobody finds me worthy enough to want to commit to a relationship, or was I supposed to men bash. Or better yet maybe I should just be honest and tell them I'm single because I'm still utterly in love with my college sweetheart who one day decided to up and marry someone else, but we still manage to fuck occasionally and so far, I've technically been content in productively sharing his time. Could that be communicated effectively without tarnishing my reputation? But lucky for me, he didn't ask. He expressed how he wanted to get to know me face to face. He didn't want to ask a million questions over the phone or have a thousand conversations via text messages; he admitted to being old school and believed in courting women and spending time with an individual to get to know them. That was the first time that I've ever talked to someone who just came out so bluntly and expressed that, it was different yet refreshing, and I liked it. I told him that I would be out here for a few more days, but I would be glad to meet up with him once I returned. We continued to talk as I prepared to head back over to the Omni Hotel for lunch. The conversation became so interesting that I even opted to take the stairs to avoid losing the call due to the lack of reception in the elevator. It was obvious he was different. Within the past several days, I've stepped out of my comfort zone, took a leap of faith, and walked on the wild side, and to be honest, I was satisfied with the results. Before I jinxed myself, I needed find a piece of wood to knock on it. The stars must be perfectly aligned in the universe because I felt my dating scene was becoming interesting.

As my phone beeped, another call was coming in from Kris. Electing to end the conversation with Brandon, I let him know that I looked forward with speaking with him again later in the day. I was on my way to have lunch with my new-found friend, plus did I happen to mention that I was looking good? My self-esteem was on 100 percent. Kris and I's phone call consisted of how my night went, how my day had been so far, what I ate, you know, normal stuff. As he ensued to tell a story about an argument between him and his wife, my mind wandered as I replayed out my conversation with Brandon in my head. Noticing that the phone call grew quiet, dammit, I missed whatever he said. He could tell that I was distracted because as I assumed, I had failed to respond to a statement that he made. "What are you doing?" He asked in an annoyed tone. "Sorry babe, I was driving, and I thought I got lost. I'm sorry. What did you say?" Irritated by the fact that I had just let him ramble on without retaining anything he said, he refused to repeat himself. I remember him saying something about the wife and something about a car which made me remember about the new car purchase that he gifted to me before I left. "So, have you taken the new car out for a ride yet?" I asked, but maybe I shouldn't have. He let out a sigh and said that if I had been listening, he had just told me about how'd he taken the car out and was driving it around when he was spotted by his wife and her girlfriend. "Wait, really? How did I miss that story?" I thought to myself. I begged for him to tell me and promised that I would give him my full undivided attention. He continues to tell me how he had been parking my car on the street, a few doors down from his house and he had woken up early to take the car to get the windows tinted, but something happened and there were a few cars ahead of him. He didn't feel like waiting so he left to run some errands and as he pulled back up to run and grab something from his house, his wife accompanied by her friend saw him getting out of the car.

He said that an argument initially ensued because she thought he had purchased a new car and didn't consult with her first, then he explained to her that he was just getting the windows tinted for a friend. She goes off on him again because she wasn't buying the story and kept badgering him for more details. Honestly, I wish I never asked to hear the story again. I let him vent because I knew he needed to, but stories that involved her almost always gave me an uncomfortable feeling. I'd sympathize with him, making him believe that his story could've actually been legit, but being the sarcastic hussy that I am, I ended my statement with, "But, it doesn't matter really because you're leaving her any day now right?" "I really am. You don't believe me? I'm just making sure that everything is straight before I leave. I'm trying to make this work this for us. It took me sometime to realize maybe I had made a mistake by actually marrying her, but I'm trying to put everything into perspective. I don't like to do this to you, you deserve to be happy. I just don't want you to be in the middle of anything. I'm pretty sure that she knows this is coming. Neither one of us is happy, and haven't we been for a while. She even says little smart things about me leaving her, I try not to feed into it though. I just have to make sure that everything is right when I go" he says. In my mind I wanted to know why he chose not to feed into it. If he knew and she knew, and what's understood didn't have to be said, what was the big fucking secret? I wish he could only see my face with my eyes rolled all the way to the back of my head. I have heard way too many of these stories, too many times and on too many different occasions. I was no longer hopeful or entertained at the thought of him possibly one day tentatively leaving.

In the event he actually chose me in the beginning and we decided to get married, I wouldn't have even required much, not saying that his wife did, but I wouldn't need any of the bells and whistles, I would have just settled for a justice of the peace license signing, nothing big and extravagant. He was all I ever wanted. Now, I've never been stupid by any means, I knew that if/when married men actually did get divorced, they're typically not in any rush to be tied down again, believe me, my mother and girlfriends have done a good job of relentlessly reminding me of it, but I considered myself to be living in the moment.

I'll admit, in the beginning when I first got wind that they were having issues and the word divorce was leisurely being tossed around, I entertained it. The thought of us being together jaded my real-life perceptions at one point, but I was brought to reality that it was probably never going to happen, and I no longer anxiously yearned for that moment. Maybe he thought that if he'd continued feeding me the same bullshit year after year, that's what continued to keep me around, but it wasn't. It was becoming more annoying than anything. At this point I'm not sure who he was still trying to convince more, me or him. Cutting him off, "Its ok, I know, I've heard this before. I can almost tell you verbatim what you're going to say before you even open your mouth, but I have to call you later, I've just arrived at this meeting. Love you", I said as I abruptly hung up the phone. I was not going to allow that conversation to affect my mood. So far, on this trip, I was having a good time surrounded by decent company and Carter didn't make me feel like my presence had to be disguised or hidden from anyone.

Valeting my car yet again, I entered the hotel as I made my way to Carter's room. Approaching the door, I could hear him talking on the phone. Due to the bass in his voice, I really couldn't make out what he was saying or figure out what the conversation was even about. Not wanting to get him in any kind of trouble or cause drama, I refrained from knocking. Instead I decided to send him a text that I was at his hotel room door to avoid disrupting his call. Maybe that was one of the side chick characteristics that I had become accustomed to throughout the years, but I wasn't sure if I should have called when I was in the lobby before I came up or not. I heard his voice stop, assuming he was reading my text, then resuming his conversation again. I still couldn't audibly make out what he was saying but I could hear his voice getting closer as he approached the door.

With the phone still to his ear, he opened the door and escorted me in. Walking directly to my favorite spot in the room I was envious of his city view. With the conversation

between Kris and I still lingering in the back of my mind, I couldn't help but to think about why I had put my life on hold thus far to basically be his hoe. Ok, I shouldn't say that, but why did my love for him run so deep that I would ultimately neglect my own needs? Clearly it wasn't about the money, that's usually always the case. There were no added benefits or incentives. The dynamics of our chemistry's foundation was genuine, yet odd. I know that I had been a handful in the past, and we'd worked the hell out of each other's nerves time to time, but we never managed to stay mad at each other for long.

He knew me back when I was a sophomore aimlessly running around partying and club hopping with my girls, maturing to the more settled version of myself now. We were all too comfortable with each other, and after failed situationships with other men, he was always there to console me and help me feel better about myself. What we possessed was deeper than anything that a title could ever give, we were in this for life regardless. Lost in my thoughts, I didn't even notice that Carter had ended his call and had complimented me on my appearance. Apologizing for zoning out, he asked me if everything was alright. Refusing to have a pity party, I brushed it off and assured him that I was fine. I wasn't going to give the situation anymore thought for now. As he put on his shoes, I went to the bathroom mirror to make sure that my makeup was still intact and that I was still looking as cute as I did when I left my hotel. "You're perfect" he said to me as I went to add another layer of mascara on my eye lashes. (Honestly, I think he was trying to prevent me from taking another 20 minutes in the mirror as some women would do, but this face was ready.) "I'm just trying to complement all this sexiness that you got going on over there", I replied jokingly, "I'm trying to match your fly. Isn't that what the kids say nowadays?" We went back and forth complementing each other for several moments before we finally came to a mutual agreement that we were both rather good looking.

The agreement was, if we had to drive, that we would use my rental since it had more space, plus I already prepaid my gas and it needed to be returned on a half tank just as I received it. In the lobby at the designated time arranged by the Morris's, they were nowhere in sight. In efforts to start this date off with a bang, I suggested to grab a drink for the bar. My alcohol tolerance hadn't been the same since my college days nonetheless I had a feeling that this lunch with Barbie and her husband was going to be interesting. I wasn't sure how well Carter knew Mr. Morris or how often they acquainted with each other, so I would make sure to be selective of how I voiced my opinions.

As I sipped my Grand Marnier with pineapple and Carter drank his cognac on the rocks, he expressed his opinion about this meeting being coordinated by Barbie and I. Who me? What did I do? I didn't even want to really go. He said that when he saw Ted in passing, Ted told him that Barbie had really enjoyed my company at the ceremony, and she wanted to invite us out. Basically, he was trying to blame all of this on me? I was just simply making small talk with the girl, trying to be a good date. Whatever the case was, we were here now so we might as well make the best of it. Toasting our shot glasses as Mr. and Mrs. Morris walked up on us. Laughing and joking with the bartender and other hotel bar patrons, I would rather stay here then go out into that heat. Feeling warm and fuzzy inside, I knew that we had agreed on taking my car, but I hoped that Carter was in a better condition to drive than I was. Lucky for us, the Morris' had a car service reserved to take us to a

restaurant that Ted really enjoyed. He claimed the
restaurant had the best tasting southern food that he'd
ever tasted, and Barbie cosigned. Carter and I exchanged
looks as if we were thinking the same thing at the same
time. What the fuck is southern food? Cow tongue and
green bean casserole, because I'm not down with that? I
know what I consider to be southern food, but I would've
bet my first-born child that him and I weren't on the same
page. Ohhhh, but then he said fried chicken, mac and
cheese, greens and cornbread and then I knew he was
speaking my language.

The ride there wasn't as awkward at I thought it would be.
Almost immediately we sparked up a conversation that
managed to keep both parties engaged for the duration of
entire ride. Arriving at the small jam-packed restaurant, I
could smell the aroma of what reminded me of Sunday
dinner at my grandma's. Waiting patiently for a table that
could accommodate 4 people, Mr. Morris quickly grew
impatient. His attitude and demeanor came off as someone
who was used to being catered to. The longer we waited
the more intolerant he grew. Suggesting that we eat at
another restaurant, I googled some places close by with a
similar menu. Shutting down my idea, Barbie tried to calm
him as he repeatedly went up and questioned the hostess
on the accuracy of the wait time originally quoted to us.
Snapping at her too, I was a tad bit discomfited by his
responses and wondered if he also had had a little "turn
up" juice before leaving the hotel. The mood changes being
revealed were nothing like the friendly gentleman that I
had met some nights ago. Now if it's one thing that I don't
play with, its people who are responsible for making and
preparing my food. Playing around with his ass I was going
to have some "extra seasonings" on my chicken. The look
on Barbie's face indicated she was used to his behavior and

knew where this was heading. In efforts not to make her feel uncomfortable or ashamed, I quickly changed the subject as a distraction to assist in easing the mood. Not working as well as I thought it would, she kept looking at him as though she was afraid of what was going to happen next, but I kept talking.

As Ted asked to speak with management, I grabbed ahold of Carter's hand and squeezed it tightly. Suddenly, I wasn't hungry anymore; show me to the closest Chipotle. Creating a small scene, I was ready to go. Other patrons of the restaurant began to stare as the atmosphere became extremely awkward. Is this how the rich entitled folks act? I've seen this type of stuff happen on tv and in the movies, but I never expected to see it in real life, let along be associated with it, and I've socialized with some real assholes back in DC. Reminiscing back to the man who made the remarks at the hotel the other night, I became irritated and the buzz that I had earlier was blown. Trying my absolute best to conceal my attitude as I looked at Carter and he looked back at me. Raising his eyebrows and shrugging his shoulders, he obviously didn't know how to react either. As the manager approached us, he apologized for the inconveniences. Barbie, trying to diffuse the situation, played it off like it wasn't as big of a deal that her husband had made it, accepted the manager's apology. I wasn't sure if she was trying to spare herself the embarrassment or spare all of us.

Assuring us that we would be seated within the next few minutes the manager offered to comp our appetizers and that's when things really went left. Ted's voice and tone escalated as he told the man that we didn't need his free food and how bad customer service could not be pardoned with $8 samples. Understanding how uncomfortable it must be for Cater and I to watch, Barbie gently touches his arm in efforts of getting him to control his actions. With a swift jerk, he pushes her hand from his sleeve, and it was in that exact moment that I was ready to go. I'm not eating anything here at this establishment and honestly, I want to get as far away from them as possible. "I'll be in the car", Barbie stated as she walked out of the restaurant with tear filled eyes. I wasn't exactly sure of what I should do. Was I supposed to go after her and console her or stay there and continue to feel embarrassed; I didn't want to leave Carter there by himself? Did she need a moment alone, I'm not even sure what is really going on right now? Carter stepped in, cutting off the exchange of words between the manager and Ted, suggesting that we dine somewhere else. With that being said, I walked out and headed to the car to find Barbie.

In the car I could tell that she had been crying. Handing her a tissue from my purse, I remained silent, not really knowing what to say. Quickly she fixed her face as I softly mentioned that the two guys were approaching. Both men got in, neither said a word. Carter leaned in and asked if I was ok, I nodded. Curious to know where the hell we were headed to now after that fiasco, I took a deep sigh. I couldn't help but to feel bad for Barbie as she fought hard to maintain a straight face. Someone needed to call this entire outing off. I didn't feel as if it was my place, but someone needed to say it. The driver still hadn't pulled out of the lot yet and Ted had his phone to his ear. I'm assuming that the driver was confused as to what transpired but without a destination or direction, we would continue to sit.

Oh God, I hope that Ted wasn't trying to make reservations for another place but I have a funny feeling that's why he was on the phone. Just as I suspected, he gave the driver instructions on where to take us. Rolling my eyes at the back of Ted's head, I couldn't help but to wonder if Barbie was in an abusive relationship. I know that the idea sounded extremely farfetched, especially since I really didn't know her, but I couldn't help but to speculate that there was something going on just below the surface of today's scene.

Arriving at our new destination, the Morris' both exited the car first and us last. As they walked slightly ahead of us, I closely observed their interaction. I saw him sternly grab her arm and though I could not hear exactly what he was saying to her, I did hear him tell her that she embarrassed him by walking out of the previous establishment. Some damn nerve he had. I whispered to Carter and asked if he had just heard the same thing I overheard. He didn't but suggested that I stay neutral and advised me to mind my own business. He was probably right, but as a woman and by nature, I was concerned. As we entered the new place, we were immediately greeted and seated. This establishment was one of those fancy places, completely different from where we had just come from. Let's just get this shit over with.

During the meal, I couldn't help but notice Barbie's reaction as her husband desperately lured her into conversation. She kept her replies short and occasionally forced a smile. Before the food came, I asked her if she would escort me to the bathroom. As a grown woman, and basically as a stranger, I'll admit the idea seemed odd, but I felt compelled to get her away from him for a few moments. The agony was written all over her face. We didn't speak as we walked to the lavatory, however as soon as the bathroom door closed behind us, baby girl lost it. I handed her paper towels as tears streamed down her face. Still not knowing what to say, I attempted to console her.

I rubbed her back as she once again tried to pull it together. I recommended her to just let it out because she wasn't having much success in pretending that everything was ok when we were all at the table. I let her have a moment while I actually needed to use the bathroom. As I came out from the stall, she was in the process of regaining herself. Uncontrollably sobbing and apologizing, I assured her that there was nothing to be sorry about. I didn't want to comment on what I thought was going on or on the actions displayed by her husband, I just wanted her to get it out of her system before this fool pops off on her and creates another commotion. I'm not therapist but I've seen "What's love got to do with it" and "Madea's Family Reunion", (with fine ass Blair Underwood), I know how that shit go, and I don't want either Carter or I to be a part of anything these two have going on. Plus, you never know how people will react, especially if you mention anything specifically close of suspecting domestic violence, her ass might pretend she's crazy and try to go off on me. I would hate to have to stretch her ass out on this Italian marble floor of this bathroom. I handed her some mascara and eye makeup that would help her face begin looking like she hadn't been crying a river for our short time away. I told her to take a deep breath in preparation to go back. I also told her that I was going to order a drink for both her and I. We both smiled and returned to the table.

Back at the table, she was able to get a drink in her system, and she was good to go. It also seemed like her husband wasn't as cranky, everyone was just a little bit more relaxed, I still wasn't feeling him, but I faked it. When the meal was complete, Ted hinted at the notion of us spending more time together, possibly going to see some landmarks, but I wasn't into it. I quietly reminded Carter that I had plans of still attempting to attend the rally. They could all go out, just drop me off back and the hotel and I could go do my own thing. Better yet, I could grab an uber and not interrupt the flow of things and they could go on their merry little way. When Carter made the statement about us having plans, I was secretly hoping that they asked what we were going to do so I could passionately tell them, but they didn't. Barbie did look a tad bit disappointed that we were choosing not to hang with them anymore. I made an effort to exchange numbers with her, I felt like it could come in handy in the event she ever needed to talk or vent sometime in the near future. Ted took care of the bill, how nice of him (side eye). Back inside the chauffeured car, we returned to the hotel. Not once was the incident that had previously occurred mentioned or asked for forgiveness, not even as both parties departed. It's almost as if it never happened, I at least thought that at the end he would apologize, but nope. That's fine, they won't get me again. I'm over Ted and his arrogant ass. Wait what am I talking about? I'll probably never see these two ever again after this. Carter has one more day here and then they'll all just be a figment of my imagination.

Upon reaching the suite, I remembered that I hadn't brought up my change of clothes so there was no need for me to go back to his room. Advising Carter that I still wanted to attend whatever was left of the rally, he revealed his appreciation for the fact that I had decided to keep the plans that he had set for us, and in return he agreed to come with me. We went back and forth about him not being obligated to go even though I just sat through "Hell Date" with his colleagues, but he insisted. He told me that he needed to change his clothes and then we could go. I figured I could always just change in the car while I made him drive. It only took a few minutes for him to change into something more comfortable, as he discreetly questioned my reasons for actually wanting to travel to the rally. He didn't know it but he was starting to irritate me. I had already told him that there was no need for him to tag along, so I didn't really feel like there was a need for him to question my motives. It was something that I felt encouraged to do for my own personal reasons, I didn't need to give any explanations besides the fact that I have become outraged by the recent disgusting acts of terrorism on the people that look like me, here in my own country. And though I haven't physically given birth to my own biological children, the people that we pay to serve and protect us, were killing our babies in cold blood without any consequences. Not only are they murdering us and our children, they're getting away with it. I am quite aware that sometimes these events can spiral out of control due to outrage and weak-minded individuals, but my mother always told me that if you're not part of the solution, you become part of the problem.

In the areas where I've recently resided, the more "successful" black folk don't seem to be as outraged or concerned since they were not directly affected, and it didn't occur in their neighborhoods. They have become mentally disconnected, considering themselves to be the exception not the rule. They fail to realize that all those college degrees, the fancy clothing labels, their proper diction and zip codes won't prevent them or their offspring from systematic racism. When these mainstream issues and incidents slowly find their ways into the counties and rural areas then maybe they too will feel outraged and inspired to want to fight for change.

Now don't get me wrong, there is nothing wrong with wanting better for yourself and your family, I get it, move into the better areas with the superior school districts, buy whatever car you desire, live as you want, but I've learned not to ever look down on people, especially the ones who look like you, who haven't had all the breaks in life that you've had, or who work twice as hard as you with half of the resources and have half to show for it. We must first identify and admit to the existence of the problem and demand change, no matter what race you are or position that you hold, or what tax bracket you're in. Wrong is wrong, until the day we stop allowing ourselves to construct divisions between one another, standing for one common goal, then we will hopefully see a change. We must learn how to efficiently and effectively make our voices be heard even if that means affecting the economy, that seems to be the only substantial way of getting our point across. Ok, that's enough of me venting. So, as we wait for the car, I ask Carter if he minds driving so that I can change my clothes. He agrees by saying, "Ooooh, lunch and a show? This must be my lucky day." I just give him the look. As we get in the car and I grab my bag out of the back and we settle in. With a 55-minute estimated arrival time on the navigation, we are finally on our way.

Pulling into the small town you could just feel the tension and smell the aroma of the burning smoke. I'll admit, the energy of the crowd was beginning to get a little overwhelming the closer we drew to the actual scene. Arriving several hours after the rally had started, the people had grown enraged and there were small clusters of residents lined up and down both sides of the main street. I looked at Carter who seemed to be driving slower than usual to see if I could gage how he was feeling. He looked calm, too calm, and I was starting to feel nervous.

Honestly, I didn't know what I was expecting the scene to look like. I had watched similar settings play out on CNN and Fox News several times, but to be up close and personal, nothing could have prepared me for this. The police were standing guard in uniforms that resembled military attire with gas masks and K9's. Numerous streets were desolate and blocked off. Protesters were holding signs and echoing chants that demanded justice. Once intrigued at the thought of the protest, I now am having second thoughts. As the police presence becomes more intense, the people are growing even more agitated and annoyed, and with the sun setting soon, I'm not sure how this movement will play out. "If we're really going to do this then I suggest that we park a great distance away. I cannot afford for anything to happen to this rental, plus not to mention I declined the insurance" I said in a joking manner, but I was dead the fuck serious. Parking several blocks away from the heart of all the action, I thought to myself, I don't plan on being out here too long.

Leaving the car and walking towards the mass of chanters and demonstrators at the scene of the murder, a slight chill ran through my body. It wasn't from the dry breeze of the Texas air that was blowing, the feeling came from the sight of the flowers and candles placed at the site encircled by the grieving family members and friends surrounding it. I couldn't even begin to imagine how it felt to lose someone so tragically and then to be forced to morn over and over in the public eye. Not even just that, but to lose a child, someone that you've put your all in to, sacrificed for and prayed over, taken away from you, slaughtered in cold blood, as if his life didn't matter. The outcries of grief and the frustration from the people were becoming tempered. I overheard that the earlier protest lead by infamous social activist, was peaceful and sincere, but I think that we arrived a little too late for that.

News cameras from major networks were there reporting the live footage. There were many different types of protesters out there, from all walks of life, not only blacks, but whites and other races, young and old. It was evident that people were fed up and had had enough.

I always wanted to be part of a revolution, be part of a generation that impacts history and makes a change. Growing up, my mother would force me to watch movies about slavery and the personal stories that my grandmother told me as a child into my adulthood, involving the civil rights movement, always inspired me to want more out of life. It gave me a push to strive harder and make my family proud. After about an hour or so, of closely following behind a tall skinny man with a bullhorn, the sun had completely set and Carter had been great at supporting my initiative. Up until this point, everything had gone as I anticipated. As we approached a line of excessively armored law enforcement, the mass of protesting marchers came to a halt; we had come to a dead end. There was nowhere for the crowd of citizens to disperse and that's what started the antagonizing and provoking of the officers. With the residents already frustrated with the overwhelming tension of national police brutality, the credibility of law enforcement was squat. In the back of my mind, I knew that things could take a turn for the worst but against my better judgement, I convinced myself to stay a little longer. I was all for the peaceful protest but honestly, I didn't feel like being amongst the crowd when the gas bombs are thrown and the crowd is lawfully forced to dissolve. The motionless crowd seemed to grow larger and a little bit unrulier with every few moments that passed. With a great number of individuals that were still actively promoting positive demonstrations, their light would soon be diminished by others who had recently joined, that didn't seem to have the same approach. The sirens of the nearby ambulances grew closer as you could hear the propellers of the circulating helicopters. Flashing lights from the cop cars speedily riding through the neighborhood lit the dark streets as the smell in the atmosphere resembled a stench of smoke which led me to believe that there were other incidents that were taking place nearby. Looking at Carter for confirmation that it was time to go, he was fully engaged, still chanting with his fist balled up and raised in the air. Lightly tugging on his sleeve, he paid me no attention as he continued to focus his undivided attention towards the defense line being upheld by the law enforcement.

Giving his shirt yet another tug, now with a little more aggression, he quickly looked down at me, placing his arm around my shoulders then refocusing his attention to where it had originally come from. I would hate to kill his momentum, nonetheless I don't feel as if he's being totally aware of our surroundings. The message we had been trying to convey to the nation was not going to be welcomed with a listening ear when this crowd becomes unmanageable. The media outlets will portray us to the world as savages who don't care about anything. They will call us thugs and perpetuate us as poor, poverty stricken, classless people. They give people like the white man back at the hotel, a reason to think that his opinions are filled with some sort of validity.

In my final attempt to get his attention, I shake his arm, we make eye contact then we both were distracted by a scuffle that ensued nearby. Not sure what provoked it or what happened that caused the movement of the crowd, all I remember hearing a loud noise and then came the reaction of the crowd. Knocked to the ground by individuals vividly scurrying in opposite directions, I took cover to protect my head and to avoid being trampled. As I watched people running and screaming, the area looked like a gang war from back in the days, almost like a free for all. Some running towards the officers almost as if they were in attack mode and others looked as if they were running from them for safety. The police were grabbing people and abrasively tossing them to the cement. During all the confusion, I was separated from Carter. In efforts to again protect myself from being trampled on, I kept my head low trying to think of an escape plan. Looked around to see if I could find Carter, I couldn't see anything but feet, broken glass and flying debris. I felt someone behind me reach for my arm but I couldn't see a face. I assumed it to be Carter, but it wasn't. I grabbed on to the strange man as he assisted me off the ground and got me to my feet. He asked if I was ok, I just shook my head yes.

Still frazzled, he holds into my arm and attempts to pull me out from the chaotic disturbance. As we both pull in separate directions, me looking for my partner and him trying to get me to safety, I notice a woman running in my direction holding a glass bottle. In slow motion, I watch as she is tackled by police. Initially, she loses the grip of the bottle as it fell from her hand hitting the concrete and shattering. As they get her to the ground, she is forced to lie in the remnants of the broken glass causing blood to splatter from her face and neck. Letting out a horrific scream of pain and agony, my body is temporally paralyzed, I couldn't move. Standing and shaking in fear and devastation as she lays near my feet with tears running down her face crying for help. The man who had once grabbed my arm in efforts to rescue me, fled and I was there standing by myself. In a full panic, the officer who had his knees dug into the woman's back advised me to get the fuck out of here. Using my better judgement and still looking for Carter, began walking away from the uproar. Thinking if I could get on the sidewalk, I would have a better view to spot Carter within the crowd.

Uncontrollably, tears began to fall to my cheeks. With filled water-filled eyes and terrible night vision, I was on the lookout for my friend in a charcoal grey tee shirt. Inadvertently, I started walking in the same direction of the scene I had just escaped from. Maybe he was looking for me within the mobs of people and that's why I hadn't seen him running in my direction.

With chaos all around me, I couldn't concentrate. I was trying to be as aware of my surroundings as possible in this situation. Thinking I spotted him or at least what I thought looked like him from the back, I saw someone with the same body build but this guy was tussling with a younger guy. It can't be him, I'm so confused to what's going on with everyone right now. Hesitant about walking up too closely to see if in fact it was actually him, I did. I called out his name but this person didn't answer or turn around. I called out to him again and still no reaction or response, maybe it wasn't him. The closer I approached the two, the harder my heart pounded. It looked like they both had something in their hands, but I couldn't make out what it was. I called out to him, this time much louder. I wished that it was him, but then again, I didn't. Now closer with a clearer view it was Carter. Close enough touch him, I pulled at his shirt. Startled as he turned around, the boy barely gained his balance, broke free from Carter's grip and ran off, leaving behind a gun that fell to the ground. "What the hell is going on? We need to go!!" I screamed and begged of him with my dry lips and tear stained face. Grasping vigorously on his arm, I pull him away. Looking out in the street for the guy who had just ran away, "just forget it, let's go", I say anxiously.

Finally giving into my demands we hurriedly start walking away when he stops and doubles back for the gun that was still on the ground. "What the hell are you doing?" I ask in a panicked tone. Why would he go back and pick up the gun with everything that is going on around us, he must have a death wish or something. It left me wondering if the gun was his. Had he brought it with him and if so, how had he managed to bring it on the plane? I had questions, but this wasn't the time that I wanted to seek answers. Refusing to say anything, we got the hell out of there. Frantically continuing to walk towards the car, sweating and out of breath, he stops and looks down, grabs me by the shoulders than asks if I was ok. Literally scaring the shit out of me, "Are you bleeding? Where's that blood coming from?" he hysterically asks he looks down at my feet, causing me to look down. I noticed that there was splattered blood on my pants and shoes. Had I been cut? Nothing hurt, and I didn't remember getting cut but with the amount of adrenaline running through my body, I couldn't feel anything. Confused to where it could have come from, I remembered the lady and the glass bottle. I replied, "I don't think it's mine. I'm not hurt. Let's keep walking please."

As we continued to walk, people stood outside of their homes and businesses with bats and other objects to protect their properties from being burned down and vandalized. Trashcans thrown into the middle of the streets were set on fire, buildings were on fire, parents were calling out for their children, it was pure pandemonium. It resembled something a scene from the movie *Detroit*. As Carter kept my hand held tightly within his, we advanced walking in route of the car. Silently saying a prayer to myself, I was in a hurry to get to somewhere safe. It was a bad idea to come down here, my mom was right. Elated to finally arrive at the car, Carter opened my door and insisted that he check my body over to make sure that I didn't need any medical attention. After physically confirming what I had already told him, he hugged me tightly, closed my door, and disappeared toward the back of the car, reemerging into the driver's seat. The crowd was beginning to trickle back to the area where we parked but it was not nearly as large of a crowd as what we had just witnessed. Locking the doors, I urged him to start driving as I programmed the navigation. Starting the car, he sustained a blank face. Naturally, I assume that he is mentally readjusting but I'm ready to get out of this town and back to my room where, sadly enough I will admit, I feel safe. Giving him a minute to wrap his head around things and to get his thoughts together, my anxiety wouldn't allow me to be patient much longer that it has already been.

Finally getting everything together, as the GPS suggested, we proceeded to the route. Riding in complete silence, neither one of us had anything to say. I wanted so badly to question him about the gun and his intentions with it, but the timing just didn't feel right. Knowing when to shut the fuck up, I used my better judgment and did just that. Reason one, we were only out here because of me, and reason two, I was afraid of what was actually going on in his head and what might have transpired when we had separated for that brief time. I would just sit in silence until he decided to break the ice. As we followed I-35E South, I remembered that this was the 33-mile road that we traveled along to bring us here, so I knew that we were headed the right direction, back towards Dallas. Relived to be traveling back, I was able to breathe and slightly relax. Closing my eyes for a second to thank the Lord for bringing us out safely and to pray for those who had no way of escaping that hectic environment, I was interrupted by the first noise that Carter had made since we had been in the car together. "Fuck!" he said under his breath. In mid prayer, I opened my eyes, only to see the reflection of red and blue police lights out of my rearview mirror. Looking at the dashboard to see how fast we were traveling, my mind immediately reflected to fact that there was a gun in the car, possibly still on his person, which as far as I was concerned, was illegal and nether one of us had a permit for it. This night was never going to end.

Normally I wasn't concerned when I would get pulled over. I knew all my paperwork was correct and most of the time, apart from speeding, I was almost positive that I hadn't done anything wrong and that I didn't have any open warrants. Unable to get myself together, my head was pounding. I was fearful for not only my life, but the life of Carter's. I couldn't decide if I should take out my phone and start recording, or to keep my hands visible at all times. I didn't want to provoke the officers, but I wanted to protect myself. With my heart beating out of my chest and Carter still choosing not to speak, I felt my body break out into a cold sweat. My chest got tight and I found myself gasping for air. How was I going to explain my blood soiled clothes and my whereabouts?

As two officers approached each side of the car, one Caucasian, one Hispanic, both with flashlights brightly

shining, I sat with my hands folded in my lap. I won't lie, I'm not racist by any means but it felt damn good seeing a brown officer, it brought me minimal relief. As another person of color, I felt that our livelihoods weren't as threatened. The officer which advanced on my side shined his light amongst the entire SUV as he proceeded to ask where we were coming from. Not knowing what to say and low-key not wanting to say anything, I just stared. Now with his light shining in Carter's face, he subliminally was demanding an answer. In his most professional work voice, he told the white officer where we had been. I think we both knew that that wasn't the best answer, but to say that we were coming from the grocery store didn't seem too valid. "Disgust" that's the word I'll use to describe the look upon the officer's face as he demanded Carter's license and registration. Shining his lights now down at my feet, he failed to acknowledge the blood splatters upon my clothing. I informed the officer that I needed to reach inside of the glove compartment to retrieve the rental car agreements and contract, and I needed to grab my id to show that I was the renter. I chose to use my government identification in hopes that he would see that I held a federal government position. Taking all the paper work, the officer returns to his car. Still silent, I look to Carter to say something…. anything.

Resurfacing from the patrol car, the officer stops and softly speaks to his partner as they both re-approach and reposition themselves on each side of our car again. At this time, the officer asks us both to step out of the vehicle. Keeping us at opposite ends of the car, they ask if either one of us has a weapon or drugs either on our person on in the car. As the officers begin to question us individually, an additional patrol car arrives at the scene. With 4 officers now present, another patrol car arrives. At this point I am extremely nervous. I never mentioned anything about a weapon being in the car, but from the amount of police presence now at the scene, I'm led to believe that maybe Carter had mentioned something. As I am further questioned about the blood on my clothing, I see them escorting Carter into the back seat of the first patrol car. "What is happening? May I ask why he is being arrested?" I ask, as the additional officers proceed to search my vehicle. Within the next 10 minutes or so, I am informed that Carter is being taken in for questioning. The officer asks if I have a license and can drive. Frantic and clearly shaken up, the initial officers took no interest in helping to ease my frazzled nerves as they pull off with Carter handcuffed in the back seat. The last officer that had arrived on the scene, who happened to be a "brotha", approached me and told me where I could find Carter when he was finally released. He explained to me how Carter fit the description of someone who was associated with some recent criminal activity and he was being taken in for questioning. I pleaded with him, explaining our prior whereabouts and explained that this was all a big misunderstanding. He then informed me that Carter had a clip from a handgun and a single bullet on his person at the time he was searched, and although Texas is considered an "open-carry" state, the types of bullets that they found were illegal.

Clearing the tears from my face, I didn't want to say too much, honestly because I honestly didn't know much more than what I had witnessed with my own eyes, but then again, I didn't want whatever I said to hurt whatever explanation that Carter had disclosed to them. Pulling myself together, the officer checked again to make sure that I was physically capable of driving and offered to give me a ride as a courtesy. I declined. I wasn't about to leave my rental car on the side of the road, plus I wanted to find where this gun was that I knew Carter had but the cops failed to find. Getting in the car, with no music or no anything, I put on my seat belt and drove the speed limit to the next exit. Directly perpendicular of the exit, sat a convenience store; I pulled over and let out a cry. Not a cute cry, one of the ugly cries where the saliva is thick, and your nose gets all stuffy, the one the Bernie Mack references as when "your soul is hurt", yea, one of those. I felt responsible for everything that had just transpired. I barely knew him and managed to potentially ruin this man's life, for what, all for what? Pulling it all together, I got out of the car trying to find the pistol. Moving the seat back and forth, there was nothing to be found. Thinking to myself of where it could be, I was almost more confused than before. I searched high and low. I searched places of the car where I knew he didn't even access, but I was confused on where it could have been. The only option was that he still had it on him when he had been searched and the officer failed to mention it.

Putting in the address that the officer had given me, I wanted to go to be with Carter. I wasn't sure how long the process would take but I wanted to be there. When he was released I wouldn't want him to have to wait and his phone was left in our vehicle so he had no way of contacting me. Arriving at the station, asking about his whereabouts, I am advised to have a seat until they were able to give me an update. After sitting there for what felt like hours upon hours, I see the African- American officer from the scene where Carter was arrested. After making eye contact, he overlooked me as if I wasn't just crying on his shoulders a little bit ago. Tired, scared and irritated, I continued to wait for information regarding my friend. Finding myself closing my eyes and praying for the fourth time today, I was interrupted by a touch on my shoulder from Carter.

"You ok?" he asked. I replied by asking him the same thing. His appearance was the same as when I last saw him, and he didn't seem to look as if he had been hurt or mistreated, so that was a blessing. Grabbing my belongings, we both walked out. Outside stood the officer who had disregarded me moments before while inside of the station. He gave a head nod to Carter as he asked," You good?" "Thanks man", Carter responded as they gave each other a mutual fist bump. "You have my contact information if you need anything" the officer responded. Again, I was lost and left out of the loop of what was happening, but I didn't care. I was happy that Carter was free and I was finally back in the car on my way home, or better yet, to the hotel. I tried to make small conversation as I drove us back. He didn't totally ignore me but you could tell that he wasn't really in the mood to small talk. Dropping him off at the hotel, he didn't ask me to come up or seem interested in looking me in the eye. In all actuality, I could use some alone time to digest what just happened but I didn't want to be alone. I felt somewhat safer with him nonetheless I understood limits and I felt as if I had habitually crossed them already. "Let me know that you got in safe" he says in an uninterested tone as he exited the car.

The drive back to the hotel is dreary and melancholy. Eager and grateful to be back, my mind was not at ease. I still felt jittery and my nerves were still actively running. In my room, I cracked open two mini bottles of liquor, texted my momma that I was safe and would talk to her tomorrow, hopped in the shower and hit the sheets. Tossing and turning for a few, the alcohol finally calmed my body down and helped make it easier for me to get some rest.

The next morning, Carter sent a message telling me how he had eventful time here in Texas and thanked me for the "experience". He decided to catch an early flight back home and would be in touch. He mentioned that I left a few of my belongings in his room and requested a forwarding address to ship it. Not sure of what items he spoke of but I was almost certain that I would never hear from him again, or at least anytime soon. Whatever items that I left were not essential and could easily be replaced. I was not about to give my address out to someone, who because of me, was handcuffed and escorted off to jail. He wasn't going to send his goons to my door to kick my ass. No thanks, I'll pass!

Now that Carter was on his way back home, I couldn't seem to get him nor the recent transpired events off my mind. Images of our better times spent together kept replaying in my thoughts, leaving me feeling extremely guilty for the way that things ended. Our personalities meshed so well and for things to end so abruptly, made this even more devastating. I blame myself, and although he wouldn't verbally admit to it being my fault, deep down he knew it was too. Originally planning to utilize this day to relax and mentally prepare for my work week, I couldn't keep focused. My mind kept drifting off, playing out last night's situation over and over. How would this affect him going further? Could this affect his job or way of living in any way? I never meant for any of this to happen. If he technically wasn't under arrest, would any of this be on his permanent record?

Within the past few days I had formed somewhat of a bond with Carter and his girls, I now fear that I may never hear from them again, and for some reason that made me depressed. To say it out loud, sounded ridiculous. To openly confess that I had deep feelings for a man whom I met less than a week ago, and his daughters that I've only communicated via FaceTime with, sounded absurd. As I sat there, in my hotel room for hours mentally and verbally abusing myself for being so negligent, I couldn't control the fact that I was also taking it out on my family and friends, including Kris and Brandon who continued to call and text my phone as they watched footage of last night's incidents replayed on live television. I couldn't bear to respond, I didn't know what to say. At this point, I'm almost positive that Kris is desperate for answers on why I've been M.I.A. for the past 24 hours and I envision his emotions to be ranging between pissed off and concerned, while Brandon just probably thinks that my time is being consumed by work. For Kris and I not to communicate with each another for this many hours was not something that normally occurred between us. There was no one that I could talk to about this. Not Sabrina or Jasmine, not even my mother who I'd shared almost every detail of my life with. I couldn't stand to hear her say that she warned me about going in the first place. No one would understand how I was feeling or could empathize with my sentiments. I can't work like this. I can't even focus long enough to power up my laptop.

Under normal circumstances this would call for a drink, but I didn't even feel like doing that. Before I knew it, the sun was setting and I was still unaccomplished and mentally numb. I hadn't washed my ass or eaten all day. Refusing to get up and turn on a light, I must have drifted off and took a short nap. Waking up and checking the time on my phone, I know that Carter should have already arrived home, but he hadn't bothered to try to make contact. I did have a missed call and text from Kris but that was it. Maybe Carter got caught up in the excitement of being back home with his family. Sitting alone in a dark room, I began to visualize how that looked. I envisioned them running into his arms upon his arrival and him hugging and holding them tightly with those same muscular arms that had embraced and protected me several hours ago. I played out the entire thing in my mind, creating an image of what their neighborhood looked like and everything. I even took it as far as picturing the interior décor of the house and what they wore as they interacted. Why was I torturing myself?

I had a terrible tendency to overthink things and situations to the point where I would give myself a headache, and I had done just that. Motivating myself to go downstairs in search of food to coat my stomach enough to take an aspirin, I slid on my sandals and left. Realizing that I left my phone attached to the charger, I decided against going back to get it since I wasn't expecting any calls and wasn't in the mood to talk to anyone. Opting to grab some light snacks, I make my way back in an attempt to be productive and try to get some work done. Arriving back at the room, I walked into the last sequence of my ringing phone.

Running to try and catch it, I desperately wanted it to be Carter. Instead, to my surprise, it was Barbie calling. What the hell did she want? I didn't really give her my number for us to be BFF's or anything; I don't want her to be calling me all willy-nilly. I wanted to let the phone conclude its ringing (hoping that she would opt in to leave a message) but against my better judgement I decided to answer thinking that maybe she knew something about Carter. As I answered the call, she was ending it. Before the call thoroughly disconnected, I managed to overhear her sobbing and sniffling before she disconnected the call. My heart dropped. Did something happen? With my hands slightly shaking and my nerves still rattled, I returned her missed call, only this time she didn't answer. I waited a few moments before I'd allowed myself to get all worked up, then I called back. Again, there was no answer. Becoming extremely anxious, I slowly began to feel the early symptoms of a panic attack coming on. At this point I wasn't sure what to think.

Pondering to myself on whether to call Carter to make sure everything was good on his end, or to wait for him to make contact. I was confident in believing that I was the last person he wanted to hear from right now though. Soon thereafter, in the midst of my deliberation, I receive a text from her that read, "I'm really sorry that I bothered you." How fucking vague was that? Like who really does that? Was I being punked? Texting her back, I asked if everything was alright. She didn't respond immediately, but instead sent a text 8 minutes later that read, "I've been married for 6 years. I have 3 sisters & 8 close girlfriends and none of them, not one, has ever seen me cry. No one has ever genuinely cared enough to ask me how I was doing or seem to take an honest interest in my wellbeing. From the first time I met you, my instincts allowed me to believe that there was something different about you. You have a genuine soul." Ok, what the hell is really going on? Is this heffa tryna hit on me or something? I don't get down with the get down. This isn't college and those days are long gone. Considering not sending a response because I'm not sure where this conversation is going, I honestly don't think I care enough. I showed interest when we were at the restaurant because I didn't want to see things escalate any further than they already had, and I ain't want to see that hoe to get slapped up in front of Carter and I, it was too much to jeopardize, so when I pulled that girl into the bathroom with me, I was basically telling her to get her shit together before she really got embarrassed. Plus, I've learned the hard way, a long time ago, to mind my business in other people's relationships. "I'm not sure if everything is alright over there, but thank you for the compliment", I replied. "Are you alright? Do you want or need to talk?" I clandestinely yearned for her to decline my offer but the good-natured part of me was curious as to what she was going through. She didn't text back. Staring at the phone eagerly waiting for her to respond, nothing came. I began to tidy up the room a little just in case she decided to accept my proposal. I also thought it would be a good idea to hop in the shower and be clean in case she wanted to meet up somewhere else. I'd figure that if she had not responded to my message by the time that I was finished washing up, that I would just reach out and call her, maybe even head over in her direction.

In the shower, my mind continued to race as I lathered my body with stress relieving eucalyptus body wash. Re-evaluating and deciphering the messages Barbie sent, I found myself dissecting each text, trying to make sense of it all. She obviously was going through something to make her want to reach out to me. All my life I had been there for others, trying to help them solve their problems or most often, being there to give love and support. The problem is, when it always came down to me and my issues, I was all I had. Don't get me wrong, there are people who sincerely care about me, however since I was such a closed and private person, everyone got the impression that I had it all together. If that's how Barbie was feeling, I could totally relate. So once again, I choose to neglect my work while tending to the needs of others. I probably wasn't going to be productive anyways with all these other distractions occupying my thoughts, so what the hell? Checking my phone, she had yet to respond, so I decided to call. The call was answered but no one said anything. In the background, I could hear yelling followed by commotion.

Attempting to increase the volume level on my phone to see if I could make out what was being said, I couldn't translate whether I was overhearing an actual conversation, or a dispute and I couldn't attribute the male's voice to her husband because of the muffled feedback I was receiving on my end. She must have accidently answered because it sounded like I was in her pocket or something. Into fifty seconds of ear hustling, I distinctively heard her voice. My heart dropped when I heard her screaming and pleading for something, what it was, I didn't know. With both voices clashing over top of one another, I oddly came to the conclusion that my call was accidently answered, but now I wasn't sure if I should hang up or not. Placing the phone on speaker while I rushed to throw some clothes on, just in case the situation got more intense; jumping the gun, I made the executive decision to go over to her hotel. Again, playing out another situation in my mind on how things could play out if I was to randomly show up at their hotel room unannounced, I needed to be cautious.

Dashing out the door, I elected to take the steps instead of eagerly waiting for the elevator. I found myself pacing, still with the phone to my ear, as I waited for valet to retrieve my car. Not knowing exactly where she is, I'm prayerfully hoping she's at the hotel. In the car as my phone routinely synced with the car audio system, I no longer hear voices, but I can hear scuffling which identifies to me that there is some sort of movement occurring. I hear a loud sound resembling a door slamming followed by more scrambling, shadowed by a dead silence. I could hear the clambering of the phone's microphone as if someone picked it up after realizing that it had been on a live conversation. Hearing heavy breathing, "Hello?" I said, hoping that Barbie was on the other end of the phone. The call disconnected. Immediately calling back several times consecutively until I detected my phone calls being forwarded to voicemail. I suddenly had a mental flashback of my homegirl who was accidently killed by her boyfriend back in high school. She had secretly been in an abusive relationship for years. Being so young and uninformed, none of us could give her the best advice on how to address the situation. In some crazy way, we just thought that was his way of showing her affection, that her flirtatious ways and simple actions would constantly anger him. Identifying his controlling and demanding behavior with the immense love that he had for her, too young and too dumb, we had become part of the problem. After her death, we experienced several therapy sessions with the school counselor and I had numerous talks with my mother about determining signs of an abusive relationships and how to seek help. Since then, I'd always hold domestic disturbances with high regards. Too deep in now, I felt that I wouldn't be able to live with that on my conscience if anything were to happen.

Accelerating the gas, I couldn't get there fast enough. My mind and heart were both racing in conjunction with my sweaty palms and underarms. With only one traffic signal away from my destination, the question was what was I going to do when I got there? Pulling up to valet, the flustered look on my face prompted the valet to miss me with the small talk. Rushing past the hotel bar, I contemplated getting a shot to help me survive the forecasted drama. With my legs a little shaky I continued towards the elevators. With a quick glimpse at the bar, giving this drink idea a second thought, I spotted Barbie sitting alone, slumped over at the bar. Lord knows I was over her and her husband since our last interaction, God please just give me the strength to be able to help this girl without getting myself into any unnecessary bullshit. Collecting my thoughts, trying to find the words to say before approaching her, I quickly reflected on my decisions in life. Concluding that I was sometimes a glutton for punishment, I have a strange feeling that momentarily I will regret this gesture.

Briefly skimming the room with my eyes to see if her husband was anywhere in sight, without saying a word, I walked up and stood next to the empty bar stool next to where she was sitting and ordered a drink. With Her head down and eyes open, as if she was staring into the bottomless pit of the glass, it was evident that something was wrong. Completely unsure of what I should do or say, should I impose or pry into what I overheard on the other end of the phone call or just excuse myself and walk away? If she wanted to talk she would've said something by now, right? Sitting in silence for several minutes, the bartender cleaned up the soiled glassware as I graciously declined an additional drink. Since she made no gesture as to acknowledge my presence, I figured that I'd pay my tab and leave, if she didn't stop me then I'd leave her be.

Preparing to leave, she slowly lifts her head and utters the word, "wait". "I'm sorry, what did you say?" I ask with a confused face. She repeats herself. "Ok what the hell am I waiting for? Obviously, she's ok, at least physically" I say to myself as I scan over her face and exposed areas of skin in search of cuts and bruises. Gulping down the remainder of her drink before sloppily standing to her feet, I can't help but to think to myself, how long had she been drinking? The car ride over to the hotel hadn't been that long so she had to be throwing several of them back within the last 10 minutes or so. With her bleeding mascara and flushed face, she reeks of bourbon and can barely stand. Assuring me that she is fine, she attempts to alter her appearance. So, what am I supposed to do with this bitch now? Asking the whereabouts of her husband, she tells me some story about him leaving to go meet up with some business partner who she thinks he is having an affair with. She includes how she called him out on it, which leads me to believe this is how and when the argument ensued. The story was long, drawn out and very detailed. She described the woman's physique, hair color, the car she drove, and the scent of perfume that she wears that her husband often comes home smelling like. In specific detail she illustrates the late, long, and often destination meetings they have, and more. Patiently listening as she rambles, the irony of the whole thing is that she is a wife who is confiding in a side chick, so the sequence of the story is extremely familiar to me.

As she vents, tears begin to form. Her voice gains volume as her words become less audible and more profane. Strongly suggesting we take our conversation elsewhere since we seem to be drawing attention from onlookers and passersby, I ask if she wants to go to her room and chat but she is adamant that she doesn't want to go back there. Not sure if taking her into public is the best idea, especially with her being heavily intoxicated, it just seems like a recipe for disaster. I managed to get her to pull it together once more and voiced to her we could go back to my room to talk. Holding onto each other's arm, I walked to back valet to request my car. We didn't wait long but the efforts of trying to keep her from leaning over had started to become a strenuous task. A gentleman working as valet asked if she was alright as he helped in assisting with

---

getting her in the car and getting her seatbelt on. Once in the car, she grew louder and more belligerent. She began conversating with herself, asking questions and answering them. She needed to vent and I was providing the outlet for her to do so, I just listened.

Back at my hotel, still leading her stumbling, loudmouthed ass up through the hotel corridors and up to the room. While on the elevator, I propped her up against the right corner and dropped her arm to search in my handbag for the room key, keeping a close eye on her making sure she kept her balance. Out of my peripheral vision I watched her raise her arm, the one that I had been holding on to, and inspect it. Wondering if I had been holding on to her too tight, I hope I wasn't the cause for the bruise she inspected. Finding my key, I looked at her to find her now inspecting the inner surface of her opposite arm. Gazing at her, I spotted another purplish bruise on her upper forearm. Unaware that I was staring, her eyes met mine causing her to immediately look away. Not mentioning it right away, I would eventually ask her about it before we parted ways.

As she sat on the bed, still venting, I handed her a bottled water to drink. She criticized herself for being stupid enough to continue to deal with her husband's consistent anger problems and behaviors. She cried, she yelled, she cried some more, trying to pull it together only to lose it again. I never said a word, just sat next to her rubbing her back and consoling her. She was so full of hurt, like hurt to the core, I could feel it. She stated how she never let people into her personal relationship and always concealed her true feelings for the sake of her family. Everyone envied her and the lifestyle that she portrayed. She often fancied of one day being able to break away from him in search of finding what truly made her happy. She told the story of how they met and fell in love, or at least what she thought was love. She'd even admit how initially money played a role in the relationship but she had convinced herself that she perpetually fell in love with him once he swept her off her feet. She never cheated and had always been a loyal and dedicated wife, making sure she played her role and kept him happy.

As of lately she found herself drinking excessively to conceal and numb the pain, emotional and physical. Laying back on the bed looking with tears running down the opposite sides of her face, she told me that she had grown too familiar with the feelings of being hurt so badly that she contemplated suicide just to end it all. With both us crying, I knew that she needed help. It was easy for me, from the outside looking in, to tell her that she didn't deserve what she was going through, that she was a beautiful person, that she was worth more than what she chose to settle for, that she deserved to be with someone who valued and appreciated her, but she wouldn't find comfort on those words. I know, because I had been there, not in an abusive relationship, but in situations when I sold myself short, when I refused to acknowledge the crown that I carried on my head, and because I couldn't recognize it, I let others disregard it.

For years, I had played second best, to a married man who I had met and fell in love with years before his marriage, but I settled and elected to be a part of his daily charades to fill a void that I was missing. My mother, grandmother, sisters, brothers, friends, they all knew. They repeatedly talked to me but they were beating a dead horse. I was going to do what I was going to do anyways, so their efforts were all made in vain. I struggled back and forth with it, taking small stands to end it with him; nonetheless being with him was comfortable to me. I knew that one day I would eventually be able to walk away, maybe when I finally met someone that could divert my attention away from him, or when I ultimately got fed up with his lies of how he was getting a divorce only to counteract it by some story about how he would need to postpone the process. But the truth was that it was up to me. No one could make me do anything, I would have to do it on my own when I was ready and that was the same thing that Barbie was going to have to go through. It's a process but I would be there for as long as she needed me to, no I hadn't known her for years, or even months, only for a few days, and you can say what you want but as a woman I felt like it was my obligation.

She continued to apologize in between her rants for what she called "burdening me with her problems", and I commended her for being brave and being able to open up to someone about her feelings and the issues surrounding her life. Before the conversation ended, I referenced the bruises. She brushed it off, blamed it on her own faults. It was puzzling to witness her be so open yet so closed at the same time. Considering our conversation as progress, maybe I was jumping the gun. I delved more into the issue, in attempts to have her gain my trust, but she wouldn't budge. Encouraging her to do what she felt was best, I reiterated nothing she disclosed to me could warrant him to place his hands on her in a harmful manner. Verbalizing the wonderful qualities that I felt she possessed, I offered my listening ear and shoulder to cry on anytime she needed. Even though I knew it wouldn't make much of a difference, I emotionally tried to build her up. If I could queue some background music during my spiel, it would've been between *Count on me* by Whitney Houston and CeCe Winans or *Aint No Mountain* by Diana Ross. Completely drained, my mouth was dry and I had a banging headache. I excused myself as I headed to get some ice from the machine and a drink from downstairs. Upon my return, she had drifted off to sleep. Quietly maneuvering around the room trying not to disrupt her, I figured I'd let her rest up for a little bit before I offered to take her back.

Attempting round 2 at trying to get some work done, I open up my laptop once more and turned on the television. Focused and exceptionally productive, I could hear the faint sound of a vibration. Quickly looking at my phone, and noticing that it wasn't me, I observed that the noise would stop for a moment and begin again. Probably Ted looking for his wife, I took it upon myself not to wake her; she had a long evening, the poor thing done cried herself to sleep. As the phone continued to ring in her bag which was sitting on the bed, I continued to ignore it. If it wasn't enough to wake her, then oh well, plus in my opinion, it wouldn't hurt to let his mind wonder for a little about her whereabouts. Maybe he had somethings to reflect on in his spare time alone. In the meantime, my phone rang, it was Kris. I didn't necessarily want to talk to him, especially after the woman empowerment spiel that I had just administered, but I did miss him, especially now since I was being neglected by Carter. Taking the call in the hallway I was being careful not to disturb sleeping beauty.

We talked as he brought me up to speed as to what was going on back home and to scold me about how I had been so distant during my time in Texas. I told him about the rally and the string of events that followed. I vaguely mentioned the story of my new-found friend and her predicament, careful to not be overly descriptive without incriminating myself and my flirtatious ways. Trying to multitask while talking to me (which he was never good at), he didn't give me any feedback after I told my story. The only thing he gave me was the advice to mind my own business. He often criticized me for always over extending myself in situations that didn't concern me. He would never understand things from my perspective. Our conversation was interrupted by a FaceTime attempt from Carter. Quickly telling Kris that I would call him back, I sat on the carpeted floor and answered the video call hoping to see Carter's face. Viewing my own face on the screen, I wanted to make sure that I looked presentable. The status of the call remained on the "connecting" screen until the phone alerted me that it was unable to connect the call. Feeling a little disappointed and still sitting on the floor, I waited a second to see if he would call back. Staring at my device, I had a strong signal for reception but there was no action going on. Should I call him back? Waiting a moment or two before placing the call, I subconsciously convinced myself that he wasn't going to answer as a defense mechanism to protect my feelings. To my surprise the call was picked up by the girls. Hearing them fighting over the phone and arguing about who was going to talk first, I listened hard to see if I could hear their father refereeing in the background, but I didn't hear him. Either way it was still a breath of fresh air to hear from them, even if they had snuck and called me without him knowing.

Coming to mutual agreement, they decided to place the call on speaker so that they both could talk. We talked about their day, how they went to church, what they had for lunch, what I had for lunch, how they excitedly waited for their dad to arrive home, and they even asked when I was coming to visit. Not knowing how to answer, honestly, I didn't know if Carter would even ever want to see or speak to me again. I simply replied, "I'll have to coordinate with your dad to see a good time for us all to hang out." "Go ask daddy" I hear the oldest one tell the youngest. "You don't have to ask him now, I'm sure he's tired" I rapidly responded, not wanting to find myself in another awkward position to getting my little feelings hurt. "No, he's not, Cuddles go ask him" Kennedy demands. When Cuddles returns, she tells Kennedy that Carter wants to talk to her, so she goes to see what he wants. The littlest one begins to tell me all the things we can do when I get there and all the places we can go. She has the cutest, most innocent voice, so enthusiastic; one can't help but to smile. Before I knew it we were on the phone for 20 mins and 15 seconds. We covered everything from her favorite movies, favorite subject in school, and her friends in the neighborhood, almost everything. There was nothing shy about this girl, and boy, could she talk but I enjoyed every minute of it.

Deep into our conversation, my hotel room door opened and Barbie stood in the doorway confused. At first, she didn't notice me sitting on the ground, she glared up and down the hallway as if she didn't have a clue where she was, she finally glanced down and saw me. At the same time Kennedy came back to the phone and said that her dad wanted to speak with me, I really wanted to speak with him too. Wanting to bring him up to speed about what happened today and I also wanted to talk about the events that had transpired the other day. Prior to him leaving, he claimed that he wasn't upset or mad with me at all, but I wasn't totally convinced. I told Cuddles and Kennedy to let their father know that I would need to call him back and talk to him later, I needed to tend to Cinderella and figure out what she wanted to do. Ending the call, I manipulated my old bones from the floor and asked Barbie if she was ok. The emotions her face portrayed didn't seem to compliment what she was verbally expressing. She looked concerned and worried as she stared into her phone but she kept telling me that she was fine. Dropping the phone from her hand, she placed her left hand across her face and let out a deep sigh. She remained silent as so did I. "How long was I sleep?" she asked. "Not too long, you kinda just passed out mid conversation. I didn't want to interrupt that's why I went into the hallway to take my call; the girls can get a little carried away sometimes" I replied. Picking up her phone again she began to look back in it as it started to vibrate. Assuming she declined the call because it didn't ring long, it began to ring again. Laying the phone down beside her, "What am I going to do?" she said underneath her breath.

So now here we were, sitting in complete silence, me staring at her and her staring at the floor. I've always been the type of friend that people felt comfortable telling their innermost feelings to and venting to, so I knew how to be a good listener and not input my feelings and opinions into prospective. And from the multiple therapy sessions that I'd endured, I've learned to not offer solutions to people's problems, but to instead assist in creating a clearer thinking space to help them rectify their problems on their own. I've had the opportunity of learning the hard way, that I couldn't force people to think like me or want to make a change based on my opinions alone. They must first recognize the problem, want to and be willing to change the situation, then comes the hard part, the follow through.

I had bit my tongue listening to her story initially because I technically didn't have any answers to give her. Of course, I could suggest that she could leave him, but I don't know her story, I didn't know anything about her. Where was she going to go? What level of crazy was her husband really? Was she scared of him or scared of leaving the lifestyle that she had become accustomed to? Did she work? Had she ever thought about leaving before? Had she ever tried? What was keeping her there? There were too many factors for me to be able to properly analyze the situation and create a reasonable suggestion or administer advice. "Tell me what you're thinking" I blurted out. Startled, she looked up. "Tell me exactly what's on your mind at this very given moment. Don't think, just say it" I spoke. She dropped her head again. I didn't want her to have to re-live what she had just expressed hours earlier, but I was curious about her thought process. I mean it was obvious that she was going to have to go back to her room and confront what she was running from, she couldn't hide forever. And I'm almost positive that the missed calls she neglected to answer were only infuriating him more. My main concern was that she wasn't in fear for her life, but how could she not be? If she wasn't scared, I was scared for her.

"Honestly" she hesitated, "I don't know what I'm thinking." She softly spoke, "I'm thinking to myself, why am I here? Why am I in this hotel room? No offense, but why am I in this hotel room with you out of all people?" I'm not sure where she is going with this statement but she better get to damn point before I get offended and put her delusional ass out. "I don't know you and you don't know me. Why the fuck am I here?" she adds. In a minute, I'm going to have to question myself on why the fuck she is here too. She proceeded with her statement, "We're not friends, you don't owe me anything. You just feel bad for me I bet. You're just such a kind person that you always are willing to help people, aren't you? Look you don't know me. You don't know anything about me yet in still you pretend to

be concerned for me. Why?" she asked. Beginning to raise
her voice, "Why do you care so much? What's it to you? I
get it, I do. I'm just some drama that you can go run and
tell all your little friends about huh? If you think that you
and your boyfriend can use this against my husband in
hopes of him climbing the corporate ladder you're wrong,
plus no one will believe you anyways. I'd never flip on my
husband." She paused for a second, as I almost bit off
tongue trying to stay calm. Who the fuck? What the fuck?
My little friends? My boyfriend? This bitch is totally losing
it. He must have bopped her simple ass in the head one too
many times. If she thought she got herself an ass whooping
earlier, she had no idea what was headed her way. The
nerve of her! I am taking my personal time out to save her
ass from being the next statistic and she flips the script on
me? Oh hell no.

Before I could even get a chance to warn her about the ass
whooping that she was conjuring up, she burst out crying. I
don't care, get the hell out. I didn't have any sympathy for
her and I'm starting to think the hoe is bipolar. Maybe all
this time I should've been having drinks with Ted instead
of her crazy ass. My grand-momma warned me about these
white women and their antics. My mind is racing and my
nerves are plucked. As I open my mouth to speak, she
continues loudly speaking, still crying, "Is that it? Do I look
like a charity case to you? Do I look like I need your damn
help?" In my mind I envisioned me dragging this heifer out
of my room by her hair and closing the door behind her
but something inside of me was curious to see how this
thing would play out. I wondered if this was all part of her
plan on how she would get back into her room. Would she
tell her husband that I held her against her will and that
would be the reason why she hadn't been answering his
calls and why she had been missing in action for the past

few hours? Either way, she was officially stranded because she was two seconds away from leaving my room voluntarily or strong-armed, and I wasn't taking her ass back, she better call her ass an Uber. "I think it's probably best if you left now. I don't really foresee this playing out too well, soooo I'm just going to stop you while you're ahead. And I truly hope that everything works out for you both" I said in a slow and calm tone so that she that could understand that I was serious. I walked to the door and opened it signaling that it was time for her to get the hell out. Instead of catching onto my very obvious hints, she didn't move but continued to cry harder and louder. I got a feeling that I'm going to have to call security on this bitch.

Honestly, I didn't sign up for all this. I guess this is what I get for always being so nice and accommodating. Kris was right sometimes I do just need to mind my own business every now and then. This entire predicament that I am in, involving Carter and Barbie is because I ventured out and stepped out of my comfort zone trying to consider other people's feelings. If I just learned to keep to my damn self, my life would be drama free. So, let me paint the scene for you, I'm standing at the open door and she is still sitting down on the bed with her face to the mattress mumbling words which I was hardly interested in hearing. As people walked passed my room I'm sure they couldn't help but to imagine what the heck was going on. My kindness had been compromised and taken for weakness. Lifting her head, she attempts to pull it together again. She wipes the tears from her eyes now putting on a straight face. I knew it, its official, she was crazy. As she gathered her belongings, still sniffling every three seconds, she walked out the door and I let it close behind her. I was no longer concerned about how she would get home or even what would happen when she got there. All I knew was that I was agitated and irritated. Pacing the floor, I thought about calling Cater back but I was over this entire situation. I just kept telling myself in less than 3 days I would be on a flight back home and all of this could be a figment of my imagination. I needed to tell someone this though. I decided to call Jasmine since she was closer to my time zone and tell her what happened. Hopefully she would answer the phone. She always wanted to act like she was so damn busy all the time that usually I would only get to converse with her spontaneously through text messages, but I was going to try my luck. Plus, I haven't chatted with her in a while, she ought to answer.

"Well, hello hussy" I said when she answered the phone, "I finally got you to answer the phone? It's probably going to snow here in Texas!" We talked for hours after she questioned what I was doing out of DC and I brought her up to speed with everything that had been going on in my life since we last spoke. As usual, we laughed and laughed some more as we exchanged stories and quandaries that we had both experienced as of lately. Our lives have always seemed to mirror one another so she could normally relate to the things that I was going through and vice versa. She also commended me on how I handled the situation with Barbie. Once upon a time, I was known to be a little hot headed and easily tempered. The old me would have definitely spazzed out on her ass but Barbie needed to be thanking God for his saving grace and mercies because I literally would have been on her ass like white on rice. I told her about Carter, the award ceremony, and everything that transpired with that protest. She agreed that I had truly stepped out of my box when I even agreed to accept his invite, but she said that he sounded like a nice guy and his daughters sound sweet. She couldn't offer me much advice but that was not what I called her for.

Giving advice was never Jasmine's strong point. In her life, she often acted on impulse, and though things more than likely seemed to work out for her, they were never chances that I personally would be willing to take. I was more of a thinker; I liked sure things, so that's where we differed. Out of my closest girlfriends, Sabrina was the most structured, taking minimal risks, Jas was the extreme and complete opposite, while I was somewhere floating in the middle, straddling the fence, that's what I did best. Upon concluding the conversation, I agreed to come out to visit her soon, with the hope of possibly convincing Sabrina that her husband was more than capable of taking care the kiddies for a few days so she could come too. Ending the call, I took off my clothes and climbed under the covers, it didn't take me long to fall asleep.

I tossed and turned all night; my mind was restless. I woke up not feeling like myself or well enough to go out and conquer the world, instead I wanted to remain in bed. For some reason, Barbie and last night's occurrence overshadowed what Carter and I had been through and was now consuming my thoughts. I managed to drag myself from underneath the covers and into the shower as I prepared to go to work. The day seemed long and dragged out, compared to my most recent days here in Texas. I spoke to my usual's, Mom, Kris, Sabrina, and even succeeded in talking to Brandon for the majority of the day. Speaking with him distracted me from thinking about everything and everyone else, and it made me look forward to returning home. He had engaging conversation, a great sense of humor, and was equally as talkative as I was. Although I vaguely omitted the details of my trip, he fully disclosed what was going on in his life. From failed relationships to his big move to the DMV, I think we covered almost everything. I wasn't eager at the idea of talking to a "new" someone and getting to know them only to have them soon disappear within a week's span but it was fun and kept my time occupied.

Day two of being here alone was pretty much identical to day one, except for the fact that I received a mid-day text from Barbie, apologizing for her actions on Sunday. The text was 4 messages long explaining how she was extremely sorry. "I know that I am probably the last person that you want to hear from right now. First, I want to like to apologize for my actions the other day. I can promise you that was not the norm for me. I had so much going on and on my mind at the time that I was feeling so overwhelmed. Honestly, I think I mentioned before, I've never been good at opening up and expressing my feelings, I usually don't tell my problems to anyone. Secondly, I would like to say thank you. Not just for coming to pick me up but for putting up with my bullshit. You chose to be kind towards me and I want to let you know that I truly did appreciate it and was extremely grateful for your generosity even if I didn't do a good job at expressing it. I'm not perfect by a longshot but I'm woman enough to recognize my mistakes. After several months of debating back and forth, you have helped me realize that I need to seek help for my relationship. I like you and was able to open up to you unlike I have been able to do with anyone else, I'm asking for your forgiveness. If you never want to speak to me again, I totally get it, but I just felt as if I needed to get this off my chest. –Barbie." I still couldn't care less. I was officially done with her. She can keep what her and Ted had going on for as long as she wanted, it wouldn't affect me none. Ignoring her text, I went on with my day, accomplishing my final work tasks for this Texas trip, very much unbothered. I was ready to get the fuck out of this place. I missed my home and most of all, I missed my own bed. My hair needed to be done; I was in desperate need of a manicure, pedicure, and an expedited trip to the spa with a Brazilian wax, accompanied by some filliacio and a forehead kiss. Yes please.

Stopping at a fast food restaurant for dinner and heading back to my room to pack my bags and gather my belongings, I arrived to a bottle of champagne sitting on the tv stand with a note attached to it that read "I'm sorry." Disregarding it, I kicked off my shoes and plopped down on the bed, eventually lying across it as I checked my phone for the time of my flight departure. In the midst reviewing my itinerary, I started engaging in a sexting convo with Kris. He was excited for me to come home especially when I mentioned the fact that I needed some "vitamin D". Texting back and forth with raunchy messages vividly going into detail of what we wanted to do to each other upon sight, followed by me deciding to take things a little further by sending over a few pics as I stepped fresh out the shower. Stashing the bottle of champagne into my luggage and making sure it was wrapped and secured, everything was packed and I was ready to bounce. This had officially been the shortest work trip that I had been on, but thee most action packed, hands down. Having checked in online, I decided to get a couple hours of sleep before waking up butt-crack early to return the rental and catch my red eye flight. When will I eventually learn not to be such a damn procrastinator?

Like clockwork, I woke up late, running around like a crazy person, pacing the floor as I waited for valet to retrieve my car, then panicking as I had the worlds slowest associate assisting me as I returned the rental; I feared that I would miss boarding the plane. After foolishly going to the wrong terminal, I made it just in time to get on. Shaking my head, I made another vow to do better. I know I made one on the way down here but this time I really meant it. Eventually, my tardiness will catch up with me one of these days and I got a feeling that the outcome won't be as pretty.

With the plane still sitting on the runway, my phone began to regain service. A message came through from Brandon asking me if I had returned to the city yet. Before I sent the request for my Uber car service, I responded and told him that we had just landed. He told me that he was had sent a car for me so after I had claimed my baggage I should lookout for an individual with a suit and a sign that read my name. How bold of him? Granted I never mentioned whether or not I had been dealing with anyone else, but how did he know that I hadn't already arranged a ride?

Don't get me wrong, hands down, it was a very nice gesture, but it was a little too forward than I'm used to. I replied "Wow, thank you" to his text. Turning on the front camera of my phone, I wanted to make sure that I looked presentable. Making sure that there was no crust in my eyes, my lips and skin were moisturized, eyebrows going in the same direction, I removed my scarf making sure that my edges were on fleek. Not sure what to expect, I got my bag and identified the gentleman holding the iPad with my name presented on it. With so many thoughts going through my head, where was this car taking me? I hope I wasn't being taken to Brandon or his Firm, I was so unprepared. Just as I felt my mind wandering about what he would look like when I saw him or if he would hug me tightly after seeing me, the driver asked where I wanted to go. As I texted Sabrina to let her know what was going on and that I might need a ride home from her office, the driver asked me again where I would like to be taken. With a sigh of relief, I asked to be taken home.

Collecting my accumulated mail and making my way to my door, I fumbled around in my overstuffed purse looking for my key fob to gain access to my house. With Sabrina calling my phone, I rushed to answer it, but missed the call. Dropping my bags on the floor of my bedroom, I laid across my bed and called her back. She said that she had some down time at work and wanted to hear the scoop of what ended up transpiring between Carter and I and how my trip ended up with Brandon sending a car to pick me up from the airport. I told her that it was a long story and that we definitely needed to sit down for drinks so I could bring her up to speed. I asked her about the kids and work and she informed me that the kids were good and work was great, but she anxiously needed to talk to me and thought that having the conversation over drinks would be most appropriate. After suggesting a few topics on what she needed to vent about, she said that she didn't want to talk about it because she didn't feel like crying at work. I immediately started to think the worst. "Did you have lunch yet?", she told me that she hadn't, but she hadn't had much of an appetite either. Extremely concerned, "How about I come over this evening after you get off? I could come over and grab some Mediterranean food and a bottle of wine, and we can just sit and chat. I could even pick up something for the kids to eat since they're so damn picky when it comes to their food. How does that sound? Will Jay be home?" I asked. If Jay (her hubby) was home, I'm not sure how productive our chat could be, given the nature of whatever she needed to say. I always felt as though he looked at me as being a bad influence towards his wife. I'm sure he would rather her hang out with other married women who had their lives much more furnished and someone who didn't live as spontaneous as I did, but oh well. He had to put up with me because Sabrina and I were practically sisters. She said that he would be home but it shouldn't be a problem, I told her that I would see her at 7pm.

So now with several hours to waste until I would start getting ready to go see her, I hit up Brandon to thank him for the car and to see how his morning had been so far. He didn't answer and as I began to send him a text, he called back. I hated when that happened, especially if I already started to compose a substantial amount of words. Answering his call, he asked if I had made it home safely and how I was feeling after my flight. I hadn't even had the chance to thank him again or ask about his morning before he took full control over the conversation and asked me to meet him for lunch. Thinking to myself "this is a bit much", I agreed to the meeting. Offering to send another car, I preferred to drive. I had some other errands that I could run while I would be out, making my day off semi-productive. Changing my clothes into something a tad bit more stylish and hitting my edges with the flat iron one mo' again, I was out the door within 41 minutes. As long as I could keep my grooming time under an hour, I would commend myself.

I arrived at the office and found street parking, lucky me. I called Brandon to let him know I was here and texted Sabrina to let her know that I would be stopping by her office afterwards if she hadn't left by then. Brandon came out to meet me in a white Burberry polo top, with the first button undone, and black pants and black shoes of some sort. I didn't know exactly what to do when I saw him so I just got out of the car stood there, hoping that he would make the first move, I would be able to gauge my reaction according to his. Walking up to me exposing his beautiful edge to edge bite smile, he extended his arms outwards to hug me. Now, I don't know if it was my excited hormones or the smell of his cologne that got my juices flowing but that hug was everything I had imagined it to be! Stepping back and looking me up and down, he asked if I had anything in mind that I would like to eat for lunch, then he mentioned this restaurant that he liked to frequent with his colleagues occasionally. Taking into consideration that I had on heels, he asked if I was up for walking as he assured me that the place wasn't far. Immediately I fell in love. He cared about my left pinky toe that would soon go numb in the shoes that I had chosen to wear. I didn't want him to think that I was one of those women, so I agreed to be a soldier and endure the pain that was soon to come, especially if this place wasn't at the end of the block. I didn't really care what or where we ate, it really didn't matter to me, I was starving, I would eat a pig's ass if it was cooked right.

Taking his suggestion, we ended up at this steakhouse. I thought it was going to be some little quaint spot with really good food, but this place was ritzier than I imagined. He must have frequented the establishment a few times prior and had been a generous tipper because the waitresses seemed to know him by name while other staff members continuously greeted him throughout the duration of our stay. I had a steak and shrimp selection cooked medium rare, per Brandon's recommendation and it was absolutely to die for. Not literally, but you get my drift. So succulent and tender, I'd never had steak that delicious and I've been to some expensive restaurants. So, an appetizer, 2 entrées, 2 side dishes and a bottle of wine later, we started to wrap up our outing. I knew that he needed to get back to the office and continue his work day, but our conversation and chemistry was so good that I could've stayed there all day just staring at his smile. When the bill came I happened to catch a glimpse of it. $230?!? For lunch? That was a bit extreme, naw fuck that, it wasn't a bit extreme, it was... I don't even know what the word for that was. Now I don't mind splurging every now and then on food, but for the most part, I try keep it sensible especially if it's not a special occasion. That was too much. I wanted to offer to help pay something on it, but I was scared that he might actually take me up on it. Lord! Maybe I could volunteer to leave the tip, that would be more manageable. Hoping that my facial expression hadn't reflected the thoughts that quickly ran through my mind after seeing it, he pulled out his American Express and placed it in the card holder without even looking at it first. Looking at him, he returned the stare and smiled, all I could do was let out a little laugh. Walking back to the building, I thanked him for the ride and the lunch, letting him know that his actions had been far too kind. He told me that a woman of my caliber should be treated as such and he didn't mind showing me how I should be treated. He was so convincing that I started to believe him.

Smiling from ear to ear, he hugged and kissed me on my cheek as he asked what I had planned for the evening. Did he want some ass? If he did, he had a good chance of getting some after he had fed me and mentally stimulated me for the past hour and 17 mins. I told him that I had some errands to run and still wanted to unpack. I omitted the fact that Sabrina and I had made plans for later just in case he threw out the idea of us meeting up again. Instead he told me that he would be consumed with work for the next few nights however he did express the fact that he wanted to talk to me later. That was fine with me. Between me catching up with my homegirl and Kris, little did he know, I was going to be occupied for the next couple of days also. Kissing my cheek again, sending a burst of tingles up my spine and causing goosebumps on my arm, we parted ways. As I got into my car, I quickly sent a text to Sabrina letting her know that I would meet with her later. I thought it would be weird running back into Brandon after he thought that I was leaving, and I didn't want him to think that I was gossiping about him to her. I wanted to be on my best behavior.

Leaving DC and heading to the Target in Virginia, I needed to grab some toiletries, food for the house, and cleaning supplies, amongst whatever else was on sale that I would purchase on impulse as I always did in that store. As I drove, I replayed Brandon and I's conversations in my mind and somehow the thought of Carter crept in. I reflected on how I had been meeting some interesting people in the last few days and how I thought that it could be a sign for an interesting future for me and my personal life. Going out on a limb, I shot Carter a text, just to say hi and mainly to see if he would respond. Within moments the little grey typing bubble appeared then went away, but there was no reply. Pulling up into the parking lot, he called. I guess what he needed to say was too much to text, so he decided to call? Answering, the conversation started off with casual small talk then progressed into us talking about what emerged when we were in Texas. Discussing everything except the rally, it's almost like it never happened. I was ok with not touching on that topic though, for now, I was just glad that there were no harbored feelings towards me. Filling him in on Barbie and her antics, I described what happened with her before I left. Making jokes about it, I did finish it off by saying that I felt bad for her and I hope that she'd find help before things got too out of hand. I sat in the car and talked to him for hours. Time had flown by and the sun was on its way down. He did mention something along the lines of him going to go surprise the girls by picking them up from school, but the time difference never dawned on me. It wasn't until Sabrina called me to ask why I hadn't returned any of her texts that I realized how late it was. With the clock reading 5:45pm, I really didn't have much time to accomplish much of anything. Still with the phone to my ear I walked into Target still carrying on my conversation. We talked until he picked up the girls and had them in the car. I chatted with them for a little bit before ending the call. Placing a food order to take over Sabrina's, I rushed to make sure that I had gotten everything including the 2 bottles of wine; I was completely exhausted.

Entertaining my God-children for a few, I noticed that her son Emmanuel had on a hospital bracelet, but I didn't pay it much attention. If it would have been something important, I'm sure that she would have mentioned it when I spoke with her during my trip. As we made our way to the basement to commence our girl talk, I had so much to catch her up on, but I was more curious to know what had her so down. Not wanting to bombard her with all my good news and events to make her feel even more depressed, I didn't know whether to tell my story first or to go last. Being the good friend that I am, I encouraged her to share. Drinking the entire glass of wine in her hand she stared at the floor and said nothing. Trying to ease the tension, I say jokingly, "so I brought my stun gun, who do I need to touch?" Looking up, she didn't laugh, nor did she crack a smile.

Really alarmed, Sabrina has never been the wild sporadic one who made brash decisions, so for her to be this deep in thought really concerned me. Sitting in silence for a minute or two, the only noises being made were those of the footsteps from the children as their father prepared to get them winded down for the night and into their beds. "I fucked up" she spoke softly. I heard what she said but I asked her to repeat herself. "I fucked up" she said again, this time a little louder. "What happened?" I asked, "At work?" She took a moment and then answered "I took Emmanuel to the emergency room because he had been running a fever, ok wait, this started about a week ago" she retracted. "Jay and I were at his parents' house spending some time with them and helping them organize some of their things around the house and his ghetto trifling ass sister was there. You already know how I feel about her. Well, she's there putting her two cents in on everything, as usual. So, me, feeling irritated and beginning to get annoyed, I went into the other room with the kids and his mother, just to get away from that dizzy cunt." I've never heard her talk like this before, so again, it caught me a little off guard, but I let her continue without disruption.

"Now I noticed that Emmanuel was a little warm earlier that day when I was getting him dressed, but he wasn't warm enough to the point where I became concerned. I mean he was running around and playing, so I had just written it off as him being overheated. I thought nothing else about it, until Jay's mother mentioned it. At that time, I felt him again and he felt maybe a tad bit warmer than before, but still not like hot...hot. So, I make him sit down for a little while as his grandmother went and got a thermometer. After taking his temperature, we realized that he was indeed running a fever, which was weird because he hadn't been sick or had any other symptoms. We didn't make it a big ordeal, in fact, I said that I would go and pick up some Tylenol or something on the way home and that was that.

To make a long story short, I managed to make it through family time without the normal bickering back and forth with his sister. We went home, I gave Emmanuel some meds to break the fever, got the kids ready for bed, and got my stuff ready for work. Next day, got the kids ready for school; I had a deposition, so I was pretty busy at work, but I get a message from Jay saying that Manny had been taken to the nurse's office during his gym period because he got dizzy and fell. He said that he was far away from the school and that he was going to get his mom or sister to go pick him up until he could get there. Already, I'm not thrilled, I cannot leave work, I mean, I could but it would be a very bad situation for me. Jay assured me that everything would be ok. He was leaving work and would be there soon. I probably would have been better off leaving because I couldn't concentrate at all, but I got through it and immediately called Jay to find out what the current situation was. He said that his mother had suggested taking the kid to the Dr.'s just to make sure that it was nothing serious since the fever had still been lingering and now that he had gotten dizzy, it raised some concerns. I agreed."

"So, I go and meet them at the hospital. Stopping at the nurse's station for an update on my son's condition. She told me that the Dr. was in the room with Jay and my sister. I cringed. I already could hear his big-mouth sister's voice. God, I thought to myself, she is so uncouth. Anyways, something in my soul told me to just listen before I walked in. Already slightly in a panic, my heart was beating so fast. From where I was standing I could see the Dr. was walking out from the room and closing the curtain behind him. As I approached the room and pulled open the curtain, I missed the first part of the statement

but what I did catch was her saying, "hopefully it's nothing serious, like him needing a transfusion or anything because if he does, then she'd be forced to come clean about you not being his father, then everyone will know that her little two-faced ass is a lying bitch." I was like what the fuck? I thought that I had said it to myself, but everything happened so fast, I must have said it out loud. I snatched that curtain open like "excuse me?" She just sat there with this dumb look on her face as he got up and greeted me with a kiss. I couldn't think straight. First of all, I don't like her for one, why did she have to be here is all I kept thinking to myself, secondly, what the fuck was she talking about, and third off don't be talking shit about me in front of my child. I didn't give a fuck if he was sleeping or not. So, she doesn't look at me or speak to me but she has this stank sorta look on her face. I give a general "hey" out of whatever respect that I have for her, but she doesn't say anything. As I go and sit on the bed with my child and rub his head, I ask what is going on. As my husband begins to tell me that the Dr. wanted to run some more tests before making a determination. Taking all of that in, I asked again, this time looking straight at her "so, what was going on?" Jay said "Babe, what are you talking about? I just told you." "No" I said in a nice calm voice, "I thought I overheard something as I was walking into the room and since everyone seemed to be talking about me, I figured since I'm here, this would be the perfect opportunity to talk." Now you know that I'm not the confrontation type, but I've grown so tired of her shit.

Up until this point, I've showed her respect because of her position as my husband's sister and I recognize that they do have a close relationship and I would never want to come in between the middle of that, but I had enough. I mean, really, enough was enough and I don't know why I felt so compelled to confront her right then and there, but I did. I'm not into making scenes, hell, I barely even argue outside of the courtroom, but I wanted to know if what I thought I heard was what I actually heard." I poured myself another glass of wine, this was getting interesting.

"So, at first, she wouldn't answer me, and he was starting to play dumb and act retarded which infuriated me more, like do not insult my intelligence, but since they wanted to pretend like nobody knew what I was referring to, I decided to be cordial and leave it be. See, Jay is not stupid by any means, he knows who I am even if she doesn't, so he knows I heard what I heard, he probably just doesn't know how much of it I heard. So, we sit there for another 4 hours as medical personnel continued to run tests and poke and probe my child. Meanwhile, all conversations were kept to a minimum. It got late and my phone reception was horrible. Everything in my soul didn't want me to leave the room but I needed to call my mother back, she had been calling me non-stop about Emmanuel's condition. I walk to the cafeteria but on my way there, I kept replaying over in my mind what I know I heard and how I handled the situation, and then I started thinking. I began to doubt myself and what I once knew I heard. Like what would cause her to say that? Maybe they were talking about someone else because if that was the case, which it wasn't, I would've been the first one to know that there was a possibility of Jay not being his father. Grabbing a bag of chips, I found a table in the corner of the dining area and called my mom back. Talking to her, put her mind at ease. They were still running tests on baby boy but I knew he would be fine. Since it was late, I didn't keep her long, I told her that I would text her when I finally got out of there and for her to call me in the morning. Still snacking, I couldn't get that statement out of my head. Evaluating the situations and dissecting them, nothing seemed to make sense."

"In the middle of my thoughts, I receive a text from Jay saying the Dr.'s had returned and that I should come back. I rush back to the room only for the Dr. to tell us that the boy has an ear infection. He scared me initially because he said he wanted to rule out meningitis and some type of bacterial infection, but he directed us to keep an eye on him and if any other symptoms began to occur, to either bring him back into the emergency room or to follow up with his primary care physician. Relieved that it was nothing major, I was still deep in my feelings. I told Jay that he could head home and relieve his mother from her duties of watching the other two and that I would wait for Emmanuel's discharge papers to be printed and swing by and grab his prescription from the pharmacy before heading home. We went back and forth about who was going to do what until we finally agreed that he would bring the kid home while I grabbed something for us to eat too.

Because there was nothing else to be done, Ms. Run-her-mouth-all-the-damn-time decides to use me leaving as a reason to walk out behind me. I didn't want to say anything to her, I don't like her, but I did thank her for being there to pick the boy up from school. Instead of this bitch just saying thank you like a normal damn person, she decides to express her opinion about my parenting skills."
"Like what? What did she say? She doesn't have any kids, right?" I asked. "I mean technically she doesn't, her boyfriend that she's been shacked up with for 100 years has a kid that he has custody of, but that's beside the point. Don't tell me how to raise my child. Ok, so let me go back.

At first, I kindly ignored her and then when she said it again, as if I didn't hear her the first time. Chile, I lost it."

"Ok but what was she saying?" I asked again. "She started off sounding like she was being sincere, telling me to thank God for things not being as serious as they could've been and how she was glad that she had a more flexible job that allowed for her to go and get to him. Low key, I thought that she was throwing shade, but I let it ride. Not to mention that her comparing her job of working at the Gap with a flexible schedule versus my husband's and my job, is laughable. Then she goes on said something along the lines of, if I would've brought him in the earlier stages of his symptoms, he might not have suffered as long as he did and that next time something like this happens, I should pretend to be more concerned about my child's health. So here we are 5 seconds from the entrance of the emergency room, going back and forth, over talking each other, creating a small performance. Security ends up coming outside trying to deescalate the situation however neither one of us was paying him any attention. As he got in between the middle of us there was some pushing and shoving and honestly, I don't know who swung first, but there we are fighting in the damn parking lot like the place where the ambulances park. She was definitely at the right place because I had been waiting nearly 4 and half years to wear her little ass out. And with this built up aggression from work and home, she might need some medical attention when I was finished with her." "I swear I called her everything except a child of God. As I mentioned before, everything happened so fast, so all I really remember was being on the ground with the security guard still trying to intervene and I could feel someone pulling me from behind. Glancing over, I could see my baby standing there watching his aunt and I act a fool. As security helped her get herself together, I then realized that my husband was the one who acted in separating the two of us. Picking up my son, I swiftly walked towards my car. I am too classy of a lady to be outside fighting like some hood rat and I was exceedingly embarrassed that my son had to witness me act in the manner. Jay let me walk away, he knew that I was mad. I could hear her still talking shit and I could hear him talking to her, but I was so mad I didn't even care to know what he was saying to her. Then that's when she said it! She yelled from across the parking lot, "that's right, take your son and go, we all know that aint Jeremiah's son anyway, trifling bitch." Too mad to even turn around and entertain her statements, I put Manny in the car and pulled off. Wide awake, he didn't say a word. Slowly the tears started falling down my face. I wasn't hurt or anything, I think that the excitement from everything had my adrenaline going. I was angry at myself more than anything, for allowing her to take me out of character. If I didn't have the boy with me, I would've gone elsewhere, but since his mom was at the house I decided to go home and send her on her way. I honestly wasn't in the mood for any of them and I had already managed to make a fool out of myself once tonight, I just didn't want anyone to say anything else to me."

"Arriving at the house, I took the kid out of the car, grabbed his prescription and came into the house. Their grandmother had cooked dinner for them and had just gotten the kids out of the tub and was preparing them for bed. I came in and spoke to her, thanking her for everything that she had done while we had been at the hospital." In a calming voice I asked, "Do you think that she knew what was going on at the time? Like do you think that they called her and told her what happened?" "I honestly couldn't have cared less if they did. If she did know, she didn't say anything or act any type of way, she was her same loving self she had always been, but I didn't feel like talking or having a conversation with her either, I really wanted to be alone. Part of me hoped that Jay kept his ass out and decided to stay at his mother's or sister's to give me time to cool off, but the other part of me felt like we needed to talk. After washing up Manny and getting him in the bed, I kissed the kids and tucked them in and his mother left, I got in the shower; put on my pj's and crawled in the bed. As I laid there, I heard a small knock at the door, disguising the frustration in my voice, I welcomed the little knocker in the room. Manny said that he couldn't sleep and asked if he could come in the bed with me. Since Jay still wasn't home, I said what the hell and let him come and get under the covers. We laid there together, in silence, watching a late night news show as he cuddled up under me. I didn't know what to say to him or even if I should say anything to him about what he witnessed. I knew the conversation needed to be had; I just wasn't sure when the right time was to have it."

"As he lays on my chest, he asked me in the most innocent voice if I was ok. It broke my heart. I lifted his head and told him that I was alright and that his auntie and I did not act appropriately. I told him that I was sorry for what he had to see but everything was going to be fine. I didn't touch on the last statement that she yelled when we were leaving because I honestly didn't know what to say. I just hoped that he wouldn't ask about it. The thought of it infuriated me more. I found it very inappropriate and inconsiderate of her to feel like she needed to say what she said in front of my child, but hey, you can't expect much from ghetto ass ratchet bitches. Feeling myself getting mad all over again, I did my best to control it without him sensing that something was bothering me. I pushed his head back down on my chest and we continued to lay there. Both drifting off to sleep, I was awakened by the sound of the alarm system signaling that Jay was home. As I followed his footsteps with my ears, I could hear him fumbling with something downstairs and then go into the kitchen; he came upstairs making a stop in the kid's room for a brief second. Once I heard the kid's bedroom door close, I heard him mumble something to himself as I could hear his footsteps coming closer to our bedroom. Trying to decide if I should pretend to be sleeping to avoid a late-night conversation or appear to be awake, I saw the doorknob turn. Making eye contact with one another through the lighting of the tv, he didn't say anything to me and I didn't say anything to him. He walked over to the bed and gently picked up Emmanuel and carried him back to his room. I thought to myself, dammit, this isn't going to go well."

"When he returned to the room, he went into the bathroom and I heard the shower cut on. He came out to the dresser and got out some pajama pants and a tee shirt and took them in the bathroom with him. Now I know it doesn't seem like a big deal, but I've known this man for years. And not to be personal or anything, but he doesn't wear pajamas, so that in itself was a little odd. Not to mention he took them in the bathroom with him too. But not to make a big deal about it, I just repositioned my body with my back facing the bathroom and his side of the bed. I remained awake until I heard the shower cut off and heard the bathroom door open. I could hear him moving around but I refused to turn to see what he was doing. I felt him pull the covers back and adjust the pillows, but I never felt him get into the bed. Hearing the bedroom door close, I heard his footsteps going down the stairs. Turning over, I noticed that he had taken his pillows and left. Even though

I really didn't feel like talking about the situation at this very moment, I expected him to say something at least. I left it alone though and eventually went to sleep. The next day everything seemed normal. I got the kids ready for school, he made breakfast, you know, our daily rituals, but his interactions with me were different, they were short and brief. Now I didn't feel like I had done anything wrong in the situation, hell, she provoked me, but I know that's his sister and he probably feels like he's in the middle, but damn he could at least have asked my side of the story, you feel me? I'm sure that he had gotten her side of the story." "I get it", I answered. "So, to make a long story short" she says once again, "after I got the kids all packed up and onto the school bus, I called in and let my secretary know that I would be in late and as he was getting ready for work, mind you still managing to avoid me, I confronted him. I asked him how he was treating me like I had done something wrong, when she was obviously the one that provoked me. Why he didn't come to ask if I was ok or anything and why he was acting as if nothing had happened. Nonchalantly he said how he had a headache last night and he had grown tired of the bickering and fighting between his sister and me. He said that he knew that I could handle my own, but he was more pissed off about the time and place that we chose to let our attitudes clash, and in front of our child at that. Now me, being the person that I am, never knowing when to shut the hell up, sarcastically added my two cents, mumbling "at least you know that that's our child", why the hell does she keep saying that it's not?"

So, he tells me that a couple years back he had a slight inclination that Manny wasn't his. To cure his suspicions, he swabbed my baby's cheek and sent off the sample for DNA testing. He says that his sister is the only person that he had told and how he truly regrets telling her. He said that at that time, he had already shared a bond with Emmanuel and that he was his son even if the DNA test proved that he wasn't biologically. He never had to test the last two because they were a spitting image of him, so he knew that they were his. He claims that he never treated any of them differently and loves them all equally. Absolutely speechless, I didn't know what to say. How could that be? Jay had been the only person that I had been with. I'm not one of those loose irresponsible women that just go around fucking every Tom, Dick, and Harry. So, I just sat there looking stupid, trying to think of any possible logical reason that could make sense of all of this. I don't understand how this is possible, I managed to say to him. He gave me this unentertained look. I was adamant that the test had to be wrong. He was truly the only person that I had been with while we were together." I sat there looking confused. She was right, she had never been that type of girl, as long as I had known her, now if we had been talking about Jasmine, this could have been a different story, but Sabrina was the "play it safe" one out of all of us. "So, then what happened?" I asked.

"I honestly couldn't give him an answer, because in my heart and in my brain, Manny was his child. I'm not one of those women who blame guys to be the daddy when he's not. If I was placed in that predicament, I honestly would just own up to my shit. Shit, I'm grown, but I honestly didn't have any explanation for why the test would come back negative. We ended the conversation by him saying that he didn't have any hard feelings towards me and that he had a very important meeting at work and that we could finish the conversation later." Sabrina just stared at me. I don't know what the hell she's looking at me for, if she didn't know, I damn sure don't know. "But if he felt that ways towards Manny, like it's his son regardless and he loves him unconditionally, then why would he even get the test done, why even tell anyone? At the end of the day, it was bound to come back and bite either one of you in the ass." I said. I knew that wasn't the best answer or better yet statement to say, but I didn't want her to feel like she was the only one who fucked up. "So now what happens going forward?" I ask.

She says that she decided not to go into work at all until today because she couldn't focus, and they haven't talked about it since yesterday morning. All I could think was WOW, never in a million years would I have guessed that to be what she wanted to share with me. This sounded like something from the chronicles of my life. We sat and talked for another 2 hours about the situation until I said something that triggered a memory from her past. I remembered her dealing with this guy we had met one night, for a very short period of time right before her and Jay had gotten together, and I asked if he could have possibly been a prospect. She was unwavering at the idea that she could have possibly gotten pregnant by him. She couldn't even remember having unprotected sex with him at all, and she said they only talked for a few weeks before she met Jay and decided to dedicate all of her undivided attention to him. I encouraged her not to stress over it too much and not to think so long and hard about it, especially if Jay had already agreed to marry her and have more children by her after knowing what he knew, she was going to be ok. For goodness sake, this news wasn't new to him, it was only new to her. I could tell that she was hurt and confused and didn't know what to think, but one thing was for sure, she had herself a good man.

Reiterating how fortunate enough she was to have Jay, I reminded her that there weren't too many stand up dudes in this day and age, willing to do such and that she needed not to worry. In my mind, I knew that was a damn lie, now had I been in that situation, Lord only knows what I would do. I'd probably just stick to my story, swab one of the other baby's cheeks and mail it off for testing just to prove him wrong, but I'm a special type of person. 2 bottles of wine down, I knew that there was no way that I was going to tell her about my adventures in Texas tonight.

After trying to make light of her situation for the past couple hours, she finally changes the topic and asks, "So tell me what's being going on with you and this guy from Texas. And also, what about the guy from my job?" Just the tone in the way that she said it, referencing me manipulating 2 guys even though that wasn't the case, well maybe it was but I didn't like the way it sounded, made me feel awkward. I told her that we would need more time and more wine for me to tell my story. Agreeing to meet up over the weekend and chat in detail about the life and times of Ms. Brooke, I got into my car and pulled my phone from my purse. 17 messages, 4 missed calls, and 1 voice message of which were from Kris wondering where I was and I why I wasn't answering. My only hope was that he wasn't at my house when I got there because I was honestly thinking of using the excuse of me being sleep this entire time. Something in my soul told me to listen to his voicemail and that's when I discovered that he was and had been at my house and was infuriated that I was missing in action. I called him and told him that I had been over Sabrina's and how I don't get good reception in her basement. Pissed off, he advises me that it would be in my best interest to make my way home. With everything I had going on, he was honestly the last person on my mind, but I am horny as fuck, so I probably should act right, at least for now. I'll be sure that he wears a condom the entire time though; I don't want a "Sabrina" situation if I decide to throw Brandon a little tail too. #NoShade

Pulling up at my condo, I see my tinted new Land Rover parked and sitting pretty. While I was away, to be totally honest, I kept forgetting all about it, but when I saw it I immediately got excited all over again. Walking into the house prepared to give him all of me, he stood in the foyer when I opened the door. His facial expression did not look as thrilled to see me as I was to see him. Walking directly to him, I immediately start to kiss on him letting him know how much I missed him while I was away. Forcing his lips to kiss me back, I slowly ran my tongue across his and gently bit his bottom lip, I know what he likes. He looked so damn cute when he was pissed off.

With that stern face, those almond shaped slanted eyes, fresh haircut, and his abnormally long and full eyelashes, I kissed him as he desperately tried hard to resist me. Asking if he missed me too, he refused to answer. Leaning down, I softly gave his nipple a gentle bite through his shirt; I knew that it was one of his hot spots. Standing and staring unimpressed, that didn't stop me. I continued to kiss while I began to undo his pants with my hands. Making my way to his ear with my tongue, he relaxed and gave in, just a little. He grabbed the back of my neck and let out a small moan. I knew he was into it. Our kissing became intense and my kitty soon turned into a slip and slide. Unable to compose himself any longer, he picked me up and carried me into the room, stubbing his foot on the luggage I left in the middle of my bedroom floor.

With my legs still wrapped around him and his pants unbuttoned, I maneuvered to getting his pants to slide down under his waist using my thighs. Dropping my legs, I kicked off my heels as he began to unbutton and unzip my pants. Pulling them off still leaving my panties slightly up above my hips, I arched my back giving him easy access to take my shirt off over my head, as he single-handedly unsnapped my bra. With my nipples standing tall at full attention, he began on suck on the right one, slightly nibbling on it like I like, alternating between the left and the right. Those were my "cheat codes", spots that would immediately get me turned on and he knew it. His dick was rock hard as the imprint protruded through his black Versace Collection briefs that I had got him from Saks for his birthday. Wrapping my legs back around his waist, I rubbed his dick though his drawers exposing it to escape through the front slit. I lifted my pelvis and positioned myself to where his genitals now rubbed against my inner pussy lips as he continued to interchangeably kiss me and suck on my breast. Intentionally grabbing his penis and guiding it to slide up and down this drenched pussy to create a small warm explosion of my juices, I could tell I was driving him crazy. He really did miss me.

As I continued to tease him by directing his penis to the entry of my "wet & wild" playground, he forcefully thrusted himself into me causing my body to quiver. The conversation that Sabrina and I had just had and all that shit that I was talking to myself in the car about us having protected sex because of Brandon went straight out of the window. God, I love this man. Even though he pisses me off and our situation is fucked up in every single way possible, no one can make my body feel the way that he does. As crazy and as juvenile as it sounds, it's almost as if his penis was sculpted specifically for me. It was a perfect fit. It hit each wall just effortlessly and made me squirt uncontrollably.

Going at it like back in our college days, switching positions, head hanging off of the bed, choking and hair pulling, & knocking the shit off the nightstand; I felt young again. 29 minutes straight in and we were still going strong, fucking and sucking, somehow making our way onto the floor. He's got me bent over, ass in the air, body fully exposed, back perfectly arched, he's making me work hard for this car. My knees are getting carpet burned but I don't care, I am begging him not to stop. Our sex is undeniably amazing. 5 orgasms in and I'm slowly tapping out. My body is doused in sweat and my hair is stuck to my face. All of my energy has been sucked from my body, literally. As he is about to cum for the second time, this time asking for my face as his new target. Usually I'm not primarily a fan of face shots but I'll make an expectation since my hair already needs to be done.

Opening my mouth, I received my "protein shake", eyes wide open and tongue extended, as he prefers. With his lifeless body, he moans and groans as he gets up from the floor. From the bathroom he yells, "Damn baby, you were making a nigga work hard." Sitting on the floor with a mouthful, I just want him to get the hell out, so I can go in, I'm way too lazy to walk all the way to the kitchen. Bringing me a warm washcloth to wipe off with, I brush past him trying to spit out his contents. He likes me to swallow but it goes against my diet. Being the asshole that he is, he catches on to what I'm trying to do to and attempts to stall me from making it to the sink. Ending up swallowing it in efforts to not to look dumb by drooling, "You're an asshole, you know that?" I said sarcastically. "What do you get out of that anyway? Damn it's not enough that I already let you cum in my mouth? Why I gotta swallow it too?" With a straight face he responds, "Do you hear me complaining when I swallow yours?" Rolling my eyes, I go into the closet and grab a towel. "What you about to do?" he asks. "I'm getting in the shower" as I go into the bathroom and close the door behind me. Usually he'd try to sneak in with me, but I knew that his little ass was worn out.

Stepping fresh from the bathroom, wrapped in a towel, I find this boy ass naked laying on top of my pure white down comforter, knocked out; he must have lost his mind. Deciding not to put any night apparel on, I pulled back the comforter and slid in the bed forcing him to move over and get under the covers. He mumbles that he needs to go but he never moves. I mention to him that my old car keys are on the kitchen bar, hinting for him to take them and leave my new toy. He says ok as if he comprehends what I just said but I know he's just talking. I have a small feeling that there will be all types of small hoops that I will have to jump through to actually get this car, but whatever. If the story that he gave me about his wife questioning the car is true, he won't be able to carry on the shams much longer anyhow. I cuddle up next to him as he puts his arm around me. Sending a goodnight text to Brandon, I set the 3 alarms on my phone while Kris is in a mini coma. He will be in for a rude awakening when he finally gets up and realizes what time it is. Oh well, that's his business. In the meantime, I'll settle for and enjoy this moment.

Waking up to the sound of my 1st alarm going off, I realized that Kris had already left. I must have been extremely tired because I don't remember hearing him moving around or feel him kiss me goodbye, as he always did when he was leaving. Hitting the snooze button, I had two more alarms that needed to go off before I needed to get out of bed to make it to work on time. Unable to go back to sleep, I scrolled through my phone reading the early good morning text that Brandon had sent wishing me a great day and emphasizing the fact that he wanted to meet up later. I followed that text with some scrolling through my social media to see if there was anything interesting that I had missed. After about 15 mins of judging and criticizing other people's lives, I convinced myself to get up and get a head start on my day. Maybe with the extra time that I had, I could put on a little makeup, a little mascara, maybe even stop by Starbucks to grab some breakfast, I was feeling good.

I got dressed, put on my favorite Ralph Lauren skirt and my Christian Louboutin "Last Empress" pumps, prayed over my hair and slicked it back into a ponytail (thank God for edge control), and headed for the door. I noticed that my Lexus keys were still where I had left them, which means he didn't take it. Walking out of the door, I doubled back to fridge to grab a bottle of sparkling water before heading for my car. The sun was out, I was glowing, and I had a little extra pep in my step; I had a feeling it was going to be a good day. Taking in the fresh air and amazing views of my neighborhood, I noticed that the Land Rover was still parked. Does someone in this complex have the same one because that would suck, big time? I tried not to stare at it too long, with the tint on the windows being so dark, I really couldn't see much of anything. I got in my car and called Kris to say good morning and to ask if that was the car. Of course, he didn't answer. I got in my car in attempts to pull off, making an extra effort to ride by the car which I thought was my new ride, wanting to check the license plates. The car had temporary Maryland tags, so it would make sense that it would be mine, but then again it was a brand-new car so it's safe to say that anyone who had the car would have a temporary tag on it, I think. Not trying to put too much more thought into it, with my windows half down and my sunroof open, I began to pull out of my community, when Kris called me back.

"Hey babe" I answered. He sounded like he was still sleep and hadn't yet brushed his teeth. I told him that I was just checking in on him and I was on my way to work. I asked him what time he left since I never heard him. I really wanted to ask the million-dollar question, but I didn't want to seem too pressed. He told me that he had left at like 5am, then he proceeded to tell me about how tired he was and how he needed to get up to get his day started. Then he says what I was waiting for "Well, I take it that you saw the key on the living room table since you're already on you way to work. I forgot the spare key at my house so be careful for now." JACKPOT!! That was my car in the parking lot. Still playing calm and keeping my composure I asked why he didn't take my old car key and just drive that car home like I suggested. "And run the risk of giving that miserable bitch something else to complain about, naw, I'm good. Plus, I had a bomb ass uber driver, he didn't talk too much. I closed my eyes and before I knew it I was back home." He said. Slightly irritated, I brushed it off and popped a U-turn. I had time to kill anyway so what the hell.

I ran into my house, found the key fob, grabbed my Gucci frames, and jetted out to the car. I felt like a kid on Christmas morning. Once inside I took a second to admire the layout of the dash and the setup of the features while taking in the scent of that new car smell. Once I figured out how to pair my phone with the car, I was out. Feeling like a teenager again, I no longer felt like even going into the office anymore, I just wanted to joyride around all day.

Feeling like new money, I headed to Starbucks to get some breakfast. Now usually I take full advantage of the drive thru service but I was feeling like I needed to step out on these hoes. Parking away from the other cars, in a corner spot, I was ready to strut my stuff across this lot. I looked down at my purse and realized that I should've probably changed it when I went back for the car keys, I mean, I was tired of seeing that bag. I had carried it each day of my trip and still had it on my shoulder. I needed a new accessory to go with my new car. Maybe after work I'd treat myself to a little gift.

Grabbing only my wallet out of the bag, I walked like I owned a chain of Starbucks franchises. Nobody could tell me nothing, I was on my shit. "Next in line" the barista called. Placing my order, I thought about how nice it would be if I picked up something for Brandon to nibble on in-between working his case. And if I got Brandon something then naturally I would need to pick Sabrina up something too. Fuck it! Food for everyone! Feeling amazing, I even picked up the tab of the lady and her small child waiting in line behind me, plus I threw in an extra cookie. I call it "paying it forward". Grabbing my items marked with the letter "B", I strutted back to my car. Calling Brandon to engage him into small talk, I thought that I should probably have called him before I had this wonderful idea to make sure he was even in the office. He didn't answer so I called Sabrina, she was there, and I told her that I was going to stop by in a few and that I had a special treat for her. Once I arrived, I didn't want to park my car in the garage, it didn't belong there, it belonged in the front of her building for everyone to see and admire it. So, for the record, I'm usually not this superficial or materialistic but it's something about this new car that was bringing it out of me. I called her and told her that there was no parking and that she needed to come down to grab the items, but shortly thereafter a spot became available. I tried to get out of the car as quickly as possible to avoid her seeing my new whip. I knew she would have questions and I didn't necessarily have any answers for her just yet. I hadn't successfully thought-out the plan to the fullest extent.

Finally parked as I am preparing to walk into her building, she comes walking out. "Don't be using me as an excuse to come here and see that guy", she says laughing. "Oh, and excuse me, you done pulled out the red bottoms on 'em today huh? You are showing off, look at you. But on a serious note, Brooke, I need him focused. He's working on a very important case here at the Firm; don't be in here trying to get in his head and off of his A-game. We really need this." Ignoring her statement, I handed her the coffee that I got for her along with a freshly baked pastry as I walked with her into her office. As my phone began to ring, I asked her to hold the cup holder that I had containing Brandon and my drinks; it was him. I told him that I had been in the area and wanted to stop by and surprise him with a small token of my appreciation for yesterday. My surprise hadn't gone so well since he wasn't available to answer my call. I let him know that I had thought of just leaving the items on his desk but I didn't know if I was being too forward or not. I didn't want him to think that I was a stalker or one of those girls that would be popping up on him; I merely thought it was a kind gesture that I felt he deserved. He said that he had missed my call because he left his phone on his desk and stepped out of his office for a quick second. I didn't let him know that I was already at the facility, something about it just seemed weird. Not to seem too pressed, I figure that I would wait a few minutes then walk around to his office.

After getting carried away trying to get the scoop on Brandon, I asked her to point me in the direction of his office. Sabrina cut her eyes at me as if she really didn't want to tell me where he sat, "You heard what I said earlier right?" she asked. "I'll call you later" I responded as I walked out. Sometimes I felt as though my friends didn't really think that highly of me. What would make her think that I was in the business of distracting him from his work? Any who, thinking about how I was going to make an entrance to his office, I decided to go back down to the security desk and have them call him so he could come down and meet me. I acknowledge that I was doing the most, nonetheless I didn't want him to think that I came to spend time with my girlfriend, I wanted him to feel special, like he had my undivided attention, I wanted to give him the impression that I was only thinking of him. I wanted to give the idea to be that I made a drive by and was now on my way to my very important job. Not going as I had planned it out in my mind, he asks security to escort me to up to the reception area of his office. Gosh, I just came from up there and though these were very expensive shoes, they still hurt just as much as any other pump I'd wear.

Enduring the rubbing and squishing of my baby toe, I sashayed my way back up to his floor as he greeted me with a forehead kiss at the elevator doors. His smile was so bright that it made my heart melt. He stood there well dressed and clean faced, dressed in a white shirt and suit pants. The butterflies in my stomach made me feel like a school girl with her first crush. I tried my very best to keep my composure and play it cool but when he kissed me on my cheek after handing him his Starbucks, my knees damn neared buckled. Inviting me back to his office, I insisted that I only came to drop off the items and stated that I needed to make my way to work. Practically pleading for me to give him at least 5 minutes of my time, he threatened to walk out and follow me to my office if I continued to refuse. Presuming that he was bluffing, I gave in. Opening the door for me like a true gentleman, he led me to his office introducing me to his colleagues along the way. He really had me feeling some type of way. I have a habit of liking to being in control of situations and my emotions, but this one was catching me totally off guard and I'm not sure that I liked the way it had me feeling. He was unpredictable.

Chatting for much longer than I initially intended to, in addition to me being physically attracted to him, I was also mentally stimulated by his conversation, plus he had a great sense of humor. Getting my morning call from the Grant girls, made me realize the time and initiated the conclusion our little chat. Answering the call, I wished the girls a great day at school. The girls and I had created a daily routine where they would call every morning before school and their father would let them facetime me in the evenings before bedtime. It was simple and effortless because of the time difference but it had become an important part of our daily schedule. After completing the call Brandon revisited the topic of whether I had kids or not. He wanted to confirm that I failed to mention whether I was a mom or not, especially since he had just ear hustled my conversation with the girls. I briefly explained how the girls were the children of one of my good friends and how they were basically like my mini best friends. He looked a bit confused but I told him that he would understand later on as time went on. Still confused, he agreed to drop the conversation and let me leave. As he escorted me onto the elevator, we made plans to meet up after work for a happy hour and/or dinner. Arriving at the lobby, he reached in his pocket and pulled out his money, he asked how much I needed for parking. I told him that I had found parking on the street and didn't need any money however I did need to retrieve my car because I was almost positive that my meter had expired 15 minutes ago. After asking if I was sure 3 times, he walked me out to the street. As we both scanned the street looking for my Lexus, my heart dropped in fear that my car had finally been towed for the numerous parking tickets I had accumulated over the years, how embarrassing would that have been? Only to soon realize that I had driven the new car. "I thought you said you parked out front?" he asked. Quickly thinking to avoid questioning, "Oh I'm driving this car today" as I pointed to the Land Rover. His face was in shock.

He wanted to say something but he just uttered "Nicccce" as we walked towards it. It was evident that he was indeed impressed but didn't want to let it show. "So, I'll see you later?" I asked, confirming our plans. "It will be the second highlight of my day, next to this, of course" he said smiling, "I'm looking forward to it." As he leans in and grabs my waist, our lips meet and that's when I became hooked. It wasn't like one of those "we're friends" or "I just met you" pecks, it was a real kiss, one that left my heart and vagina pounding afterwards. He opened my door and held it until I was fully situated in the car, leans in, plants another kiss on my lips and shuts the door on some player type shit.

Saturated in the moment, I sit there for a second to analyze what I was feeling, both mentally and physically. This guy is good, he almost got me, almost had me open, caught myself slipping for a second, but I gave myself a pep talk and took my talents to work.

My day at work absolutely dragged. Choosing to stay at my desk for lunch in efforts of balancing out my tardiness from earlier made the day go by that much slower. I fought hard to keep my eyes open as I stared at the computer screen trying to summarize the data I collected from my trip. My fatigue had me starting to consider rescheduling my evening date with Brandon, I was tired. In between fighting my sleep and being useful at my desk, my mind was sidetracked with thoughts of my new beau. From the car to the kiss, the lingering tingling feeling that my body was experiencing, was the only thing that was keeping me alert. I needed someone to talk to. Sabrina was busy, Kris seemed to be in some sort of important meeting that he couldn't answer my call, and after my mom rushed me off the phone to clean dishes, Jasmine was my only other choice.

Talking to her always was a fresh breath of air, she was always so energetic and full of life. She was a go getter and lived her life on the edge plus I hadn't talked to her since I left Texas. I needed to update her on the outcome of the trip and what had emerged from the Carter situation. Chit-chatting with her was just what I needed. Chile, this crazy girl had me dying with the stories of her recent dating experiences. She made Los Angeles seem like the land of OZ. She told me about this property her company just expanded into their portfolio and she was so hype. She sent pictures to my email as I gorged over the lavish lifestyle I felt I was missing out on being over here on the east coast. As I quickly brought her up to speed on what was going on in my life with the new car, Carter and Brandon, she asked about Sabrina. She said that she tried reaching out to her a few days back but she got no answer or a return call. She asked if I talked to her and how she was doing. I told her that I had seen Sabrina the other day and that she was extremely busy working and I joked about how this big case that she was working on was going to make "us" lots of money. Towards the end of the call, Jasmine had again persuaded me to come out there and visit her. She said she could show me around and even introduce me to some millionaire residents. With a perk like that, who wouldn't want to go? After I shoved the last cookie into my mouth, I swore off sweets from now until I went to Cali so that a bitch would look snatched when she stepped off that plane. Wrapping up my catch-up session with her, it was time for me to clock out. Yeah, it's true, nothing really got accomplished that day but I damn sure wasn't finna get in trouble for falling asleep at my desk. Better luck tomorrow.

Ready to go home and crawl in the bed, I get a text from Brandon saying that he had to stay later than he earlier estimated and was wondering if we could push our date back to a later time. Thank you sweet baby Jesus! Little did he know, he was about to be assed out anyways. He said that he would check back in with me by 8:30pm and notify me of his progression, which was fine with me. That gave me a chance to go home, throw a load of clothes in the washer and take a nap. I was exhausted, I didn't even need to eat dinner, plus I was still full from entire pack of cookies I had eaten at my desk. Back in the Rover, I called Kris to see what he was doing and forced him to talk to me on my drive home. Conversing for a few until he put me on hold forever and I finally hung up. Just plain rude, that's what that was.

With a load of dirty clothes in the washer and stripped down to my underwear, I crawled up in the bed and begin scrolling on my social media, only to see that a mutual friend of Kris and I's was tagged in a picture with Kris and his wife. I get it, their married, but the bullshit that he constantly feeds me paints a picture which leads me to believe that they can barely be in the same room at the same time because that's just how much that they don't get along, but these 1,000 words that this picture is saying tells me otherwise. Oh, they're hugged up, very much looking like a happy couple, both proudly displaying their wedding bands which I never even seen him wear before. When was this picture taken? I wonder what excuse he gave me about his whereabouts when this event occurred. A part of me wanted to be petty and comment on the pic, but I'm not a fan of drama. At the end of the day, I would look like the dumb one for actually becoming involved with a married man in the first place, not to mention, forming and carrying on a relationship with him built on the empty promises that he would consistently feed me. I could just like it though. Then he would know that I saw it, but I won't. Oh, but what I will do is save the picture to my phone. If I hadn't learned anything else from Kris, it was that you would need cold hard evidence to incriminate his ass. He was a fast talker and one of the slickest motherfuckers you would ever encounter when it came down to you accusing him of something, but he always knew how to make it up to you, he was a great ass kisser...perfect for a businessman in his profession.

Seeing that picture sparked my interest, what else had I been missing? I have not been an avid social media partaker, however when I got bored enough or had some downtime, I would log on and see what was going on. Lying in bed clicking my little heart out, searching, stalking and investigating, I went through everyone's pictures, finally ending up on his wife's page. Although her page was private, I could see the pictures that Kris and our mutual friends were tagged in. My momma always told me that if you go looking for something, you're bound to find it and that's exactly what happened. So ok, maybe he's the only one in the relationship that's not happy because she sure as hell seems to be very happy and in love with my man.

Too excited to sleep from my new-found information, I desperately needed to find something to do with myself before I went crazy. Fuck him and fuck anyone else who has something to say about my situation. I was in my feelings, even though I was well aware how situations like this play out every day. Preparing to wash another load of clothes, Carter calls me just to check in. He was still at work but he needed to vent about something. I listened and gave my opinion like the good friend that I am, but I couldn't stop thinking about the picture that I had just seen. He could tell that something was up because he kept asking me why my voice sounded so down. I shrugged it off blaming my lack of energy on being tired. I mentioned to him that I had a girlfriend in LA who I was planning on making a trip to visit in the upcoming weeks. I wanted to see if I could coordinate some time to see him and the girls if they weren't too busy during the time I would be there. I would have a hotel so he wouldn't need to worry about accommodating me with a place to stay. He thought it was an excellent idea and believed that the girls would really enjoy meeting me face-to-face. He went on to say how the girls had been begging him to bring them to DC ever since I told them that I lived near the White House. They were interested in seeing where the President lived and see where Martin Luther King Jr. delivered his "I have a dream" speech on the Lincoln memorial. I thought it was a great idea. Maybe if I called in a few favors to my homeboy over at the White House, I could surprise them with a tour. By the end of the conversation, we had agreed on some dates that worked best for both of our schedules. I got on the computer and booked the flight. I had plenty of vacation days that I needed to use before the end of the year, so why not? Excited to see all of my friends, this trip couldn't come fast enough.

The next couple of weeks were a breeze, work was tolerable, Kris was on time out due to my internet lurking, but I blamed it on PMS, waist was slimming, and my hair was growing. Carter had become one of my closer platonic friends talking almost twice a day, Kennedy and Cuddles had become my new BFF's, my skin was radiant, and Brandon and I's relationship was beginning to flourish, I was mentally in a good place. He loved spending time together when he wasn't in the office. If he had work to do, he'd lure me over with food and wine and convince me to bring my work over and we'd both just both sit there in silence doing...work. Kris always knew when I was trying to distance myself from him and that made him more agitated and act needy, ultimately causing our interactions to become more limited. All Kris and I did as of lately, was argue and bicker about irrelevant shit. I still loved him and was very much still in love with him but deep down I knew the truth no matter how many times he would tell me otherwise, he was never going to leave his wife and the pictures that she constantly posted of them together steadily reminded me of that. I wanted to believe him as I had for the past couple of years and if he were to show up at my door, right now with divorce papers or ready to make this official, I'd drop everyone I was entertaining for him, but since he couldn't give me what I longed for, Brandon was there, playing his role. Brandon sincerely cared for and about me, he took interest in things that I enjoyed and made me feel like a priority in his life, all the qualities that led me to fall in love with Kris. When it came to allocation of Brandon's time, the only factor I had to compete with was his job. Everything between us was great. Great chemistry, great kissing, great sex, but there was one problem, I got tired of always driving over to his house. I would make sure that I always had a bag packed and ready to go and from me being there all the time, I was neglecting my house for constantly being at his. For weeks, I wouldn't go home for days at a time. Once he gave me a key, he expected me to always be there. There were times when I would want to invite him over to my luxurious bachelorette pad, but there I ran the risk of Kris popping up which he sometimes liked to do primarily when we were on better terms, but I knew that one of these days he'd try it. One late night Kris called my phone while I was sleeping over at Brandon's questioning my whereabouts because he was at the condo and I wasn't there. Several times he has accused my recent attitudes and rants to be acts of distancing myself from him, attempting to try to leave him and be with someone else, so it was only a matter of time before he came to pay me another visit.

As the month ends, I find myself back at the Ronald Regan Washington National Airport yet again, this time I was flying out to visit my best friends in California. I was going to need every last one of these 7 days to relax and clear my mind. Although I was enthusiastic to catch up with Jasmine, Carter and the girls, I was still going miss my 2 favorite men Kris and Brandon. I'm not sure of which one I would miss more, probably Brandon, just for the simple fact that we had been spending so much time together as of recently, but Kris still had my heart. Arriving at LAX, waiting curbside for Jasmine, this hussy pulls up in a cherry red Mercedes Benz E350, hair just flowing, looking ever so flawless as usual. My bitch was winning! I didn't want to seem too excited because I didn't want the other people who were standing there, also mesmerized by her haughtiness, to think that we weren't accustomed to this here lifestyle. I grabbed my shades (the gift that I gave myself when I got my new car) from my other new gift to myself, my Alexander Wang tote, squished my luggage into the back and got in. We both remained extremely cool until we were out of the distance of people being able to hear us scream. Both very excited to see one another, I yelled, "BITCH!!! When the hell did you get this?" as I started rubbing the dash board and leather arm rest. "Oh, this old thing? You know I like to treat myself every now and then. This girl here works very hard, I deserved it." She says as she places her sunglasses on the top of her head to control her hair from blowing, "When we closed our last 2.3 billion dollar deal with Sydencorp, I couldn't be pulling up in my Ford, girl, I needed an upgrade. Plus, I be pulling everything driving in this, they be on ya girl." Both letting out a laugh, I was so happy to see her, I had missed her so much. I was even happier to know that she was doing her damn thing out here. I always loved to hear about people, my friends in particular, doing well. Years ago, when we were all college students and broke, we all set a plan and we were executing it to the fullest. Turning up the music, I removed my jacket exposing my very low-cut shirt and applied some MAC lip glass, next stop...DRINKS!

Taking a selfie or 20, I narrowed it down to the perfect one. Sending one to my momma, Sabrina, Carter, and both Kris and Brandon, I informed them that I had touched down safely. Everyone except Sabrina responded with the same texts saying how good we looked and to be careful. Sabrina replied that she desperately needed to get away and should have come along with me. Inviting her and convincing her via FaceTime that it wasn't too late, she said that she would consider catching a flight in 2 days if the case she had been working diligently on, finally concluded. I asked her to keep in touch with whatever she decided to do. I didn't necessarily think that it was a good idea to leave her family at a time like this, but I understood her need and want to get away. Mentioning to Jas that Sabrina was considering coming, she asked what had been going on with her. I briefly gave her a synopsis that included how Sabrina and Jay had been having some marital problems and that things had been a little rocky at her palace. I didn't go too much into detail because I wasn't sure how much info Sabrina was willing to disclose about the situation, but either way it was enough to heighten Jasmine's curiosity. Arriving at our destination, the outside patio bar was packed with some international cuties who had triceps and biceps exposed, turn-up ready. I was prepared to let loose and cut all the way up.

Catching up on the details surrounding Jas's career and love life, I could finally share my recent string of interesting events including my new ride and boo. We stayed at the restaurant forever, talking and flirting, mixing and mingling, that is until her prospective boo came by to pick up our tab and treat us to some more drinks. He was fine, looking like an Arabian god. Golden skin and full jet-black hair. He was polished, very gentleman-like, poised, and intelligent. From what I could tell, Jasmine was winning all around the board. I've never dated outside of my race, but he had me forgetting about my situations and wanting to ask him if he had any brothers or single family members that looked like him.

With the change of the day air to night, I realized that we had been in the very same spot for hours. I hadn't had this much fun in forever, LA had me feeling like I was 25 again, I may never go back.

As we wrapped up our night at the patio bar, I was feeling no pain. I wasn't fucked up but I was undeniably nice. Jas had more to drink then I did so I know she had to be messed up. Grabbing a cup of water to go just in case I needed to drive, I would feel awful if something happened to either one of us because we got too wasted celebrating my visit. And goodness knows that I wouldn't want anything to happen to that gorgeous car of hers; I couldn't afford for anything to happen on my watch. As we left the bar I called to touch base back home. Brandon answers, his voice was low and sort of dismal. Asking him if everything had been ok, he told me he was tired. I offered to call him back later but he wanted to know about my trip so far. Carrying on a full-blown conversation, I walked in the direction of Jas's car trying to escape the loud noises and thinking that we would be heading out soon. I told him how much fun I was having, and I let him know how much I was missing him.

"Brooke!! Brooke!!" I heard a male voice hollering my name. I turned to look, obviously nobody would have been talking to me, I didn't know anyone here, but it was Jasmine and her boo calling me waving me in the opposite direction of the car. Brandon, overhearing the deep voice calling me, questioned what was going on, I told him that I didn't know but I remained on the phone with him as I walked over to them. Mr. Arabian Knight told me that Jas was going to leave her car and he was going to drive us to the next destination. Brandon got silent as he was trying hard to listen in on what was being said. Asking if I was ok, he wanted to me give him the details of what was going on. Walking to the dude's car, I quickly explained who was who and what was what, and to my understanding, what was going on. He instructed me to be safe and to let

Jasmine and her male friend know that I was precious cargo and to make sure they took great care of his "woman". His woman? He was talking about me? We didn't discuss any of these title things before. Maybe he didn't mean it quite like that, maybe he meant his woman, like his "woman friend". Let me not get too excited and overthink it before I get my feelings hurt. He'd fuck around and have a bitch walking around on my best behavior like I'm in an actual relationship or something. I laughed it off then told them I would call him back when I arrived at my hotel.

Climbing into the back of his SUV, I rolled down my window, taking in the sweet smell of the night air as he drove. Suddenly realizing that all of my bags were in Jasmine's car, I wondered where we were going. Not wanting to yell over the radio, I sent Jas a text message reminding her. It took her a while to check her phone as we pulled up to what appeared to be a gated community of some sort. Now, I'm originally from the hood, so you know my head was on the swivel trying to check out my surroundings. Everything was dark except the lit venue that I could barely make out looking through the trees. Now, I heard about these LA people and the shit that they are into. I hadn't been in close in contact with Jasmine since she moved out here but I hoped that she hadn't fell for the old okey doke and get my ass caught up in some coke sniffing bullshit. I've never been one to judge and I'm all for having fun but there's some things that I'm just not particularly in to and don't care to try. I know that in the past, she had always been on a quest for shiny things, but before she relocated out here, she found herself in a little trouble which humbled her and taught her the hard lesson of learning that everything that glitters aint gold; I just hoped that she remembered that.

As her guy made small conversation with the security guard about sports, she turned around and gave me a look. I'm not sure what that look was indicating but I could only imagine. As we pulled in the driveway, he hopped out the running car and walked into this building, I'll call it that because it was big as shit, too big to be a damn house in my opinion. Curious about what was going on, once he was out of sight, she turned the music down and turned back around to look at me. Unable to contain myself, I asked her if the palace we were sitting in front of was a house or not. She laughed and said that it was but it wasn't his house. She went further into detail stating how her man friend did indeed have a big house that he stayed in also, but we were here to make a stop because he had some business to take care of. Too scared to ask what he did for a living, I felt like the less I knew, the better.

I never pictured myself being good in an interrogation room. All they would have to do is keep me in there long enough with no food and freezing temperatures and I'd sing like a canary, but fuck that, I'm too old to be caught up in some BS, so I asked. She said that he had his hands in a few things but he made most of his money from real-estate. She said that he came from money; his entire family was well off. I asked her if I needed to fear for my safety and again she laughed it off, but she never gave me a defined answer. She did however, mention that she would discuss the whole luggage thing to him when he got back in the car, but she told me not to worry about it. She was still intoxicated. It was almost pointless talking to her as she slurred her words and laughed in-between her statements. "Only me", I thought to myself. I could not find myself in trouble every time I decided to leave the state.

Sending Brandon a quick text followed by another one with no reply, I shot a text to Kris and he didn't reply either. I almost caught an attitude because I knew that both of them couldn't have been sleep, I just talked to Brandon not that long ago, then I realized that I was on west coast time, meaning I was 3 hours behind them. With that information now being taken into consideration, I texted Carter to see what he was doing plus I had missed a call from my girls while I was out turning up. Immediately responding, he asked how my trip was coming along so far and checked to see if I was enjoying myself. Not wanting to alert him, I told him that everything was fine and I was having a ball. I told him that I was just checking in with him and the kids. He asked what day was best for us to meet up. I told him any day was fine with me and that I could either come to him or he could come up this way. Suggesting he could come to me to prevent me from going through any extra trouble of having to rent a car and being stuck in traffic, I carried on texting as Jasmine kept nodding off. Breaking my concentration, I heard the car door open and the lights inside of the truck turned on. At the front passenger door stood her boo trying to wake her up and assist her with getting out of the car. Looking toward the house, there was a woman standing in the doorway calling Jas by name, trying to get her attention.

Getting her attention, Jas yelled out to the woman in response as she signaled for us to come in. Grabbing my pocketbook, I helped her turn off the engine and get out the car. I was confused to what was about to happen, I thought we were here to handle business, why were we going inside? Exiting the vehicle, I took notice that there were several other luxury cars parked out front, did they all belong to the same person or was there something going on inside? Something about this situation raised my antennas nevertheless it was too early to question things. My intuition told me that something felt a little different, but at the same time my curiosity was peaked. My plan was to send my location to Carter just in case anything crazy popped off while I was here. Now that I think about it, I mean for goodness sake, I didn't even know the name of Jasmine's boy toy. I couldn't remember if she ever told me or not, I don't know where the hell I am, I was in bad shape, but I trusted that my friend wouldn't put me in harm's way.

Walking up about 10 steps, the woman met us half way to grab the hand of Jasmine as she led us into the house. Ok, so this house was absolutely freaking gorgeous! I had never seen anything this amazing before, except for on tv of course. The foyer was the size of my entire condo! It had the most amazing marble floors with a dual staircase. The chandelier, ohh My Gosh, it was to die for. Usually I am very modest but I couldn't stop looking around. The paintings on the wall were exquisite. I don't know much about art but I'm sure they very worth a pretty penny. Casually dressed people informally stood conversing with glasses in their hands as I watched several people embrace Jasmine as though she was one of their good friends. As homeboy introduces me to his friend and his wife, I couldn't help but to let them know how fascinating I thought their house was. They smiled and thanked me as the wife offered to give me a quick tour following a glass of champagne. Not wanting to seem too eager and excited, I agreed. Leading us out to the back of the house where other people were mixing and mingling with a DJ playing on the patio in front of an Olympic sized pool, what had I done wrong in my life to not have all of this? I'm clearly not brushing shoulders with the right people. Boy, I tell you, I thought that I was doing pretty damn well for myself over in the nation's capital, until I walked up in this bitch; I might as well live in the projects as far as these people are concerned. Don't get me wrong, I'm extremely grateful and blessed for what I do have, but this, this shit that I'm witnessing, I couldn't even begin to tell you what was going on in my mind. I felt like getting pregnant by someone here tonight, just kidding, but not really.

As I grabbed a glass from one of the hired servers dressed in nipple pasties and thongs, Romeo, Jasmine's guy (that's what I'll call him), he asked if I was ok and told me that he needed to run upstairs and would be right back. He told me that Diane, was coming to show me around. I wasn't completely comfortable with being left alone but what's the worst that could happen. Immediately I used the setting on my phone to share my location with Brandon, Kris and Carter. I didn't care, I just needed someone to know where I was. Glancing around the room, I made eye contact with a decent looking white male, maybe in his late 30's, early 40's. Trying to hurry up and turn away, I could feel that he was walking over towards my direction. Introducing himself as Sutton he asks for my name.

Questioning if I live in the area and how I knew Diane and Ashmel, I could tell that he was trying to make small talk but I didn't know how much information I should disclose. I wanted to come off as friendly but not naive. As Diane approaches me, she says, "Oh, I see that you've met Sutton. He is our adorably single neighbor" as she places a kiss upon his lips and turns around and winks one eye. "I'll let you two continue your conversation, I didn't mean to interrupt. Drink up" she says as she sashays away. "How embarrassing?" He says as he begins to blush, "she just had to mention the fact that I was single huh? That lady is truly unique." Unique was the last word that was coming to my

mind. It was hard to overlook the fact that this married woman just kissed this single man on the lips, there are basically naked employed servants walking around leisurely, this was far from unique. This was something I wasn't used to seeing, but I guess hey, when in Rome....

"This house is remarkably stunning" I said, changing the topic but still trying to make small talk, "Diane said that she was going to show me around but I guess she changed her mind once she figured I was being entertained by you." "I can go and get her for you if you would like or I could show you around myself" he says with a smirk. I wasn't feeling the smirk. With my guard and antennas still up, I trace the room with my eyes to see if there is any sign of Jasmine or Romeo but I don't see them anywhere. As I finish up the contents in my glass, I say fuck it and take Sutton up on his offer. He says that he's going to get another drink and asks if I want anything before we begin.

Removing another glass of champagne from the hostess' tray, "I'm ready when you are." I'd be damned if I take a drink form this guy so he can slip me something and have his way with me. I think not! As he walks away to go get his drink from the bar I take a good look at the people attending this event. Majority of them are white but there's a few of us filtered in too. Not to sound racist, there is an abnormally large presence of foreigners too. I've never really been good with geography so I'm not exactly sure which region they may have migrated from, but if I had to guess without sounding as ignorant as I can possibly sound, I would assume they were Arabs. Either way, I knew that I was in the presence of big money and I've witnessed (on a much smaller scale, back in D.C.), the more money they make the more weird shit that they are into. Did I really trust Sutton to give me a tour? This place was big enough that I'm sure nobody could hear me scream if we were alone but there were people around so someone would help me, right?

Walking from room to room, this house was even bigger than I had initially imagined. Each undiscovered room was filled with more people, laughing, drinking and having an openly good time. Although I did see some people participating in what I will classify as sniffing what I presumed to be white lines of cocaine among other things it didn't make me feel uncomfortable. This is almost exactly how I had always envisioned a Hollywood party to be, just a little calmer and minus the celebrities. I could happily check this from my bucket list. As the tour concluded, we ended up taking a seat along the edge of the pool. Sitting with only our feet in, we discussed and analyzed relationships, soul mates, money, music, life, existence, U.F.O.'s, and all other random shit that people talk about as we continued to toss back drinks and puff on a little marijuana. I don't consider myself to be a smoker or someone who smokes. I can't roll a blunt (or top paper), I don't know the special names, genus and species of the different kinds; I just socially partake in it occasionally, that's how I'd originally formed a relationship with Reece some years ago.

We moved our conversation from the side of the pool as the party grew a little wilder and the music grew louder, to the patio couch that surrounded the fire pit. There we finished our conversation as I fought hard to keep my eyes open. The combination of smoking and drinking, combined with the jet lag had me feeling like I needed to rest my eyes before getting up to find my friend. I'm not sure what time it was when my bladder and intuition finally made me open my eyes, but people were still vibrant and full of energy, up laughing and still having a good time. There was also a good amount of people passed out in some of the most random places. Sutton was sleep at the opposite end of the sofa with his legs intertwined with mine. I didn't want to wake him, but I needed to find my friend and get to my hotel where I could sleep comfortably. I didn't want to be a party pooper but I'm sure the sun would be rising soon, and I wasn't going to sleep squished up on some patio furniture when I was paying for a deluxe king size bed. Trying my best to move my interlocked leg, he repositioned himself and opened his eyes. He asked if I was alright. I told him that I needed to find my friend and a bathroom. Trying my best to describe what Jasmine looked like and what she was wearing, Sutton was unaware of her existence. Frustrated, I attempted to describe the guy that had brought us here. He repeated that he wasn't familiar with Jas but might have seen Romeo a time or two before. Unwrapping his leg from around mine, he stood to his feet and stretched as I fumbled through my bag looking for my phone. I had 2 missed calls from Jasmine and a call from an unfamiliar number with a 424 area code. As I went to return Jas's call, my phone battery died. What a fine time for the dumbass battery to die. I will figure out something after I use the bathroom, someone must have an iPhone charger around here.

As Sutton leads me to the bathroom, I catch a glimpse of the gentleman earlier introduced to me as Diane's husband. He is in the corner with a female, who should I say, doesn't look like Diane, not in the least. Keeping it to myself, I let Sutton show me to the bathroom. He said that he was going to head home soon but before he left he would check and see if anyone knew the whereabouts of my friend while he waited for me to come out. Inside the bathroom, I sat on the toilet as I let the several hours' worth of alcohol exit my body trying to contemplate why I had been left alone for so long by my best friend who I traveled across the country to see. I know she did try to call me but why did she not come looking for me? I had unanswered questions but I'm too tired to think; I want to find her and get going. Washing my hands and I attempted to fix my hair in the mirror as I thought of a plan. A plan that would get me out of here, to somewhere I considered safe, just in case I couldn't find this girl. With no phone, I couldn't call an uber and I vaguely remembered the name of the hotel I was staying at. The more I thought about it, the more worked up I got. A soft knock at the bathroom door right as I was preparing to open it, Sutton was there staring at me, "Are you ok?" he asked. "I'm fine. Any luck finding my friend?" I rebutted. With a look of disappointment on his face; my stomach dropped.

Sutton offered me his phone to use if I could remember her number off the top of my head. I dialed what I thought I remembered to be her number but all I got was a generic automated message. I knew he felt bad for me, he just didn't know what to say or do. This entire situation was completely insane however I was tryna stay as positive as I could. Even though I told him not to worry about me and granted him permission to leave me and go home, secretly I hoped that he wouldn't necessarily take me up on my suggestion. He was the only person that I somewhat knew here, and I didn't want to be left alone. As he asked me simple questions about Jasmine, I felt extremely stupid for not to be able to answer them. He asked if I knew where she stayed, who she lived with, the guy's name that she was with, typical information that I should know about this girl that I've referred to as my "best friend". Any respect that he once had for me was slowly withering away with every "I honestly don't know" response I gave. But it was the truth, I didn't know these things about her or her newfound life. Being that this was my first time out here, I didn't know much of anything. I might've had her address saved in my phone from sending her a housewarming card from when she first got here but what good was that going to do me now. I could call Sabrina, but I know she was sleep and probably wouldn't answer. Maybe I could catch a cab and tell it to take me to any nearby hotel, at this point I really didn't care. There had to be something decent in at least a 15 to 20 mile radius from where I was, but then again, I don't even know where I would hail a cab in the neighborhood and at this time of night. If I could find somewhere safe and comfortable to sleep, I could go out and find a phone charger once the stores opened in the morning. Pissed off to the highest pisstivity and irritated beyond measure. "Listen you don't know me, and I don't know you, but you do have some options here" he says. I knew what he was about to say. He's going to invite me over to his house and I knew for certain that I didn't want to go. I'm already in a strange place with strange people, but I don't want to leave one bizarre place to go to another one, especially a secluded one at that. "My daughter has an iPhone so there may be a charger in my car or house, I can go get it for you and bring it back if that helps. I also have some friends that own some hotels, so I can take you to one of them and give you my number just in case anything happens, or you need something, you could give me a call." I was not expecting him to say that but at this point I had run out of options and ideas and I was willing to take him up on his offer and check into a hotel. I figured there I would be able to emotionally vent, clear my head, and properly gather my thoughts.

"So, what are you thinking?" Sutton asked. Just as I was about to give him my answer, a cluster of loud talking individuals walked through the front door. Amongst the group were Jasmine and 4 other guys that I hadn't seen before. My first intention was to cuss her the fuck out.

 How could she just leave me like this around a bunch of people that I didn't know? This wasn't college anymore, I'm grown, it's just some shit that you don't do as a responsible adult. Part of the problem that I have when dealing with certain people from my past is realizing we're not on the same page anymore when it comes to certain things. I would have never, in a million years, had done that to her or any friends of mine for that matter. As our eyes locked on each other, she walked right over to me like nothing was wrong. I was so livid that I couldn't even say anything. Sutton turns and asks, "Is this your friend?" Friend? Shit, after I leave here and get my bags, I'll probably never speak to her ass again in life, ok well maybe not for life but it will take a while for me to move past this. "How'd you sleep, sleeping beauty?" she turns and asks me. Too irate to say anything, I know she could tell how pissed I was, but she is trying to diffuse the situation like she has always done in similar situations.

With an annoyed "eat shit and die" face, I chose not to answer. I can feel Sutton looking at me as I refuse to make eye contact with him. "And thank you handsome for looking after my beautiful, did I mention, single friend from D.C.?" she says as she turned her focus toward him, rubbing his shoulder. "It was no problem really" he says to Jas, "I was on my way to check my car for a charger for her phone and to drop her off to a hotel so she could get some good rest, in a bed, not on some outdoor pool chair. I was trying to help her look for you for a while now, but I'm glad she found you." "Oh, I told Diane, to let me know when you guys were done with the tour, then I guess I lost track of time. The next thing I know, someone told me that you two were outside hitting it off, so I decided not to intrude, just in case you two were making a love connection, you know what I'm talking about?" she says as she hits him with her elbow and winks one eye. What is up with this winking shit? "I stayed for a while and then you guys fell asleep. Oh, did I mention how cute you two looked on the couch? You looked so damn adorable. Any who, I knew that she was tired, so I let her get some rest, plus I had to make a run really quick, so I left. I knew that she was in good hands. While I was already out, I figured that I would just go and pick up my car so by the time that she woke up, we could leave."

This conversation is literally making me sick to my stomach. I'm trying so hard not to make a scene in here but her nonchalant and careless demeanors are strongly provoking me. After all these years, she continues to prove herself to be implausibly irresponsible and never takes ownership for her bullshit. Like honestly, it is impossible that she couldn't see anything wrong with what she had done? I had expected that to be something that she had learned to outgrow but I guess old habits die hard. She lost track of time, my ass. Ha, bitch not for no 7 hours you didn't! The more I repeated the incident in my head, the more ill-tempered I grew. "Well, even though Brooke and I shared some good conversation, I don't think that she felt 100% comfortable here with me alone. I mean I don't know and maybe I'm wrong, she says she came all the way out here to visit you, and she clearly was excited about that, but being with her for the last 45 mins, I felt a shift in attitude. I think she was more concerned about you than anyone else. And though I'm a safe guy to be around and I'm not sure how long you've lived here, but I've seen you around a time or two, and you and I both know how these parties can get. It's probably best that you don't leave her with strangers next time. Stranger danger, isn't that what they say?" as he laughed it off coming to my defense.

Letting out a loud laugh, "She's fine, she was alright. My little princess can be shy when she first meets people, but she eventually opens up after a while. Isn't that right?" as she looks to me for confirmation. "And she's not with strangers" she says sarcastically, "I know a good number of these people here, nothing was going to happen to her. I got eyes everywhere. But where have you seen me around at? I meet a lot of people. Was it here at one of Diane's events or are you a friend of Ahmed?" She is tempting me to say something per every comment that she responds with. My tolerance is truly being tested. "I see you around. People talk" he says vaguely and casually with a smile. As she stands there with a baffled look on her face, Sutton turns to me and asks, "Hey, so I'm about to get out of here, are you okay?" Thinking quickly, I really don't want to be with her right now but I don't want to inconvenience him anymore than I already have. It's bad enough that he's had to entertain me for the entire night and has had to help me look for Jas, now I'm going to take him out of his way to drop me off at a hotel? But then again, my clothing items were still in her car. I needed to make a decision. My extended hesitation gave Ms. Jasmine the green light to answer for me on my behalf. "She's fine, I got her. I'm going to say my goodbyes and then we can be out. She'll be with me. I won't let her out my sight this time. If she wants to talk to someone, she can talk to me now. This way she can get some sleep because I have an eventful day planned for us tomorrow, we gonna tear the stores up. Aint that right B?" she says loudly and full of energy. Butting in, "Or, as soon as I can get my phone charged, I can tell you where I had a reservation and you can drop me off there" I added.

"Well its really up to you, let me go say bye" she says as she walks away. Sutton looks at me with a raised eyebrow as if he's asking if I am really going to be ok. Shaking his head in disappointment, he hands me a business card, "my number is on here if you need anything." "Thank you" I whisper.

Patiently waiting for another 10 minutes as Jasmine continues to work the crowd, increasingly growing even more irate and ready to leave, I walk over to where she is standing making my presence be known to her once again. Acknowledging me by introducing me to those whom I'd hadn't previously met, politely I greet them and excuse myself from the conversation expressing how exhausted I was and how long of a day it had been for me. Finally catching the hint, Jasmine withdraws herself from the discussion, making the announcement that she needed to take me home. In the car there was nothing that I felt like saying to her; she was well aware of my emotions and was conscious of me being vastly annoyed. Trying to make small talk as conversation ice breakers, I reclined my chair back, closing my eyes and covering my face with my forearm; I pretended to be sleep as I waited for my phone restore. "I honestly didn't think that you would be staying at a hotel knowing that I had a place. You really don't need to get a room, I have plenty of space for you to be comfortable" she says humbly. Now the only reason I got the room in the first place is because I never want to intrude on people's lives, I mean you never know what people have going on and sometimes you just like to have you own space. She's my girl and all, but I had no idea if she was shacking up, if she had a roommate, etc., and I'm too old to be sleeping on somebody's floor; these aren't 20 year old bones And not to mention, so far I feel like I have been a burden to Jas's social life, impending on whatever she maybe had planned before I decided to come. "The hotel is fine, it's too late for me to cancel anyway, and not to mention, according to the hotel's cancellation policy, I'm positive they've already charged my credit card". As the phone finally cuts on, I immediately search in my email for the hotel's address to give this girl so she could stop with the chit chat. After giving her the address, I repositioned myself and laid back in the chair as she drove me to the hotel. I was hungry as hell but all I could think about and all I really wanted to do, was to get out of these clothes. As we arrived, I hoped that she wouldn't want to come in and talk any more. I had enough of her and her damn shenanigans for one day; if I was going to get over this attitude I had, I was going to need some alone time. Retrieving my bags from the back, she ran off the itinerary of what she had planned for later in the day. I told her that I would call her when I got up and got myself together, and at that time I would let her know how I was feeling.

After checking into my room, I shut the curtains (as I knew that sun would be brightly shining through momentarily), found my charger and plugged in my phone as I extended my body across the bed and kicked off my shoes off, quickly falling asleep. The knock at the door from housekeeping interrupted my slumber, ignoring them, I continued to sleep. Before I knew it was early in the afternoon and I still had absolutely no motivation to move. It felt good to lay there and do nothing. Picking up my phone to check for missed calls and text messages, the only person to have seemed to be thinking about me was Brandon. Calling him back, we talked for about an hour as I deliberately avoided the details of last night's activities. Keeping it simple by simply telling him that I enjoyed myself, I didn't want him to know that I had a dysfunctional group of individuals that I consider to be my closest friends. I didn't want him to believe that "birds of a feather, flocked together" because that has never been the case in my friendships. Vastly different from one another; we all had different thought patterns, different views and opinions which ultimately made us a great team when we needed to put our heads together, occasionally.

After speaking with him for a while, I decided not to be a bum anymore and to get up and do something with my life. Glimpsing out of the window, the sun motivated me to throw on my sundress and breakout my newest Gucci shades that had come in the mail right before I left DC. Calling Carter to see what he had planned for the day, I wanted to know my options before I would even consider taking Jasmine up on any of her offers. He told me he was waiting for the girls to finish up at gymnastics and planned to feed them afterwards, but he didn't have anything else on his agenda. He planned on making the drive to me the following day so that he didn't interfere with the bonding of my friend and I, which he referenced to as "the intermixing of our black girl magic". Not wanting to alter his schedule, I kept the plans as they were. I called Sabrina to tell her what happened and to bounce the situation (involving "her friend") off her and to get her take on things. "I understand your frustration" she told me," but she is who she is, aint nothing new. She's been pulling the same stunts since college and it's a bit funny that you still get mad about it, she aint gonna change. If nothing else, she is consistent." She was right, it was foolish of me to assume that with age came maturity and acceptance of responsibility. Quickly changing the topic, I asked how she was doing and how the situation at home was panning out. Emmanuel's health had improved but besides that things at home were pretty much the same. Conversations between the two had still been at a minimum as she could feel the tension was still there. At this point, she wasn't sure if the hostility was coming from her end or his.

With most of the day almost gone, I ignored Jasmine's calls and decided not to take her up on her offer. Even though I had talked it over with Sabrina, I still didn't like the feeling of yesterday's occurrences. Making the decision to show myself around town, I had a few places in mind that I knew I wanted to see that were close to where I was staying. Once dressed, I put on my sneakers and strolled towards the Hollywood Walk of Fame. Stopping to grab food, I entertained myself as I took selfies and asked people to take candid shots of me in front of landmarks. Traveling mostly on a Hop-on Hop-off tour bus, I relaxed on Venice Beach and wandered on its Boardwalk until it grew dark. Grabbing another bite to eat, I concluded my night on the rooftop pool of my hotel. Video chatting with the girls until I would eventually fall asleep, they were equally, if not more excited to finally meet me as I was to meet them.

With the rising of the new day, I still was in my feelings as I refused to communicate with Jasmine. She sent texts expressing her concern but what she failed to do was to apologize. Not that any of that mattered because I would still be pissed but she somehow neglected to see fault in what she did; I don't need that type of immature negligence in my life. In her last text, she notified me that I had left a pair of sunglasses and my jacket in Maliq's car and she was trying to return them to me. The boyfriend had a name! Normally, I would've said F it, but I had just bought both items and paid a hefty price tag for each. Letting her know that I didn't plan on staying at the hotel for much longer, I offered to meet her somewhere to grab the items. Looking forward to Carter coming to pick me up, I knew that he was traveling a great distance to come and

213

get me. With almost a 6-hour drive ahead of him, I was certain that we wouldn't meet up until midafternoon which gave me time to do some more sightseeing. Sitting by the phone waiting for her to respond, nearly 40 minutes had passed before my phone rang. Carter was calling to say he was approximately an hour out and asked me if I had eaten already. He was more prompt than I expected; he must have set out early to make this voyage to see me. Texting Jasmine back to let her know that she could send the items to my home when she got time, she called. I didn't want to physically speak to her, texting was fine for me. Accepting the call, a male's voice was on the other end. Taken off guard, Maliq said that he had Jas' phone and to meet him outside of my hotel in 10 mins. Why the hell would he have her phone? Was she with him?

Making my way to the lobby, through the hotel's front window I see the SUV that took Jasmine and I to the party the other night. Walking outside, Maliq approaches the entrance, awkwardly embracing me with a hug. His friend sitting in the passenger seat, compliments me on my beauty as they both pose questions surrounding my itinerary for the day. I don't know him for him to be questioning me. He offers the idea of hanging with him and his friend, guaranteeing that they would show me a good time much like he had the other night. He references Sutton, but he doesn't call him by name. He mentions the company I would be among wouldn't be as boring as the "homey in the Bermuda shorts" that I was hanging with. Politely declining, I'm beginning to feel uncomfortable. Maliq attempts to put his arm around my shoulders in efforts to lure me inside of his vehicle. Irritated and apprehensive, I sternly request my items. Reaching in the back seat, he hands me my belongings, asking once more if I wanted to roll with them, this time offering to take me to see Jas. He offers me money and I think he offered me drugs. He says that anyone who a friend of Jasmine's was, was a friend of his, leaving me to question this entire ordeal of why he was here with her phone and she wasn't. With my items in my hand, I excuse myself as his friend inappropriately suggest the act of preforming a bump of cocaine from my breast. Returning inside of the hotel with a peeved expression on my face, a hotel employee asks if I'm ok. Ignoring him, I'm ready to get as far away from here as I can. Stuffing the remaining scattered items from around the hotel room into my luggage, my phone rings. Hoping it was Carter saying he was here, it was a call from a private number. Letting it go to voicemail, I felt the urge to screen my calls. Instead of leaving a message, a text came through reading "There's a little something special for you in the pocket of your jacket. There's more where that came from. Call me when you're ready." Perplexed and highly disturbed, I immediately check the pockets of my jacket. Inside I find a $100 bill and a tiny zip lock bag with a white powdery substance. Flushing the matter down the toilet as I've watched in movies, I was starting to get paranoid. I'm not sure what Jasmine was into, but I knew I didn't want to be a part of it and more importantly I didn't want to be associated with this activity.

Once Carter arrived, I felt so much better. The girls were perfect, just as I envisioned them to be. Friendly, outgoing, and eager to discover the City of Angels, we had a good time together. With it being their first time in L.A. I suggested taking the kids to Disneyland since I had extra days to spare. Carter reserved a room and we made it a two-day trip full of laughs and love. Since the falling out with Jas, I changed my departing flight from Los Angeles to San Francisco, catching a ride back home with Carter. His house was beautiful, simplistic but very nice; he had done well for himself. Had I had my own family, and/or kids, I would probably have been interested in increasing my space back at home, but since it was only me, I had no need for the extra square footage. The spending of 8 days in his home and around his daughters, gave me "family fever". In my current situation, the only prospect that I currently had was Brandon, but it was too early in our relationship to even consider.

The day we said our goodbyes was bittersweet. I knew that I would miss them, but Carter and I agreed that they would make a trip over to the east coast for another reunion very soon. And though I talked to both Brandon and Kris every day, I wanted to see them. I missed them. The relationship between Carter and I was strictly platonic. There was no intimate chemistry we just enjoyed each other's company. Returning to DC, we talked every day. I could talk to him about any and everything and vice versa. Unlike Sabrina, he knew about Kris and Brandon and although it would be natural for him to judge me, he didn't, or at least didn't do it to my face. He truly became my best friend right along with Kennedy and Cuddles.

Over the next year, we would grow even closer. He and the girls made frequent trips to visit during school breaks and we all had become very familiar with each other. He'd give me advice and be my sounding board in the times that I needed, and I would be the same for him. Imagine the pain and grief that I endured in learning that Carter was in a horrific car accident that resulted in 3 fatalities. I received the information from his Nanny after he went off the radar for 3 days. Growing concerned after not hearing from him or the girls; it wasn't like him, let alone the girls to go missing in action for that long. As I persistently continued to call both his cell and home phone, I finally got an answer from Ana informing me of the loss. The nanny/housekeeper said that the girls had been with a relative and had returned home only once to gather some of their belongings. She provided me with a contact number for Carter's sister to gather more information.

News that he had succumb to his injuries was irrefutably devastating. Not only had I lost one of my closest friends, but the girls had now lost the only other parent that they had. Tirelessly I repetitively called the number that had been provided to me, but I would never be able to speak with anyone directly. I would leave message upon message, but no one ever returned my call. Refusing to take days off, work was the only thing that kept my mind distracted as I began depending on sleep aids to rest. I distanced myself from each of my love interests as Sabrina became my shoulder to cry on. She'd check on my daily and used her resources to help me find out more information surrounding the accident and info of the girl's whereabouts. Desperate for answers, like clockwork, I called the number which was associated with the girl's aunt; the voice of a child answered the phone. I introduced myself as a friend of the family and asked if Kennedy or Cuddles was around. The child informed me that they weren't there but should be back in a little while, I cried tears of joy; I found hope.

Calling every hour on the hour for the remainder of the day, no one answered; the hope that I felt earlier was slowly dissipating. In the office the next day, I burst into tears as I updated my co-worker on what happened when I called, and the child answered. She prayed with me and encouraged me to not give up. Now calling the number, for the first time today, from my desk phone, since I fell asleep without plugging in my cell, it rang and rang as usual and then the voice of a woman answered. With joy, I explained who I was and asked if they were familiar with any of the individuals I was looking for or had any information on how I could get in contact with them. "Oh, Brooke" she says "I have heard so much about you. I know exactly who you are." Tears run like a faucet from my eyes. "When the phone rang, I said out loud, now who would be calling me from Washington D.C. with this weird number that shows up with all of these 9's attached on the end. I thought it either was a bill collector or the IRS, and in any case, I didn't need to talk to either, but Cuddles overheard me and her little butt got excited at the thought that it could be you, so I answered." I could hear Cuddles in the background, "Calm down, calm down before you hurt yourself or break something" the woman chastised. Too overjoyed, I could barely get a word out. All I could do was cry. As she put Cuddles on the phone, I broke down even more. "Ms. Brooke? Ms. Brooke?" she called "There's no one on the phone" she told the lady in the background. "I'm here Cuddles" I say in between gasping for air.

Hearing her voice has brought me so much delight. She told me that Kennedy was sleep and that they had wanted to call me but didn't have access to her father's phone and didn't have my number. She told me about her daddy's accident and how it made her feel. We talked until the lady whom I had spoken with initially, asked if she could speak with me again. Before letting her go, I prematurely urged her to write down my number and advised her to call me anytime she wanted. I wasn't sure if her aunt had long distance or not, but I didn't care; I would pay her entire phone bill if it meant that the kids could call anytime.

The lady and I spoke on the phone as she introduced herself as his sister Sharon. She opened up about her version of the incident involving Carter and a teenager who was texting and driving. Exchanging cell phone numbers, she advised me that I had been calling on her house phone explaining why I hadn't been able to reach anyone. She said that she would urge the girls, especially Kennedy, to call and talk because she felt like it could be therapeutic for them, little did she know it was therapeutic for me too. As Sharon tended to other family members and friends who were stopping by to pay their condolences, she promised to keep contact with me as the arrangements were finalized. Thrilled to have finally made contact with them, I dropped to my knees in my carpeted cubicle and thanked the Lord that they were safe.

That evening, I called in efforts to speak to Kennedy but I was informed that she was sleep again. Sitting in my bed wide awake, my heart broke for her. I thought of all the ways that I could cheer her up but being all the way on the other side of the map, there wasn't much that I could do. I could obviously send toys, but I don't think that would help; she needed her father. As the wheels turned in my head, I had an idea; maybe I could adopt them. Carter had mentioned before his adopted sister had kids and it was overwhelming for her to take care of everyone. Giving this a great amount of thought, I decided that this was something that I really wanted to do. I could change everything about my lifestyle to give these girls a place to call home. With my mind made up, I ran the idea by mom as I spoke with her the next morning. "Brooke, I'm not sure that's the best decision baby. They don't have any other family they can go and stay with? I know how open and kind hearted you are, but you don't even really know them all that well. And besides, what do you know about raising a kid, let alone 2 kids. Lord knows you aint babysat in 20 years. You don't even go and get your sisters kids when

you come in town, and now you want to go and raise some strange man's kids? You might want to give that a little bit more thought. How you gonna balance your life, with work and all, and theirs? Where they gonna go to school? Where they gonna live?" She went on and on, "Children are a lot of responsibility, it's not like the dog that you died to have and then returned after the first week. It's more to just dressing them up and having them look nice. They're not doll babies you know, and they cost, they cost lots of money, big money. They require sacrifice, do you even know what that entails? Lord knows I struggled to raise you all on my own but that was only by the grace of God and only him. Plus, did you take into consideration that they may have a hard time readjusting with all that is going on? It's gonna take time, lots of time, and patience, and hard work. Just think about it, really think. Think long and hard, pray about it, I know I am, but ask the Lord for some direction and clarity."

Biting my tongue and choosing not to debate with her, I simply excused myself from the conversation, letting her know that I would call her back later. She had got up under my skin. She has never thought that I was capable of handling a shit load of responsibility, even in my younger days. But boy if she only knew all the shit I had been through and never told her about, maybe she would give me a tad bit more credit. I had fully considered all aspects of the burdens that I was choosing to endure. I had weighed my options and figured that I knew, for the most part, what I was getting into. I had built such a boundless relationship with the two little girls and had grown to love them so much that they were a major part of my life. I knew how much they loved their father and the story behind their mother; those girls needed a break in life. Of course, I didn't know how they would react with all they were going through, but I would be here to love them and be there with and for them. We all were hurting from this loss and if they wanted to be here with me, I would do everything in my power to make it happen. I was ready and willing to make all the sacrifices to raise them with love, care, and stability.

Even though I tend to bounce a lot of ideas off my mother and take her words of advice into consideration, she wasn't a main factor in my evaluation. I had spoken to Sabrina about it and she encouraged the idea, offering help whenever I may need it. I had run the idea pass my boss, who seemed to be extremely supportive, but for some reason I wanted and felt the need to talk the idea over with Brandon. Although, he had known me the least amount of time, we had been inseparable as of recently and I was curious to see how this could or would affect our relationship.

Inviting him over to my place, I planned to put my thoughts out over dinner. Since we were always going out to eat, this would be something different. I figured that in an intimate setting, he would be relaxed and feel inclined to tell me his true thoughts and opinions. Coming over that evening after leaving the gym, I had the breakfast bar set with an empty wine glass next to each setting. The food was still in the oven keeping warm and his towel and washcloth were in the bathroom, so he could shower before dinner. Earlier I had picked a small fight with Kris, so I knew the coast would be clear for this overnight endeavor. I sat on the couch letting the tv watch me as I texted Sharon, Carter's sister, to check on the girls. I didn't really know what to say, I was concerned and wanted to make sure that everyone was ok. I offered to take some time off and fly out there, but Sharon said that they had everything handled as far as the funeral arrangements went and they were in the process of organizing paperwork and insurance policies. She said that she would be sure to contact me when the preparations were finalized so I could plan accordingly. My ideal plan would be to fly down a day or two before the funeral and possibly bring the girls back with me, but I didn't know to express that during everyone's time of grieving. It was pertinent that I have this conversation with Brandon sooner than later. Up until now, throughout my life I had always been accused of making selfish decisions, I didn't want this to be yet another incident.

Stepping fresh from the shower, smelling so fresh and so clean, I fixed our plates as we began to talk about his day. I hadn't been to work since the situation occurred, so his days had more going on than mine had. He asked how I was holding up with everything and I began to run my ideas by him. I didn't know what I was expecting him to say or what his reaction would be, but I knew that it would be nothing shy of honest. Finishing our meal, we sat on the couch, leaving the dishes to be cleaned later. I continued to fill him in on what was weighing heavy on my mind and heart for the past few days. I told him everything. I told him how Carter and I met, how we hung and communicated the bond they we built and just went into detail of our platonic relationship. As I talked, he just sat and listened not asking any questions or butting in. He looked as if he was extremely intrigued and irritated at the same time, by what I was saying to him. In hind sight, maybe the idea of Carters and I's interactions in Cali and here in DC concerned him, since he was never aware of us meeting up or Carter's existence at all. In too deep, I couldn't stop the story to explain all the details. Not yet mentioning anything about the idea of taking custody of the girls, he asked, "So what about his daughters? How are they holding up?". I go on to tell him how I've been keeping in contact with Carter's sister and checking on the status of the girls and how I planned on going out to California for the services. That's when I hit him with my grand plan. I passionately explained how I had been giving major consideration to the idea of bringing the girls back to the East coast with me and I asked him how he felt about the idea of me taking the girls in.

Although I had already had my mind pretty much made up on what I wanted to do, I wanted his unbiased point of view. Right off the back, he agreed that I should bring them here. He explained that if the children didn't have anywhere to go, no family members that wanted to take responsibility for them, and if there was actually an opportunity for me to get them, that I should at least try. Surprised by his response, I hesitated. Honestly speaking, I didn't expect him to say anything of that nature. I think that I expected him to ask more questions and give alternative suggestions. I mentioned the idea had crossed my mind a time or two, but I hadn't confirmed anything, nor had I even expressed the idea to Carter's family. I told him that I had been given mixed reviews from my friends and family. I told him what my mother had to say about the situation and then contradicted it by saying how Sabrina encouraged me to go through with it and lent her support as well. We sat in silence for 45 seconds as he sat and just stared at me. For the first time during this conversation I was feeling a tad bit uncomfortable. What was he thinking about? Maybe he really didn't believe in the things that he just told me, maybe he felt as though that was what he needed to say just to be nice and to seem like he actually cared. Like when I would give Kris advice on how to please his wife and encourage him to stay and work things out.

Deep down I didn't mean it, but I felt like I needed to say it and he needed to hear it. Maybe this was one of those times for me.

"In the event that I step out on a limb and take on this huge responsibility, how do I know that they are better off with me? My mom is right; I don't know the first thing about taking care of two children, especially two that are going through a very pivotal time in their lives. What if I can't give them what they need? What if my love isn't enough?" I asked. He took my hand and held it in his own and replied, "In the short span of time that we have known each other, I've learned quite a few things about you. I learned that your strong, independent, brilliant, funny, responsible, and caring. We don't always have the answers to everything God throws our way, but they say that he doesn't give us more than we can handle. You have more than enough to provide those little girls, and you have a wonderful strong support system... and you have me. I don't know anything about parenting, although I did have a carnival goldfish for about a week and a half, but I loved that little guy all the way up to his death. I will be here to help you if you need it. When I tell you how I feel about you, I'm not just talking to hear myself talk, I really mean it. You are amazing, and I love you." Chill bumps went through my body and my arm hairs stood up when I heard him say that. My facial expressions must have reflected what my body was feeling because he leaned in closer to repeat himself. "Yes, I said it. Brooke, I love you." My eyes began to tear up as I enlarged my eyelids and turned away trying to prevent the tears from falling. Gently grabbing my chin, he turned my face back towards him and kissed my forehead. The feeling was definitely mutual, I had grown to love him, but my life was so fucked up and discombobulated that I just couldn't afford to let someone blindly walk into this mess that I had got myself in. "Listen" he said, "whatever I can do to help, just let me know. I'm here for you, and if you come with 2 little additions, then I 'll take them too."

That was all I needed to hear. For 12 years, all I ever needed and wanted was to hear and genuinely know and feel, was that someone wanted to be with me, all of me, even the parts of me that weren't so put together and full of confusion. Pulling me in as close as I could be without being a part of his flesh, I unwaveringly let the tears flow. It was a combination of tears of joy, confusion, and grief. Being so strong all the time finally took its toll and broke me. I wasn't embarrassed or ashamed like I normally would be, I felt relaxed and safe all while in the comfort of his arms. Wiping my eyes, he reassured me that everything would be alright and work itself out.

Once the funeral arrangements were made, I let my boss know that I planned on being out for a week or so but told her that I would keep her updated. With well wishes and condolences from my friends and family, I picked up a few things for the girls and caught the next flight out to be with them. Brandon volunteered to go and be by my side if I needed him, but I didn't. I was just charmed with the idea of him being there to support me and my endeavors, not like Kris who was too selfish to care about anyone else but himself. When I had told him about my dilemma of bringing Kennedy and Cuddles back with me, he told me that I was doing too much and how he didn't think it was a good idea. His main reasons were more along the lines of how it would affect solely him and our continuous rendezvous. In reverse of Brandon, he suggested that the girls needed to go and stay with their real family, "You don't even know them" he claimed, "I mean if their dad wasn't trying to fuck you, you wouldn't have even had a relationship with them at all." He can be such an asshole at times, which makes me question how I've managed to be so attracted to him after all of these years.

As the plane traveled through turbulence, I spent the entire time imaging how the girls would react when they saw me, then I reminisced on the times that Carter and I shared together. Before I knew it the tears began to flow down my face as I searched my bag for tissues and my sunglasses. I had never experienced death this close before, I didn't know how to handle what I was going through. I realized that all the kind words and sympathetic gestures that people expressed to me meant nothing. They were just words and almost nothing could ease this pain that I was feeling. All knew was once I got to the house, I would need to put my feelings to the side and be strong for these babies. Sharon had told me that the girls were both handling it very well, but she was unsure about how they would react seeing him at the funeral. She offered to pick me up from the airport as she also extended an invitation to stay at her house. Not wanting to inconvenience anyone, I got a hotel room so that their family could be properly accommodated. Once landed, I got a rental car and made up in my mind that I wanted to see Kennedy and Cuddles right away. I wanted to wrap my arms around them and hug them tightly. Not sure if that's what they needed but it was definitely what I needed.

As I pulled up to the house, I could easily envision why Carter may have decided to move away. The environment was very different from the one where he decided to raise his children; I wonder if they felt out of place. Parking my car, I called Sharon's phone to make sure I had the right address. This didn't look like one of those neighborhoods where you should be walking up to the wrong house, knocking on the door, asking for someone whom you've never met before. Just my luck, she didn't answer. Sitting in the car, I said a small prayer asking God for the strength to be resilient enough to endure whatever I was about to walk into. Just as I opened my eyes and lifted my head, 3 kids burst out the door laughing and screaming. Right away I identified Cuddles so I knew I had the right house. I don't know if it was the luxury car that the gentleman at the car rental place upgraded me to or if I just looked that out of place, which made them notice me. Making sure the car doors are locked (after declining the renter's daily insurance), as I approached the house all the kids and the individuals standing on the outside porch stopped and stared. Feeling a little nervous to be the center of attention, it was too late to turn back. The closer I got, baby girl finally recognized me and ran straight to me. The force of her energy when she reached my thigh almost knocked me off balance in these skinny 6-inch heels. As I hoisted her into the air, she held me tightly as I squeezed her back.

After she loosened up her grip, I stared into her innocent eyes. "My daddy's not here" she reminded me. Sensing my eyes beginning fill up, "I know baby, where's your sister?" I asked changing the topic. "Come on, she's inside" she replies. By this time the other children whom she had previously agreed to play with are now standing in front of me, probably wondering who I am. The little boy bluntly asks, "Can we ride in your car?" Not wanting to totally ignore him or say anything rude, I simply reply "maybe later". Cuddles tell the kids that she will be back and forcefully leads me into the house, as I speak to the bystanders on my way in. Once inside, she drops my hand and runs to get Kennedy's attention. "Kennedy! Kennedy! Look who's here! Ms. Brooke is here!" says the excited little one. Kennedy turns around and slowly gets up off the floor, where she was watching television, and walks towards me. Before she makes it to greet me an older woman comes out of the kitchen "It's finally nice to be able to put a face to the name" as she extends her arms towards me. Assuming this is Carter's sister, Sharon, I receive her with open arms. She continues to talk as Cuddles puts up her arms to be lifted. With Cuddles on my hip and Kennedy by my side, this lady goes on saying how she's heard so much about me and what a pleasure it was to finally meet me. She begins to introduce me to other members of their family as the kids continue to stay close by my side. Mostly older patrons, with pleasant things to say, either complimented my attire or referenced something that they had heard about me. Everyone seemed to be very welcoming.

Finding an empty chair, the girls and I have a seat as we began to talk. It was hard trying to find things to talk about other than their father or their current living situation, but I wanted to liven their spirits and see where their heads were. The youngest one had no problems opening about new toys that she got and the new friends that she had made since their relocation, but I could tell that Kennedy wasn't as excited. She was taking the circumstances much harder. She wasn't as talkative as she normally would be, and I noticed that she barely cracked a smile the entire time. The distress and hurt on her face was apparent but I didn't want to damper the mood. I figured that I would talk to her more in depth when she was alone to see if I could get her to open up. While sitting there with Cuddles doing most of the chatting, her friends from outside returned looking for her. She started to brush them off, but I encouraged her to go out and play, letting her know that I would be here when she returned. This would give me time to talk to Kennedy and see what was on her mind.

Conversation between her and I avoided the obvious. I told her that I had picked some things up for her and that they were in the car, but she insisted that she would get them later. I felt so bad for her and with every long blink she made and deep sigh that she took, my heart broke a little more.

I stayed until the late hours of the night listening to people reminisce about stories involving Carter and/or the girls. He was indeed a kind and generous soul and would be truly missed. The kids had already passed out watching TV and Miss Cuddles aka "Hang all night", fell asleep in my arms. As the crowd of visitors and family members dispersed, Sharon showed me where to lay down the heavy dead weighted child. It was a small room with two twin sized beds and an inflatable mattress in the middle of the floor. Laying the baby down, I went out to the living room to grab the eldest. She was too big to be picking up, but I would be willing to do so if needed. As I got her up in attempts to get her to walk, she opened her eyes and headed towards the room where she had been sleeping for the past few days as I followed closely behind her. She and her sister had been sharing a bed. I asked her why she didn't sleep on one of the other beds. She said that she wanted to be near her little sister. Pulling the covers over her, she asks how long I am visiting for and if I can stay here with them. Jokingly I laugh at the idea of the twin bed fitting all three of us. She proposes the idea that she is willing to sleep on the floor if I agree to stay. I told her that I won't stay in the house but I'm staying extremely close in a hotel and I will talk with her aunt to see if one of the days they can come over to where I am staying for a sleepover. I kiss her on her forehead as I stroke her cornrowed hair. I remind her of how much I love her and encourage her to get some sleep. She doesn't say a word, she just stares at me as I watch a tear fall to the side of her face. "What's wrong?" I ask, as if I don't already know. "I want my daddy, I didn't want him to leave us. It's not fair." she says as more tears stream from her little eyes. What do you say to a child that has lost her entire world? I couldn't find the words to say to make her feel better. There was a pain in my throat from fighting back my emotions, so in turn I just agreed with her. It wasn't fair. It's not fair that these children have to endure this type of pain at such a young age. We sat, and we cried together, trying hard not to wake her sister. Wiping her face with my shirt I tell her that it's ok to cry and that she needs to let it out. I give her the generic spiel that everyone gives, you know the one about him not being in any pain and in a better place, but I know it's not true? He wouldn't want to be anywhere other than here with his girls. "I'm so happy that you're here Ms. Brooke" she says with a stuffy nose. "Now you know I had to be here with my girls, ya'll are my BFFF's" I replied. "BFFF's?" she asked. "Yeah, my best friends forever forever" I responded, "and I'll be here for as long as you need me to be, ok?" "Ok" she says. "Now try to get a little rest, I'm not going anywhere" I add, "I love you both."

Back in the kitchen, I helped Sharon clean and straighten up the days' worth of disposable plates and cups. She opens the conversation up by talking about the kids and how much they adored me. She told me how excited the kids were when they returned home from their trip to DC and their visit to the white house and national monuments. They had told her all about our road trip up to Philly to see the liberty bell and the cheesesteaks "They were crazy about those cheesesteaks and something called water ice, or something like that." I just smiled. She began to delve into asking me questions about my life back in DC and what I did for a living. We stayed up for another hour or so discussing politics and points of views, what I like to do for fun, and Carter of course. She told me how Carter felt about me, how he bragged and put me on some type of imaginary pedestal. I told her how I, too, cared for him and the girls and how I was deeply hurt by the news of his passing. I thanked her for opening up her home and heart to me. Once again, she offered the option for me to stay, but I again declined. I told her where I was staying and asked that if it was ok with her if I returned in the morning. She said that I was more than welcome and that there is an open-door policy when it came to me. She thanked me for traveling out here and being part of the girls' support system. She explained her efforts on trying to get the girls adjusted and ways that she had tried to make them more comfortable with the unfortunate turn of events. I wanted to pitch my idea right then and there, but I wasn't sure how well it would be received. Would she think that I was in it for money? After just meeting me, could she understand that my heart and intentions were pure?

As the next few days progressed, followed by the funeral, these girls were taking the situation much better than I could have ever imagined. I spent every day with them, even allowing them to come sleep over at the hotel with me. I wanted to ask them how they felt about coming back to D.C. with me, but I didn't want to prematurely mention it without any follow through. At one point, Kennedy did ask me if I could ask their aunt to let them come and visit me sometime; if she only knew, I was trying to get them permanently. I didn't know much about children but what I did know is that they were like elephants, they never forget. Before I spoke on the issue, I would feel more comfortable if it was potentially already in the works. I knew that I adored those little girls and everyone else including me, knew that the feelings were mutual.

One evening, as the girls slept in the king-sized bed, during my nightly phone check-in with Brandon, he asked me if I had given the situation anymore thought and if I had expressed my strategies with Sharon yet. I had been in California nearly two weeks already and was still walking on egg shells, not knowing how fragile anyone's feelings were. I confided in him, telling him that I honestly couldn't figure out how to best approach the topic without it being taken as offensive or overstepping my boundaries. He encouraged me to sit down and have a heart to heart with Sharon. He thought that as a woman and as a mother, not to mention someone who cared for and wanted the absolute best for her nieces, that she should understand, and at least be able to consider my proposition as an option. He even suggested drawing up paperwork that could solidify the arrangement if I needed him to.

His interest boosted my confidence. I was almost positive that she isn't going to want to part ways with these little angels who are a daily memorial of her brother whom she just cremated, but her plate is full. Hopefully Sharon would be able to see things the way that Brandon and I are envisioning them to be. Before Brandon and I changed the conversation to a lighter situation, I swallowed my pride and silenced my doubts. I shot Sharon a text asking if I could speak with her regarding the girls whenever she had some time. Without hesitation, she responded "Yes. I have been reluctant in speaking with you regarding some things also but please feel free. You can even call if you'd like. Either method works well for me." Feeling more relaxed now, I let Brandon reassure me that this was a healthy decision to make. He even engaged in a mock phone call with me in efforts of trying to ensure that I could efficiently get my point across without surpassing my position. With everything in place, I decided that tomorrow morning would be the day when I would have the chat with her. I was more than confident enough that I could plead my case via telephone, but I honestly felt it would be best if we'd talk face to face. Therefore, she would be able to see how passionate and sincere I was. There was no doubt in my mind that she didn't already know how I felt about the girls, but I wanted to be able to see her facial expressions and use that to gauge how receptive she was, or wasn't, to my ideas. Finishing up my conversation with Brandon, I told him that I loved him and thanked him for being such a positive factor in my life which brought me so much joy and encouragement. My racing mind barely let me get any sleep, thinking about this conversation that I was preparing to have with Sharon. What if she said no, or thought that it wasn't a good idea? What if she thought like my mother and considered me to be incapable of providing what the girls needed? What type of life style would the girls have staying there with her? What would Carter have wanted?

Finally falling to sleep, I woke up to the happy faces and laughter of Kennedy and Cuddles as they watched morning cartoons. Looking at them and their bright smiles further reassured me that I was making the right decision. Even if this didn't work in my favor, I would do my very best to make sure that I would always be there for them and maintain an active relationship in their lives at whatever costs. Allowing them to lie around for a little bit longer as I used my shower time to mentally prepare, I was ready. I got them dressed and picked up some breakfast for them to eat as we ventured back to their new home. Not wanting to seem too anxious, Sharon and I made small talk as she worked to straighten up her kitchen from what looked like breakfast that she prepared probably before sending her kids off to school. As she rested herself in the seat across the table from me, she asked me how I was doing. Not like for the moment, but she wanted to know what I was feeling, emotionally. She had watched me be strong for everyone else for the past week and some odd days, but she wanted to know how I was truly feeling. I told her that I attributed the success of my healing process with being able to spend time around the girls. I knew how much he loved them and basically lived for them, so although spending time with them made me miss him, it also made me appreciate him more, it made me appreciate life as a whole more, as weird as it sounded. With those explanations of words, it allowed me to introduce my reason for asking her to sit down and speak with me. I first excused myself for being too forward if she felt that I was, then I began to flood her with my feelings and ideas. Her face remained emotionless throughout my entire discourse, leaving me in confusion for not knowing where the conversation would go next. She looked down, she looked back up at me, and down again. I covered my forehead with my hand as we sat in there with only the sound of the Disney channel playing from 2 rooms over. I didn't know what to think, I started second guessing and doubting my "already spoken" expressions.

Quietly standing up from the table, Sharon pulls a paper towel from the roll, tore it at the perforated point, walked to the window and gazed out of it. Meekly watching her every move, the emotional atmosphere of the room had drastically changed. Should I keep talking and maybe retract my prior proposal or should I just wait for her to begin speaking? At a total loss for words and ideas, I heard her sniffle and watched as she took the paper towel and dabbed her face. With her back facing me, I assumed that she was trying to conceal the fact that she was crying but I couldn't fathom why. I hadn't said anything to offend her and if I did, I feel like I initially offered her a disclaimer that those were not my intentions. I continued to stay seated only to have my mind wander about how I was going to make my next move and what would it be.

Turning now to face me, she sat back down, confirming my idea that her eyes were in fact filled with tears. Sitting down, she still said nothing. Our eyes meet, and her mouth opens, but she can't get the words to come out. "I apologize if what I said offended you in any way. I want to promise you that was never my intent" I softly spoke as I reached across the table and placed my hand on top of hers. The very thing that had me leery and hesitant to ask in the beginning, had me now regretting that I had even said anything in the first place. Sharon finally spoke. She first apologized for her emotions that were currently getting in the way of her being able to verbally express what she was feeling, and then she redirected. "The last conversation that I had with my brother was about him needing to stop living on cloud 9 and to come back down to earth and open his eyes to the real world's injustices and shit like that. I criticized him for being out of touch and sheltering the girls lives so much that they wouldn't be able to cope once they got out into the world. I fussed at him for a good 5 minutes and he never said a word back. I almost thought that he had either hung up or put the phone down and walked away, but he didn't. He'd listen to me go on and on, I was just running my mouth and although you don't know me well enough, I've been told that I can talk. I could probably hold an entire conversation by myself if I wanted to, but that's who I am and it's my role, it's always been. I was his big sister, I should know things and tell him what to do. I'd been protecting him since he was little. See, my mother, God rest her sole, she didn't know what she was doing when she took custody of us. I raised Carter and basically the entire neighborhood. Nobody talks about it much, but she had a drug problem. She battled with it for years. How the social worker never caught wind of it, I'll never know. Oh, the good Lord knows that I've seen some things that no child my age should've ever had to see but I protected my brother from seeing it. I was his shield. I always knew that there wasn't going to be much that I could do with my life because I had taken on so many of other people's burdens, but I was determined that I wasn't going to let Carter waste his life taking care of other people."

As she continued to talk, I just listened. "When he became old enough to start getting into trouble, there's nothing that knuckle headed boy aint do. U name it, he's probably done it. I'm sure it's some stuff that I don't even know about. I wouldn't put anything past him. I remember having to go physically pull him from off the corner some blocks over because he thought he wanted to be down with the neighborhood gang. Oh, I've had grown ass men step to me, the motherfuckers aint scare me though. They couldn't have my little brother. He wasn't the streets, he was mine. He was all I had, and selfishly, I didn't want to be alone. Although he could walk the walk and talk the talk with the older guys, he was different. Those other guys knew it too, he just wanted to fit in. I would be late to school making sure that he was in school and that he stayed in school all day. I made excuses for our mom, her absences, her inabilities, and her shortcomings. The older he got, the more he got to see the situation for what it really was. He lashed out a bit, but not for long. He would always tell me how much he hated me and would be quick to remind me that I wasn't his mother, oh and he'd be quick to remind our mother that she wasn't his real mother either, but I didn't care." I could tell this story was going to be a tear jerker, but I didn't want to see her to break down, my heart couldn't handle it. "I remember his 9th grade teacher, Mrs. Reynolds, she used to wear me out. She was always on my case about being late and sleeping in her class. Until one day she pulled me to the side and had a talk with me. At first, I wouldn't say anything because I didn't want anyone to get in trouble and I didn't want to go to another foster home, but each week she'd find a new way to have a conversation with me until I finally opened up. I never told anyone about our situation at home because I was worried about what would happen to us. But on this day, I finally told her. She was such a sweet lady who you could tell really thought that she would be able to help me but there was literally nothing that she could do. So, when Carter got her as a teacher, she already knew what I had been going thru with him and she made sure to give him extra attention. She recommended him for programs and extracurricular activities, sometimes even paying the cost associated with them out of her own pocket. As she helped make my plight easier, I was able to focus enough to get my ass a diploma. That boy really wore me out, and honestly speaking, with these kids I have now, I'm not sure how much more fight I have left in me. When all the commotion around here dies down and when the masses of people stop flooding through these doors extending their comforts, I don't know how much of me I will have to give to anyone else" she finishes as she shakes her head.

The story of the boy that she just described sounded nothing like the refined gentleman that I met in the Texas airport, who despite my arrogance, treated me with nothing but kindness. The guy who rolled the dice and politely asked me to escort him to a banquet when he was

being honored for his success in corporate America, was she talking about the same person? As I sat and reflected over the features that she had disclosed to me, not only did I have a new and upmost respect for Carter, but also for her. See I thought that I had it rough but sometimes when you hear someone else's story, you become much more grateful for what you had or in some cases, what you didn't have.

The vibration of my cell phone sounded on the table where I was sitting, reaching into my bag, I saw that it was Brandon. He probably was calling to see how things had gone with Sharon since I had been quiet for a few hours now. Neglecting his message, I was waiting to see if Sharon had anything else to say. I mean, she had yet to give an answer, but I guess the most logical thing would be for her to go and converse it over with the rest of the family before she made any brash decisions. I didn't want her to feel as though her back was up against the wall or I was strong arming her. Although I hoped she would make a decision now, in all actuality she had time. With all these feeling overwhelming my heart, and thoughts consuming my mind, the real question was should I say them out loud or not? I don't know if my speaking would further confuse the situation or add fire to the flame. I wanted to give her time to think, but I was leaving in 2 days and I wanted to spend as much time with the girls as possible while I was here. Giving her time to think the proposition over, I left with telling her and the girls that I would be back later on. The girls weren't thrilled with the fact that I was leaving and not taking them with me, but I sat down and told them that I think that they needed to spend some time with their aunt. The truth was, I needed time to be alone with my thoughts. In the event that she would counter offer my deal with something that didn't allow me to be in their lives as much as I would've like to, I would be totally devastated. I got in my car and drove back to the hotel. As I sat on the edge I the bed, I spotted an article of children's clothing on the floor. One of the girls must have left it. Picking it up and smelling it, I missed them already. As I sat there holding onto the shirt like some sort of weirdo, my phone rang. Looking at the screen I saw that it was Jasmine calling. What the hell did she want? We had only spoke a handful of times since the stunt that she pulled stunt the last time I was out here on the west coast, so what would be prompting her to reach out this time? Was she in trouble again? Did she need to borrow money? I decided to answer her call (because I am often gluten for punishment). She claimed to be calling because she had spoken to Sabrina and was informed that I had experienced a recent loss, she wanted to extend her sympathy and condolences. If she had spoken to Sabrina, I'm sure she knew that I was out here on her side of town too. Unfazed by her knack of fishing for details of my whereabouts, I caved in and told her where I was staying. I had no intentions on driving out to meet her but if she wanted to connect she would have to come here. Surprisingly she agreed although I hoped that she hadn't.

Now Jasmine has always been my girl. She was a very caring person, one of the kindest spirits that you would ever meet, but if things weren't about her, nothing else mattered. I equally admired and was disgusted by her actions at times, but at the very least, as Sabrina said before she was consistent. With her coming, I would at least have my mind temporarily distracted for a few hours.

Not too long after giving her my location, I checked in with Brandon to tell him when happened over at Sharon's and told him how Jasmine had reached out to me and wanted to meet up. Talking to him always calmed my soul but I didn't want to necessarily mentally burden him with my issues all the time. For goodness sake, after all he was a lawyer; he had much bigger things to put his focus towards. When Jasmine arrived, she greeted me like nothing had ever transpired a year prior however I embraced it. I wasn't going to focus on the past anymore because if I didn't learn anything over these past couple of weeks, I learned that life is really too short and tomorrow wasn't promised. And though people graciously use that saying, we often walk around in our 20's, 30's, and 40's, thinking that we have plenty of time, taking life and those around us for granted, not knowing what life has in store for us the very next day or even hour.

Sitting down on the sofa, she removes a bottle of wine from her bag and begins rummaging the room for some clean cups. Finding an unused glass, she pours the wine and hands it to me. I take a sip as she extends her condolences once more and asks me the details of my emotions. Well into the night, after several hours of conversing, I have literally brought her up to speed on everything. Extending some advice, she mostly just listened to me as I went on and on about these little girls. "I have never heard you be so passionate about anything in your entire life" she said to me. "Well I really hope that everything works out for you and those little girls. I think that you are exactly what the girls need in their lives and if I can do anything to help, let me know." Before letting the night get away, she apologizes for her actions from when I was last out here to visit. She briefly explains how she got caught up in a situation involving drugs, money laundering, and Ponzi schemes. She mentions that in the months prior she had hit rock bottom, lost her job, admitted herself into rehab and moved to Concord,

California to escape the life that Los Angeles had provided to her. She adds the information that Maliq had been arrested and she too would likely be facing criminal charges in the months to come. With already too much going on in my life right, I found it hard to empathize with her. I wished her well and congratulated her for getting out of her situation and finding help. As she gathers her belongings to leave, I get a call from Kennedy asking me if I was coming back. Because it was so late, and Jas and I had finished up the entire bottle of wine, I figured that the kids were sleep and that I would just get them in the morning and maybe take them to breakfast at this spot not too far from here that Jas raved about. Kennedy said that Cuddles had fell asleep trying to wait up for me, but she was still waiting and wanted to know if I would be coming or not, primarily because Sharon was making her put her pajamas on and she was stalling. I told her that if she asked and aunt Sharon didn't mind, I could come get them, but I also expressed again to her how Sharon loves them and that she should consider spending some quality time since Sharon was still grieving and deeply missed their dad. I suggested that her presence of being there might ease the pain. She eventually agreed to stay there but made me promise that I would be there bright and early in the morning to get them. I agreed.

The next 2 days were filled with hugs, laughs, calories and ice cream, and most of all, special memories that would last a lifetime, but I still hadn't received any feedback from Sharon in regard to her decision, but I wasn't going to push either. Throughout my plane ride, I scrolled through the pics on my phone of all of us together while convincing myself that what was meant to be would be.

Returning home and back to my normal business schedule, I filled my days with work and constructive activities that would keep my mind busy. As usual, I spent most of my time with Brandon and those other days which were far and few in-between with Kris when Brandon would be consumed with a heavy workload. Brandon was everything that I wanted in a man, but without the kids here in DC with me, the picture that I had once painted in my head, and the dream that he blindly sold of us being a blissful makeshift family, was slowly disintegrating, making it easier to fall back into Kris' clutch. Maybe God didn't designate me for the family life. I mean after the abortion, I wrote off the miscarriage as a sign that God was slightly punishing me for killing one of his own, but honestly, maybe I wasn't cut out for the motherhood bid.

For months, I kept in touch with the girls. I bought them both phones so we could facetime every day. We talked on the phone all the time; Sharon even allowed them to come to DC when Jasmine would come home to visit. It felt odd that she never said anything more about our last real conversation but I was pleased and appreciative that she allowed us to maintain a relationship. While they were visiting, they got a chance to meet Brandon and Sabrina and her boys. We had some really good times. Things for me were taking a turn for the better. I received a promotion at work, lost 10 pounds, my hair was growing, butt got more toned, Brandon and I had grown much closer, we had taken a vacation and had another one planned in a few months. We had surpassed the honeymoon stage of the relationship and were unofficially cohabitating, at his place. I needed to keep my place for my own personal reasons, of course, but things were looking up for me and those around me.

At 1am on a Tuesday, my phone rang, it was Sharon. She said that she wanted to know if I was still interested in what we had discussed when I was back in California. Quietly crawling out of the bed, trying not to awaken Brandon, I closed the bedroom door behind me and took the call in the other room. She said that she had been thinking about it for a long time and it weighed heavy on her heart but she ultimately thought that I could provide the girls with a better life than she could. She loved them to death and said that she was selfishly keeping them as a reminder of her brother, but they deserved more than to just be trophy kids. Again, she reminded me of how in awe the girls were of me, how they looked up to me and how I am all that they ever talked about. This was a lot for me to process at 1am and given that my current living situation was different now, I couldn't calibrate everything in my head. Once she realized how late it was on my time zone, she apologized for waking me and told me to let her know after I had given it some more thought. Returning to the bed, I was unable to return to sleep. Instead I twisted and turned as my mind wandered. I secretly hoped that Brandon would wake up, so I could tell him, but he slept peacefully.

Catching the alarm clock before it went off; I got out of bed and took a shower. By the time I finished, Brandon was up making him some coffee. Neither one of us were "talkers", per say, in the morning, so I didn't want to overwhelm him with the latest and greatest news, but I couldn't contain myself. Walking out into the common area, I found myself following him from room to room bombarding him with the full details from my late-night call. "There's a hint of excitement in your voice, are you excited?" he asked. Of course, that's what I wanted but the problem is, I wanted it when I wanted it. Now that the reality of it all was setting in, I'm not sure if it's still what I want. In efforts to distract myself months ago from overthinking the situation when I didn't receive an answer, I altered my life in such a way that it might not have made my life conducive to take care of 2 children anymore. Throughout the day, I created about 101 pros and cons of the girls coming to be with me, eventually resulting in the bad outweighing the good. I couldn't bounce my ideas off of Brandon because he would just support either choice I made and help reinforce my justifications. I already knew Kris's opinions from prior inquiries and when he thought that I decided against getting them, he further lavished me in expensive gifts to emphasize why he didn't think that me taking them on as a load, was a good look for us. Besides I knew how my closest friends and family felt especially since they had made a connection with the girls during their visit. This was going to be solely up to me and totally on my own recognizance.

After several days of going back and forth with the idea in my head, I decided that I was just going to go through with it. After all, almost all the reasons that I could come up that were "anti-kiddies", derived from extreme selfishness and those girls deserved a chance. Jasmine assisted in helping the girls prepare for the transition and helped organize their flight situation, while Brandon helped on the legal end. The closer the day came for them to arrive, the more the excitement built up inside of me. I had everything situated, registration for school had been completed, equipped with tutors for both girls, I bought them beds, child proofed my condo unit, bought snacks, and sugar filled treats, things that I figured kids like. My friends and family prepared a small gathering to officially welcome Cuddles and Kennedy to DC. There were banners, balloons and cake. I think the girls really enjoyed themselves. I knew it was time to buckle down and become much more responsible than I had ever been in my entire life.

As the next few months flew by not everything had gone as expected. The girls and I hit a few rough patches, but we made it through. While I literally became a mom overnight, Brandon stepped up his game and attempted to be an equal partner. Living quarters were tight and during my down time, I would search for properties that would give us enough space not to live on top of one another. The waters of my relationship with Kris had been troubled since I had absolutely no time for him anymore. He lost his freedom of being able to randomly stop by for mind blowing sex sessions and our rendezvous experiences had become non-existent. We barely conversed via phone anymore and when we did converse almost always resulted in an argument or me having to call him back. He stopped consistently paying the mortgage and car note causing financial frustration and inconvenience on my end, but Brandon was there to help when needed. I tried not to let him intervene in things that dealt with money, but he was supportive emotionally, physically, and financially. Our situation had almost become something like a 2-parent household, minus the cohabitation. I wanted to be the best role model and set a great example for them to follow, so much that the Kris predicament didn't really affect me. I mean, I knew what I was doing was wrong and frowned upon, but it's one thing to have my skeletons in my closet, but when I am literally sharing a closet, I couldn't afford for those skeletons to fall out.

After months of washing my own hair in the bathtub and wearing my hair in nothing but a ponytail, I was finally graced with a few hours of alone time while the girls and Brandon went for a walk through the park. I called my long-time hairdresser and pleaded for her to fit me in. While sitting waiting to be serviced, I overhear one of the other clients mention how she was desperately trying to find a tenant for her single-family home in the county. After speaking with her and telling her my story, she agreed upon giving me the lockbox code and letting me come and view it. She said if I was satisfied, that I could move in immediately. Ever since I had graduated college, I vowed never to rent again because I considered it to be a total waste of money, but my back was against the wall, literally. Renting for a year shouldn't be bad. It would give me time to get the condo sold, research some new school districts and neighborhoods, and do all that good stuff responsible parents do.

After leaving the shop I had Brandon and the girls meet me at the property, so I could get their opinions too. Resulting in a total win on everyone's behalf, I called the lady and arranged to meet so we could work out the details. With a new house in the motion, that meant more bills, a longer commute, and more sacrifices. I now fully understand the saying, "a woman's work is never done."

A year into the deal, my little family is thriving. We're winging things, but they're working, and I could not be prouder of myself. With Kris' absence lasting a few months, I receive a call from him out of the blue one day while I was at work. He wanted to know how the girls and I were doing and of course he blamed the fact that we hadn't spoken on me. He claimed that there were more than plenty of single mothers who made time for other things besides their kids, as he accused me of overly dramatizing the circumstances. Quickly irritated by him and his antics, I broke down all the recent changes that had been occurring since he had been on a hiatus. He was surprised to know that I had moved but was quickly intrigued by the fact that I had an empty property that was readily available for us to utilize without the company of the kiddies. Annoyed and bothered, I let him know I was peeved that I had even gave him opportunity to disrupt my flow of work. Apologizing for his reactions to not having spoken to me and his withdraw from seeing me, he asked if it was at all possible for us to meet up one day just to talk. That was an almost impossible task. Agreeing that I would try my best to fit him in my schedule was the best option I had to offer him before I ended the conversation. Sitting back in my chair, I began reflecting on everything that we'd been through and had he been a standup guy years ago, had he not acted a damn fool, we could have been sharing in this experience. Instead of Brandon, Kris (the man that my heart once literally only beat for) and I could have been what I always wanted. And although I still loved him very much, I had new priorities. And just as he neglected to consider my feelings when he took his nuptials, I could no longer consider his.

Making the decision to find a day to take him up on his offer, I sensed the need to explain who Brandon was and his position in my life as my fiancée and his role in the girl's lives. Some might say that he didn't deserve to know but I wasn't as fucked up and cold hearted as I'd sometimes like to think I was. I figured, after all that he's done for me and all that we'd experienced, I owed him that much.

That night, our daily routine went as normal, but I spent a large portion of the evening wondering what I was going to say to Kris and how I was going to say it. Brandon stopped by, as he most commonly did if he didn't have to work late and he noticed that something was a little off. I so wanted to be truthful with him because he has truly been a blessing to not only me but the girls too, nevertheless I could only be honest to a certain degree. I couldn't look him in his face and tell him that this woman that he thinks so highly of, who maintains this good girl image for so long, has been sleeping with a married man for years, even during the duration of us being intimate. I couldn't tell him about the gifts and jewelry, the car, the mortgage payments, and the long list of other services that Kris has sponsored. Any man in their right mind would walk out and be perfectly right in doing so. So, I brushed off my abstract attitude as a result of being tired and blamed it on the stresses from work. I knew the conversation needed to be had but I would need to plan it out. I didn't want to be with Kris because he ultimately couldn't give me what I wanted or needed right now. His sole position in my life was designated for playtime and I wasn't getting much of that as of lately.

Two weeks passed before I was able to take Kris up on date. We met up after work in a little quaint park. He looked good, not like I was looking, he looked well rested. He smelled great like he hadn't preformed any type of work earlier in the day. His jeans and sneakers were crisp, and his shirt still had the iron creases in the sleeves. The agreement was just to meet up and talk but somehow, we ended up in a dive bar. One mixed drink and 4 shots later we're kissing in the bathroom of the bar like teenage love birds. GOSH DAMMIT! There's no doubt that he is evidently my weakness. Our session was interrupted by a bar patron who kept banging on the door to utilize the facility for its actual purpose. Laughing and stumbling out, we make it back to his car, where he slid his hand up my dress and began to circularly massage my clitoris. Already in heat from the bathroom session I didn't put up a fight.

Instead, I began to feel on my own breasts, intensifying my hormones. He knew what he was doing to me and he could have me right in this car as people walked past and looked in, I was ready. I wanted him to fuck me like he used to, and I wanted it badly. As he removed his 2 fingers from my pussy, he licked them as though he was tasting the sweet nectars of fruit. "Let me taste you" I commanded of him. Unbuckling his Hermes belt, he pulled out my very best friend of 15 years. Goodness knows I loved his penis. After deep throating it several times, I realized that I wasn't going to be able to go home like this. Requesting him to take me to my car, I had him meet me at the condo. I had about 30 mins before tutoring was over and I could call Brandon, tell him that I was running late and ask him to grab the girls. I'd agree to get dinner, so nothing seemed suspicious or out of the ordinary. I know this is fucked up, but my pussy was hungry and needed some of that daddy dick Kris had.

Slipping off my more than saturated panties, I placed the call to Brandon. In running down my itinerary to him, I mentioned how I would be stopping by the condo to look for some of the kid's items I claimed I couldn't find at the house. With no reason to doubt the validity of my whereabouts, he ends the call with "I love u" as I struggle to say it back. Feeling guilty, I sat in my car with the A/C on blast, rethinking my intentions. I wasn't a bad person and I knew better. My better judgement was telling me to take my ass home but the reformed inner hoe in me figured that I was wasting valuable fucking time. Riding to the condo, I had mixed emotions, but I settled on the original plan of telling Kris about Brandon, in which I purposely omitted in our earlier conversation. Kris' car was already parked when I entered the lot. Taking a deep sigh and reminding my pussy to behave herself and to curb her craving, I walked towards the building as he closely followed. Making it inside he immediately started kissing on my neck. Giving him total control of my body, we switched several positions ultimately resulting in my knee having a serious carpet burn. As he brought my body to a total sweat, I was satisfied, as always, he aims to please.

As we both lay on the floor with our exposed bodies facing upwards, panting and breathing heavy, I tell him about Brandon. Although I downplayed our relationship, I made it known that he has been a counterpart in helping with the girls, but I more so painted the picture of him being more of a friend other than a significant other. Trying to convince myself that I didn't care what he thought, in all actuality I did. As I confessed my truths, if that's what you call it, he revealed how his situation at home had grown more distant and that he had been consulting with a lawyer regarding proceedings in a divorce. Kris had talked about getting a divorce for some time now and has always been in the process of handling paperwork, so his stories don't impress me. He just wanted to let me know...again.

Expressing his praises of my recent personal growth, he was impressed with the maturity of me taking on such a big responsibility with the Kennedy and Cuddles. I knew I was doing a good job, but for some reason, it meant much more coming from him. As he continued to talk, he caught me by surprise when he inadvertently interjected possible ways for him to participate in our lives. He normally was everything opposite of the family type, but today he was showing interest? Had he had a change of heart? Had things at home become so bad that he was considering this chaos thing called life that I was intertwined in? Instead of being impressed, I'm a tad bit concerned.

Realizing that I had let the time get away from me, we quickly had another session in the shower and air dried. Redressing in the same clothing I wore to work, I needed to support my little white lie about staying out late. Walking me to the car, he sends me off with a kiss but not before taking noticing of the princess cut diamond ring on my left hand. Quickly questioning the connotation of it, he asks if it was a gift from "my friend". Nonchalantly brushing it off with a laugh, I eased his mind by telling him that he had nothing to worry about. Giving me a questionable look, he knew there was more to the story. But he also knew that he wasn't going to get a straight answer out of me either, at least not tonight anyway.

Going our separate ways, I drove home completely disappointed in my words and actions. I knew better and needed to do better. Going against my God given common senses, I did exactly what I wanted to, selfishly taking only myself into consideration. Picking up a pizza and wings, I was too embarrassed to even look Brandon or the girls. Instead I kept myself busy setting up the plates and cups with ice as the girls made their way downstairs from their evening baths. Excusing myself from eating with the family, I wasn't feeling well. Hopping in the shower once again with intentions of washing some more of the shame away, I laid in the bed as my fiancé brought me up some ginger ale and the kids came in to say their goodnights. Feeling sick to my stomach, why would I choose to jeopardize everything that Brandon and I had worked so hard for? All of this for a married man, whom a few months ago, fell back because he was too immature to handle what I was trying to do in my life. As Brandon returned to our room from tucking the girls in, he asked me if I needed anything, as he gently kissed my lips.

With the passing of the next few days, the guilt eased up and I mentally made a commitment to never put myself in that situation again. The next time I decided talk to Kris, I would have to break the bad news to him. I mean I don't know why I felt so uncomfortable with the idea, it's not like he extended the same courtesy to me. And in his case, the situation was slightly different because opposite of me, he was the one who made the decision in asking her to marry him.

About a week passed since our little escapade when I received an invitation to meet for lunch. Kris was in the area for work and wanted to meet up again. I told him that my time was tight due to my heavy workload and that there was no possible way that our meeting could result in any other typical lunch date "nooners" that we've shared in the past. Laughing it off, he obliged. He told me that he didn't have much time either, so with that being said, I asked myself what was the point of us meeting? If we're both pressed for time, what was really the purpose? Not wanting to put too much thought into the idea, I needed to get up and stretch my legs anyway. Plus, I figured that this would be the perfect time to discuss what had been eating me up since our last encounter. As I came outside from my building, his car was double parked in the street with his emergency hazard lights on. Sliding into the passenger seat, we greeted each other with a quick kiss. Holding hands as we always did, we drove around the corner in search of quick food options. Raising my palm to kiss the back of my hand, my engagement ring caught his attention once more. And once again, he felt the need to question it, suggesting that if it didn't mean anything that I needed to change it to another finger or change the hand completely.

For a second time, the cat had caught my tongue and I was at a loss for words. "When did you get this?" he asked "Niggas is still giving out promise rings? So, what, he's promising to be with you?" He asks in a condescending tone as he laughs, "tell buddy to go ahead. What is he, 16?" Becoming slightly irritated, I roll my eyes as I tell him that Brandon had in fact proposed and asked me to marry him. With a blank stare, Kris confirms if I am serious. Sanctioning my confession, I tried to avoid going into detail. Looking me in the eyes, he looks back down at the ring; I guess the cat had his tongue too. He begins to question the particulars of Brandon and I's relationship and asks why I chose not to say something sooner. Accusing me of betrayal and eluding the truth when it came to Brandon, I defended my actions. Cutting me off in the middle of what I was saying, he told me that none of this mattered as he demanded I tell Brandon that I couldn't marry him. So, what was he expecting me to do exactly? Wait around and let him waste another 10 years of my life with all the lies and empty promises that he continued to feed me over the years? How was that fair to me? I had found a man that loved me and supported me through all my recent undertakings and though he didn't shower me with extraordinarily fancy and expensive gifts, he was there for me when I needed him and even when I didn't. He had a genuine selfless humanity that allowed him to love me and the girls unconditionally.

Unwaveringly expressing how he and I needed to sever our ties with one another, he receives a phone call. The call was short and simple with him giving only one-word responses and closing the call with a "thank you". Turning his attention back towards me, I felt no need to continue this conversation. I found myself getting emotional and with the pile of work waiting for me back at my desk, I didn't need to have anything that could alter my mood. He informs me that the call he just completed came from his lawyer. He was calling to inform Kris that his wife had been served with divorce papers. Now the reason for this meeting and the reason for his drastic mood change suddenly, started to make sense. He said that he had come all the way to my job to share this good news with me. Good news for whom? It didn't matter to me either way if they stayed together or not. I had become too distracted to worry about his "home situation" with everything that I had going on. In no way would I feel responsible or feel like he got the divorce because of me or for me, no, that's not how Kris operates. Somehow this would all benefit him. Everything he does always benefits him. Claiming to have been miserable for years and never left before, that was his problem, not mine. He knew that I was happy now. He knew that we had grown apart by my lack of participation when it came to him and I was almost over our entire situation with all my new interferences. He wanted to ruin my bliss. The idea that someone else was doing what he should have done years ago didn't sit well with him and he was pulling out all of his big cards to interject it from going any further. I wasn't buying into his stunts; I honestly believe that he would almost say anything at this point to interfere.

Without finding a place to eat and still driving around aimlessly, I recommended he take me back to work and mentioned that we could possibly continue with this conversation later. Being in denial, he convinces himself that I would appropriately handle the situation. Insisting that we pick up some food to-go instead of dining in, he wanted to ensure that I ate. He was caring but in an egotistical way. Little did he know, my appetite had been suppressed by our conversation and at this point I just wanted to get back to work.

Throughout my workday, I reflected on what he told me in the car. I mean, even if he was telling the truth about having his wife served, there's no telling how long the process after that would still take. I knew, from the times that she would call my phone seeking information and details of Kris and I's relationship, that she loved him, so there's no way that she would make this easy for him. Plus, in the state of Maryland, they needed to be separated for a minimum of a year before anything could be finalized. It was still a long process ahead and I wasn't sure if I was willing to wait and make that sacrifice once again.

Managing progress throughout the next few months, Kris meticulously tried his best to be more proactive in my life and the girl's lives. He'd buy them toys and gifts thinking it would win them over as it had done with me in the past, but I kept him away from my girls. The situation was confusing enough for me, I didn't want to incorporate them into this foolishness that I had created. I'd make numerous excuses for why Kennedy and Cuddles were unable to meet him, blaming it on dance recitals and extracurricular activities. I painted the portrait which reinforced the actual schedules of family life, giving him a chance to really consider if this was the lifestyle that he was willing to take on. As much as I pushed him away, he pushed back harder, trying to attest that this was what he wanted and that with us is where he wanted to be. Honestly, I'm not sure how the kids would even take to him. All they knew was Brandon. They were loyal to him and he was the closest thing to a father figure they had since their father. I didn't want to introduce a new male into their lives, especially one who I didn't know would be around for long.

Kris was extremely patient with me and my full plate of responsibilities. Naturally, I had expected him to give up and throw in the towel by now, but he didn't. He randomly sent flowers to my desk with beautifully written notes attached, edible arrangements, cookies, etc. for weeks on end. In the meantime, Brandon and my family had been pressuring me to finalize details of our wedding.

Overwhelmed and suffering from recurrent anxiety attacks, the thought of having to conceal information from both of the men I loved and cared for was physically taking a toll on my health. Kris was under the impression and confident that I was handling or would handle the Brandon situation and Brandon knew absolutely nothing about Kris. With every gown fitting and cake tasting, I recognized that I would not be completely happy either way knowing the pain I would eventually cause one of them. I attributed my filibustering and decrease of body weight to being abnormally busy at work and the mismanagement of my free time, but I knew those excuses would only take me so far. People close to me began to volunteer their services in assisting the wedding in their individual areas of expertise. What I really needed was someone to vent to because I was slowly losing my mind. I couldn't just pick anyone to listen to my woes, no one would truly understand my condition without knowing the history between Kris and I, and me summarizing the past 12 years of my dealings with him, wouldn't do my argument any justice. I was going to have to confide in one of my closest friends, but which one is the question? Sabrina is more logical, and level headed; she would be utterly disappointed in me. On the other hand, Jasmine, well, it's hard to say. I didn't need someone to take my side, I needed for them to listen and contribute the best advice possible. And given Jasmine's past track record, I'm not even sure that her opinions would be useful. I'm not passing judgement but right now we were neck and neck with winning the award for most fucked up ideas. I had hidden the truths of my dealings with Kris for so long, that it will ultimately be a shock to anyone I told. Unable to determine who I should talk to, I continued to hold everything in until I felt as though my head was going to literally explode from over thinking.

Exactly a month until that day that Brandon and I would exchange vows, I still found myself contemplating on what I should do. Kris knew nothing about the forward progression of the wedding plans, but I couldn't hold it in any longer. Meeting for dinner, we'd connected in Laurel and I finally came clean. I told him that I was having inner battles within my heart and my mind about who I wanted to spend my life with. Wanting to be with Kris throughout my entire adult life, he has been all that I ever wanted, but I loved Brandon. And though the love that I had for Brandon wasn't, and will probably never be, as strong as it was for Kris, he is where I needed to be. Falling from my eyes, tears flowed as I passionately told Kris how much I cared for and about him, but I was genuinely scared of making to wrong decision. Defending my feelings, he justified my fears claiming to have found himself in my position when he was in my stance. He wanted me to make the best choice for me, but he strongly relayed the idea that he considered himself to be the best choice for me. Apologizing for every pain that he caused, he promised to never to hurt me again. Offering to marry me once his divorce was final, his goal was to make me happy; he was at a point where he would do any and everything to keep me. Unfortunately, he was a little too late. I didn't want him to be forced into being with me. I didn't want him to feel like he had an ultimatum and was pressured into making a choice to keep me from leaving. I wanted him to want those things with me because that's what he wanted, not to offer them out of fear that someone else wanted to have me. Going in our separate ways, neither one of us was in the best of spirts. It hurt me to see him like this, I would never intentionally cause anyone pain. Although years ago, he disregarded my feelings and chose to ignore my hurt when I found out about his marriage, I didn't operate like that. I was a thinker and I hated being the reason for someone's miserableness.

For the next week, I struggled. I struggled with the fear of making the wrong decision. I wasn't motivated to do anything, and I wasn't excited like most brides in my position would be. With my bachelorette party in a few days, my girls constantly called with ideas and events planned for our weekend getaway. Even though I selectively presented a smile towards anything regarding the wedding or Brandon, I was unamused and uninterested. People close to me attributed my emotions to having "cold feet" as they convinced me that everything would be ok. Before leaving for my trip, my girls and I heading to Miami while the fellas headed to Vegas for our last turn-up as single people, Brandon asked if we could have a talk before going our separate ways. Assuming that it would be a dialogue outlining rules for behavior while out celebrating, it wasn't. He questioned my recent attitudes and behaviors and asked if I was sure this marriage was what I truly wanted. He divulged thoughts and concerns and asked me mine. Brandon wanted to know how I was feeling and if there was anything that he could do in helping me to feel more secure. He was a true gentleman and undoubtedly loved the girls and me with all his heart. There is no doubt in my mind that there wouldn't be almost anything that he wouldn't do to make any of us happy. Looking me in the eyes he told me if I wasn't ready, he was prepared to wait because he wanted me to understand and embrace our perfect imperfections. Thinking long and hard about how I could innocently introduce him to what I was battling with, I was unable to find a suitable way to disclose that I was having doubts and I had been cheating on him this entire time. There was no nice way of saying, "I wanna marry you but I'm kind of in love with this other guy too, but he's married, well technically in the process of getting a divorce, but he loves me too and wants to be with me. I'm truly considering taking him up on his offer because he's been leading me on for years now, but I can finally have him to myself now. And yes, the girls haven't met him but I'm sure that they'll love him too because he's that fucking awesome" without looking dumb as fuck. Just as I'm thinking that this conversation is coming to a close, he asks again if there's anything I wanted to say or needed to vent about. "Oh God, he knows something!" I thought to myself, do I just continue to carry on the lie or come clean? I got to think fast.

Assuring Brandon that I wanted to be with him and that my feelings for him were equally as strong, if not stronger, for him as his were for me. I built him up with the wonderful qualities and characteristics that I loved about him and how I admired him for all that he contributes to make us a family. I did casually mention that I had ran into and recently spoken to an ex of mine a few days back and that we had a deep conversation that had me in my feelings, but I guaranteed him that there was nothing to worry about. Asking me if the guy's name was Kris, I was nearly fainted. My body broke out into a cold sweat and my stomach dropped. My body became hot and jittery, and I felt a little dizzy. Was my vertigo acting up again? How in the hell did he know that? I had made sure that I was extra careful, erasing texts and emails, saving pictures in hidden apps in secret folders on my phone; I never brought the flowers, cards or gifts home, so how could he have made such a precise accusation? Playing it as calm as possible, I agreed and decided to leave it alone and not ask any questions that could further lead to me incriminating myself. When he asks if I had been back to the condo anytime lately, my heart plainly hit the floor. If he knew about my escapade, this would ultimately be the end of my fairy tale. Other than the time that I told him I needed to look for some of the kid's items, I told him that I had been there to store some of the wedding decorations more recently, but that's all I was willing to admit to. He tells me that he had gone by the condo and there was a handwritten letter that he saw. He didn't give much detail about his findings, he just sort of left it at that, leaving me in an awkward state of confusion.

Before ending the conversation, he says "Brooke you know how I feel about you and I've listened to how you say you feel about me, and I believe you. I believe everything that you tell me and have ever told me and I'm not going to start doubting you now. I think that you're a wonderful woman with amazing potential. You're generously always thinking about others. Even though Kennedy and Cuddles refer to you and their BFFF, you're an amazing mother figure to them and for that I love you even more. Beyond the unprecedented amount of love I have for you, I trust you. I'd like to think that I've made myself easy to talk to, free from judgement, and I think that we have an open-door policy. Just know that you can always talk to me if you need to. I don't want to have secrets between us. I want us to talk things out. I want to believe that what we have will last forever but we must be on the same page. Not just when it's convenient or if I pressure you into telling me things. I want you to tell me when things are affecting you, because once we do this, it's no longer all about you, we all become one." With watery eyes, I've become more and more emotional as of lately. Lifting my tear streaked face, he gently wipes my face with his thumbs and kisses my lips. His touch and the way that he stares into my eyes makes me fall in love with him all over again. As I assertively profess the love that I have for him, I reassure him that I am in this for the long run.

As he grabs his bags to go catch his Uber to the airport, he hands me a printed sheet of his flight and hotel itinerary. "This is my information just in case anything happens. You can give it to your mother too in case she needs to reach me regarding the girls." "I've forwarded you mine already, it should be in your inbox" I replied. Exchanging one more kiss, he leaves out as he prepares to celebrate the finale of his days as a bachelor. Once he leaves, I sit there like a deer caught in headlights, on the edge of the bed, contemplating. I've held so much in for so long that I was forgetting who I was. What was I doing? How could I be so egotistical to even consider deliberating my so-called choices when there other people involved who are equally affected? Even with the thought of all of my girls flying in to turn up like the old days, I was tempted to be a "no call, no show" at my own bachelorette weekend because I knew that there was no way I was going to be able to irresponsibly enjoy myself with so much on my mind.

Attempting to mentally motivate myself, there still were some loose ends that needed to be taken care of before my mother arrived to watch the girls. I needed to run some errands, pick up some groceries and maybe a few movies that could keep the girls attention, so they wouldn't drive my poor mother crazy. I needed to pick up the girls from their extracurricular activities and stop by the ATM, so they could have some spending money while I was away.

Finally, in route to the airport, I had accomplished all my goals with a little time to spare. Sabrina and I met in line as we both checked in our bags. It was extremely rare that I had leisure time to calmly stroll through the airport, so we decided to grab something quick to eat as she influenced me to get a drink to officially initiate the festivities. Standing up after the second shot of Tequila, I was starting to feel more at ease. I wanted to desperately tell Sabrina about the conversation between Brandon and I before he left but I thought to myself the less people that knew our household woes, the better. Plus, I wasn't in the mood to hear her lecture me for the entire trip. In addition to all those things, with me being slightly inebriated, I was liable to say something that I would later regret. Making a pact with myself, on this trip I would let my hair down and celebrate the fact that in less than 2 weeks, I would be someone' s wife and that my story book life would finally become a reality.

As my fabulous girls and I gathered for dinner, looking like our own rendition of the real housewives, we graced the streets of the superficial beach town, becoming our own paparazzi as we took endless selfies and group pics. It had been years since all 8 of my bridesmaids had been together in one place at the same time and we were enjoying every minute of the childless, family-free vacation. We drank, club hopped, and danced like we had no cares in the world. I admit, my liquor tolerance isn't nearly as high as it had been back when I was in my prime, so I decided to turn in early. I didn't want to ruin the good time that everyone else was having, so after I purchased a few bottles for our

VIP table in the club, I headed back before I became the "drunken hot girl". Almost making it back to the room, I had the urge to vomit. I was at that point when being tipsy is no longer fun. Unable to contain and overcome the nausea feeling I was experiencing, I leaned over relieved my upset stomach in the hotels landscaping. Feeling like shit, I got myself together and made it to the room. Throwing myself onto the bed, I was able to peacefully fall asleep, waking up at 7 am sharp, hungry enough to eat a horse.

With the girls still sleeping off their night of partying, I grabbed a fruit salad from the lobby and wandered down to the beach and sat in the sand right beside the water. The views and sounds of the crashing waves were calming and allowed me to contemplate upon the issues that were awaiting me back in DC which I had pushed to the back of my mind by being on this trip. All my life I've waivered and procrastinated making it almost impossible for my brain to make a logical decision. It was like my heart and head spoke two different languages and the translation was not clear. At this point, there was too much invested, in every aspect, for me to still not have a solid or concrete resolution. I needed to pick a side and own it. I choose Brandon! I would literally be stupid not to. I would learn to fight the urges of Kris and would need to totally disconnect myself from him (something that I hadn't been able to do in the last decade), but I was going to put on my big girl panties and make it happen. Relieved at the idea that I had firmly settled upon a decision, I placed all of Kris's numbers on the block list of my phone. Calling Brandon, I awaited the sound of my future husband's voice. He didn't answer so I left a sentimental message explaining to him, how I much I was in love with him and how I couldn't wait to be in his arms later that evening. The last hours of our trip practically flew by. Going our separate ways, we all were eager to see each other in the upcoming week for the long-awaited ceremony and all of its glitz and glam.

3 days until the wedding and I can barely wait. My boss suggested I take a couple days off from work to make sure that everything was running as smoothly as possible. Stopping by the office in attempts to not drastically fall behind in work, I noticed that I had several missed calls on my desk phone and 4 emails in my Junk inbox from Kris. After an hours' worth of deliberation, I decided against calling him back. Although it wasn't fair to him, it wasn't fair to me either. I didn't want to have to contemplate or give this messy situation anymore of my focus, I was over it and I was content. After tying up some loose ends in the office and receiving dozens of well wishes from my coworkers, I was out. Running on time for my weekly afternoon spa appointment, I could significantly benefit from the 2-hour sauna and deep tissue massage that I was scheduled to get. On my way to the spa, Sabrina calls me. She planned to pick up Jasmine from the airport later this evening and I assumed she was telling me that she was either on her way or something happened. Jasmine was always slow as hell, so it wouldn't be uncommon if she had missed her flight. And with our relationship still a little shaky, I'm not even sure if I would be upset if she didn't attend.

"Girl, so I'm on Facebook, doing my normal scrolling, and I get a message notification" Sabrina enthusiastically says. "The message was from Kris, I almost thought it was spam. I haven't heard from him in about 9 years. Hell, we aren't even friends and we have about 3 total mutual friends on there, including you." As I'm waiting for her to get to the point, I pull up to the spa. As she rambles on, she says that he contacted her asking her how she was doing and how he wished that everything was going well in her life. She says that after several exchanges of messages, he asked about me and asked how I was doing. While I listen to her talk, I slowly shake my head in disbelief. He is taking drastic measures to get my attention. A few years back when I found out that he and his wife were planning on tying the knot, I didn't bother to interfere. What gives him the right to do so on my part? I find it to be very inconsiderate and intrusive. Could I have done a better job of communicating to him what was going on? Yes, but for my mental health and sanity it was easier for me to divert my vulnerability from even speaking with him. Even though Sabrina didn't know that Kris and I had been carrying on this rendezvous, it wouldn't take her long to draw up a conclusion. I sincerely wanted to understand why she sounded so excited as she told me this story. She goes into detail of how she bragged on my progress and my plans of getting married in the upcoming days. See, I knew that deep down, neither Sabrina nor Jasmine, actually, my entire family or anyone that was close to me, liked him, especially after he broke my heart and married that girl. She boasted to him as if she found pleasure in informing him that my life was great despite the hurt that he once caused me. Little did she know that she was taking the dagger and piercing his heart deeper with each message of his she replied to.

As I calmly pretended not to care or be interested, I excused myself from the call as I went to partake in this massage that I needed now, more than ever. As I laid on the table, letting Charissa knead her palms into my back, my mind wandered. Although I had decided to stay with Brandon and go through with the wedding, what was I doing to Kris? Yes, he had treated me badly in the past, but we've both moved on from it. Well actually, I didn't really have a choice in the matter, but with the lavish gifts and monetary financings it provided, it cushioned my emotional fall quite a bit, making it easier to look around the bigger picture. I'm not a ruthless person and we were so much more than me dodging his phone calls, pretending like we didn't have something less than a month ago, like he never existed. Maybe I should at least contact him? He should have heard about the wedding arrangements from me, the person that he has slept next to for the past years, confided in and loved. He didn't deserve to hear about it from Sabrina, over a social media site, the way that I heard about his. Once I left the shop, I decided to call and talk to him, I would answer any questions that he had and hopefully put his mind at ease.

With the setting of the sun and dinner time approaching, I made the dreadful call. To my surprise, he didn't answer though. Unblocking his number in case he called back, I immediately thought to myself that he might not even want to talk to me anymore. I'm not sure how much information that he gathered from his conversation with Sabrina earlier, but maybe that was enough to satisfy and settle him. Calling Brandon to see if he had made dinner or if I should stop and grab something before heading home, with our out-of-town relatives starting to arrive at the house; I didn't expect for him to cook for everyone even though most of the people staying at the house were from his side. He didn't answer either. Having been out most of the day, I didn't want to show up to the house empty handed. It's never a bad thing to have extra food people could snack on if they got hungry later. I called in my order to a poplar soul food restaurant in the southeast region of DC and I sat outside in my car as the 20-minute estimated wait time approached. Kris crossed my mind again as I imagined how his face looked as he read Sabrina's message thread. Just as I began to tap into my feelings of guilt, Kris calls. Hesitating to answer, I knew I couldn't avoid or prolong this conversation any longer than I already had. Plus, it was better to take the call now then to have him blowing up my phone later. Confidently, I answered, cautious not to sound too happy or too sad, too concerned or too relaxed. I needed this to be done right.

He spoke in a solemn tone. He didn't sound distraught or anything, just calm. He eased into the conversation, avoiding the giant neon yellow elephant in the room. After making small talk for several minutes, he asked if we could meet. I couldn't bring myself or allow myself to be put in any situation that could potentially make this process more difficult than it has already been, so I declined. Even if I wanted to see him, honestly, I didn't have the time. The ceremony was in 2 days, I had things to do, tasks to complete, family and friends to tend to and I didn't have any spare time to fool around or entertain him. Begging and pleading, he referenced our history and the way that we felt about each other, as leverage for his argument. Out of frustration he slowly fell deeper into his feelings as he called me out for being a coward, refusing to face the drama that I created. "I left my wife for you!" he said "I love you. I've always loved you. Our story is predicted to end with you and me together and you know it. As hard as you try, you can't deny this, you can't deny us. It doesn't matter how far back in your mind you have pushed me or what you plan on doing. Whether u marry dude or not, deep in your soul you know that you two will never have what we have, and he'll never be able to give you what I have over the past years." Oh yea, what the hell would that be? Besides hard dick and bubble gum, maybe some financial dependence, 1 abortion and a miscarriage, an annoying (yet curable) sexually transmitted disease, what had he really given me? I'm sure that I could easily find 10 niggas that would literally kiss my ass, wastefully splurge me with nice things and worship the ground I walked on if I agreed to let them continue their marriage as I silently and faithfully played the background side bitch for over a decade. As I concluded the call, I informed him that I would not let myself feel guilty for him leaving his wife. That was a choice. We all have choices and I was choosing to get married to someone who undoubtedly wanted what I wanted and wanted it with me. Kris hung up.

In my attempts to convince myself that I wasn't the biggest piece of shit walking the earth, I would not feel bad for making a decision that upset him. Realizing that I was not responsible for his happiness, I was solely responsible for my own happiness and those of my girls. Hours after I had retrieved the food for my family and guests, after everyone had eaten, kids bathed and in bed, guests situated in comfortable sleeping arrangements, and Brandon sleep, I found myself sitting all alone, deep in my thoughts. As I've stated before, I am not a hoe. I just happen to be intensely in love with a man that I've known for over 15 years, 7 months, 3 weeks, and 2 days....and by circumstance he just happens to be married with now a strong possibility of divorce. 1 day. 1 day and 7 hours until I walk down the aisle to marry "the guy". "The guy" that I have admirable respect for, who has accepted me despite all of my flaws, my $137,562.84 worth of student loans, and my lower than average credit score. "The guy" who has assumed all responsibility for not only me but also the 2 beautiful little girls that have permanently developed into a part of our everyday lives, a guy who manages to love me more than life itself, and here I am, mentally assaulting myself and second guessing my life choices. The depth of this glass of

Moscato is too shallow for me to drown my sorrows, insecurities, and indecisiveness. With my eyes fixed on these with H lettered monogrammed wedding party favors and table seating cards, I couldn't help myself from thinking about my other "guy". Why was I second guessing myself?

Wedding Day.

With the vigilant help from my maid of honor and wedding planner Sabrina, and not to mention my overbearing, control-freak mother, I entrusted everything was set in place. Messages from within the text group chat began popping off at 8am. With barely any sleep from last night, the mere thought of today's events made me jumpy and apprehensive. I needed a few more hours of sleep but that was wishful thinking. What girl isn't excited and ready to seize her wedding day? I couldn't wait for this day to be over with, maybe then my mind would be at ease and I could eliminate this unrest in my soul. I'm not sure how much longer I would be able to conceal my feelings, but I knew that I was going to have to be careful not to alert anyone of my indecisiveness.

With time barreling down, my bridal party and I checked into the hotel that was located a few blocks from the church to begin our preparation. The make-up artist and hair technician were on the premises ensuring that we all looked flawless for this majestic time that we were about to experience. Feeding off their energy, I convinced myself that everything was going to be fine. As Kris crossed my mind for the last time, I hoped that I was truly making the right decision. Was I marrying Brandon because I was in love with him or because it was comfortable and convenient? When I read these vows that I wrote, would they be an accurate reflection of my definitive and true feelings? I did love him, but was I in love with him or was I settling for him because I once thought that I would never be able to have Kris all to myself? I didn't want to hurt him later down the line. Out of everyone involved in this love triangle, he was innocent and didn't deserve to be hurt or embarrassed. What happens if I had chosen Kris, what type of life would Kennedy and Cuddles really have? Brandon and I had created this life for them that allowed them to open up, feel free, comfortable and protected; it wouldn't be fair for me to snatch that all away from them. But then again, they are kids. They would eventually get over it and adapt. I'm sure that their father had dated before; I assume that they should have at least been introduced to one or two of their father's love interests. The senseless thoughts consuming my mind must have visually reflected on my face because when my mother walked into the room she immediately called me out on it. As she asked for the room to be cleared so that she could have a word with me, I knew that this situation was taking a turn for the worse. I could never hide anything from her; her motherly instinct that could always sense when something was wrong.

Quietly sitting next to me, she placed her hand on my leg and inquired about what was concerning me. I said nothing. I dare not tell her that I was contemplating marrying Brandon for the opportunity to possibly be with Kris. She would've smacked the shit out of me but maybe that's what I needed. As she continues to pry, probe, and interrogate me, she took it upon herself to speak words of encouragement as she shared her story of having cold feet when she married my father thirty-something years back. As she reminisced, I felt my eyes fill up as they grew heavy with tears. Wiping the tears from my face, she softly spoke her praises of me and how proud that she was of all that I had achieved. She raved on the wonderful job that I was doing with Kennedy and Cuddles and even spoke on the positive characteristics of Brandon. Reassuring me that everything was going to be fine, as always, she encouraged me to seek the Lord for clarity and strength, now and throughout my future. Praying was her answer to all things. And not that I didn't believe that prayer worked, I'm just not sure that God would be willing to hear what I had to say right about now. She also didn't hesitate to mention how she had an impressively substantial and sacrificial financial contribution to today's occasion and reminded me of her fixed income.

A knock at the door from Sabrina updated me that guest had begun to arrive at the church and that the limo would be arriving momentarily, in other words, it was show time! My stomach dropped. As the makeup lady retouched my face, the girls led a toast in my honor. As they all shared special words and short stories about how I have left positive impressions on their lives, I felt the need to run. The words they used to describe my character did not represent the person standing in front of them today. They descriptively used words and phrases that represented someone of a finer womanhood with outstanding and commendable morals and values. Someone who was ambitious and knew what she wanted. A woman who was kind and generous, with a heart of gold. One that suppressed her feelings and needs as she assisted in making lives healthier for those that sought assistance and support from her. They described a woman who had played by the rules, worked hard and was finally getting an opportunity to lather in love and happiness, with the blessings that God hath bestowed upon her life. The woman that they spoke of was not me. I've spent years creating this illusion of myself that they didn't even really know who I was and what I was truly capable of. Had they known the exact thoughts currently lingering in my mind, I'm confident their statements would have been rescinded.

"Toast to the bride", they chanted as we gulped down the champagne realizing that we were officially running behind schedule. As the girls rushed downstairs to pile into the limo, Jasmine lagged. I had noticed during the morning she kept trying to get close to me and I would oddly catch her staring at me at times, but I shrugged it off, trying not to give her too much of my attention. If it weren't for Sabrina vouching for her and reassuring me to truly practice forgiveness, she might not have even been here. Before I walked out the door, with Sabrina holding the train of my dress and Kennedy and Cuddles in front of me, Jasmine spoke. She acknowledged that she was appreciative for me forgiving her and allowing her to be a part of my special day. She also complemented me on how beautiful of a bride I was and stated that she was immensely overjoyed for me and my new family. Putting my pettiness to the side, I embraced her and thanked her for coming. I had too much on my mind to be dealing with some extra bullshit on top of my pre-existing bullshit. Plus, Kennedy and Cuddles absolutely adored her, and I didn't want to alter their image of her.

As we waited for the next elevator to arrive, I watched Kennedy and Cuddles as they looked undeniably cute in their flower girl dresses as they practiced the petal laying techniques. At a young age, they had already experienced so much yet they still seemed to remain so full of innocence. At the arrival of the first elevator, Jasmine took the girls and piled in, Sabrina and I decided to get on the next one. On the elevator, Sabina breaks the news to me that the woman who originally agreed to sing as I walked down the aisle, had come down with a cold and was unable to keep her commitment. Before I had a chance to comment, she assured me that she had found a replacement with an equally angelic voice as a substitute however, the song had been changed. Not showing much emotion, Sabrina grabbed my hand and asked if I was ok. She claimed that she had known me for years and accused me of not seeming like myself. Assuring her that I was fine to prevent myself from messing up my make up once again and to avoid the embarrassment of showing up in the car with red eyes, I knew that she knew I was lying but she didn't push, she just continued to hold my hand as I struggled to save face.

During the short ride to the church, I glanced down at the impressive ring that Brandon used to propose with. Rationally dissecting what this ring represents and what it took for him to consider me to be worthy enough of deserving his last name? How long had he pondered on whether I was the one? Being involved with me was a risky situation. Amazingly he transparently chose to overlook everything that labeled me as a liability and planned to want to spend the rest of his life with me. Although I hated to compare Brandon and Kris, the truth of the matter is Kris had his chance and didn't think that I was worth the risk, so in hindsight he practically missed his chance, and though I'm sure he has since comprehended it, in all reality it was too late. And though I could give 100 reasons on why I should marry Brandon and tell Kris to kick rocks, I still believed, beyond a shadow of doubt, that we had something real and though I'd hate to admit it, Kris was right. Brandon and I didn't share what Kris and I had. Our love was different, it was resilient. It was strong enough to keep me lingering onto his every word since I was in my late teenage years, and somehow still captivating my focus even as I stood here in my white wedding gown on my wedding day. Some people would call me a fool, hell I would call me a fool too had it not been myself in this situation, but the saying goes "the heart wants what the heart wants" and I couldn't deny that my heart was with Kris.

Positioned in the procession line, my legs grew weaker with each step I took towards the sanctuary doors. I watched as my mother and Brandon's mother were escorted to their seats, next the bridesmaids and groomsmen, closely followed by each of the flower girls. Sweating profusely, I whispered quietly to myself "You can do this, you can do this." Just as my uncle extends his arm to escort me down the aisle, my aunt Denise halts the proceedings to pat my face dry. "I can't have my baby out here all sweaty. These pictures will stay with you for life, believe me, I know. I'm forced to look at your Uncle Burgess's receding hairline every time I pull out my wedding album" she says in efforts to get me to smile, as she kisses me on the cheek. "Nowadays ya'll young folk got this Facebook and Twitter and junk. So, you got to stay lit, that's what the young kids are saying, stay lit." I struggle to crack a smile as I now envision the soon to be uploaded pics that will invade social media momentarily, being broadcasted for everyone, including Kris, to see. Reaching out for my arm once again, the doors of the church open and the crowd stands to their feet in my honor. As the pianist begins to play, I anxiously wait for the soloist as my queue to proceed down the aisle. The chords being played sound vaguely familiar. Oh, my sweet fucking baby catfish! My heart drops as I identify the song. The substitution song was *At last* by Etta James, which was made popular to the younger generation when Beyoncé sang it. What are the odds that this would be the choice? Don't get me wrong, I loved the song, especially when Bey sang it at the Inauguration Ball for our first black President and First Lady, but it was a song that would always remind me of Kris. When we were in college, we would often stay up late talking, like extremely late, until the infomercials and paid programming would come on. Every night there would be this commercial where they would try to sell you a cd with all the hits from 60's, 70's, and 1980's. The commercial would advertise about 10 different old school songs but the catchiest one would be the Etta James version of *At Last*. When these commercials would come on, it would signify that we were up too late and needed to get some rest. But in the morning, it would be stuck in my head, so I would sing it in the shower as I would be getting ready for the day. I literally ran that damn song in the hole. We always said that if we ever got married, it would be our song. So why is it playing now? There's no way that Sabrina would've known because it an inside joke between Kris and me. I had prayed to God just as my mother suggested, maybe this was the sign that I prayed for?

With every step I took, my head felt lighter. Ultimately approaching the alter, my uncle passed me off, or to be politically correct, he "gave me away" to Brandon. He looked amazing as he stood 6 feet 3 inches tall in his tailored navy-blue tuxedo. His skin was flawless, and his barber did an impressive job on his shape up. His brown eyes glistened, and his smile lit the room. My eyes grew full as I stared at him and he stared back at me. Tears of joy? Nah. A tear of emotional unrest was more fitting. The butterflies in my stomach were becoming unbearable as I feared that I would have an anxiety attack at any minute, and I needed to poop. What would be the odds of me getting a Xanax or Lexapro at this very moment? The voices in my head grew loud enough to drown out the words and scriptures from the minister. My attention averted, and my mind wandered, regaining focus when I heard the minister prompt for Brandon and I to exchange vows. Speaking directly to me as if there were no one else in the room, Brandon spoke proudly and confidently. He compiled a list of attributes and stellar qualities that attracted him to me.

With his articulate and eloquently spoken words of kindness, our friends and family are brought to tears. Continuing to profess his love, he reaches out for my hand. My palms, moist with sweat, cause an abrupt pause in his speech. Without me uttering a word and my heart beating out of my chest, he looks at me as if he knows that something isn't right. Bowing my head in shame, as the tears rapidly fall down my face, "You're not ready" he says in a low tone. Pretending not to hear him, he says it again only this time he gently gives my hand a tender squeeze. Now both silent as he feels uncertain to complete his vows, the minister clears his throat as he quickly tries to get both of our attentions. Refusing to look up, I whisper "I'm sorry. I'm so sorry." I know that sorry is not enough and means nothing at this very moment, but I don't know what else to say. I was not only about to humiliate myself, but I was going to embarrass Brandon in the presence in his entire family. I wanted my cake and I wanted to be able to eat it too, I wanted Brandon and I wanted Kris. I was with them both for two very different reasons. Brandon helped me to increase and improve my maturity, while Kris was something that, over the years, I had become more comfortable with embodying the more fun, materialistic, more superficial aspects of life, but I loved them both.

I recall the time that I confided in Sabrina early on in Kris and I's extended relationship after he had just gotten married. I took that her advice always came from a good place but when she told me to cease all contact with him because he was married, I felt like she truly didn't understand our chemistry. She couldn't begin to imagine my emotions towards him and how distraught I was when I got wind of his engagement. Suppressing my emotions, she'd constantly lecture me about my dealings and friendship with him. Sabrina found his actions of actively keeping in touch with me to be disrespectful to myself and his wife. She accused him of being selfish and egotistical. Her assertive thoughts and overly opinioned feelings is what allowed me to secretly carry out my actions with Kris for so long.

Whispers of the guests made it evident that things weren't going as planned. Reminiscing on the words that Sabrina instructed me on in the past, I wanted to believe in what she had told me. Quickly making eye contact with Brandon I assured him once again, that I wanted to do this, and I wanted to do this with him. It was evident that his mood had changed and that my uncertainty had caused him to have a change of heart. Still soundless, he needed to complete his vows. The look on his face illustrated the struggle that he now faced. Fighting to convince himself that I was still truly the one for him, he stuttered and inconvincibly forced the words out of his mouth. His grip on my hand loosened as he progressively began to lose interest. He no longer believed or felt confident in what he was confessing to me. In the event that he decided to go through with the ceremony and marriage following my meltdown, what would our quality of life be once we left this church? When all our friends and families had returned home, what would he feel? Would he be able to trust me?

With everything going on, I forgot my vows in its entirety, but I figured that I would be able to freestyle it. I knew what I loved about him and how he had been an intricate component in the process of restructuring who I was, so I would use that as my focal point. With a deep breath, I would attribute my recent actions to the brush of emotions that my heightened excitement. Declaring my oath, Brandon looked uninterested in what I had to say. Unmistakably he was the one having second thoughts about the situation. Light chatters in the atmosphere led me to believe that our audience gained a strong sense of our uncertainties. Desperately I tried to convince him that I was still in it and that he could believe in my promises of being faithful and true to him. With the ending of our vows, the minister gains back control of the ceremony, now to proceed with the exchanging of the rings. Eager for this part of the ceremony to be over with so that I can get a drink, Brandon interrupts and asks for a minute alone. My body freezes. Really wanting and needing this to be over; I can't believe that he decided to halt the services to step aside and talk. I can't be allocated more time to think.

"I'm sorry, this will only take a moment" he says to the guests as he takes me by the hand. Sabrina attempts to grab the train of my dress as I swiftly follow his lead. Making our way to a small room right outside of the side sanctuary doors. Placing his hands on my shoulders, I had never seen this side of him nevertheless I cannot claim to be the victim. I provoked all of this with my tactless indecisiveness; I couldn't blame him, but I was going to. I could accuse him of psychological deflecting. Maybe he was unsure too. I had spent so much time thinking about how I felt, that I never stopped to consider his feelings, better yet, the sacrifices he's made. Maybe his feet were cold, and I was providing an outlet for him to walk away.

"What the fuck was that in there?" he sternly asked as he began to pace back and forth. "Shit! In front of my mom? My family? My boss? Why did you even bother to show the fuck up? Everybody was right about you" he said. "Nooo, I just couldn't see you for who you really were. I continuously defended you time after time, now I look like a got-damn idiot! You want to be with him?" "You want to be with him?" He asked again, now raising his voice, "Then go! Get the hell out of here." I sobbed, and I continued to plead my case, I had never seen him so mad and he had never spoken to me in this tone before. "I don't want to go, I want to be here. I want you. I want us!" I screamed, "This isn't about anyone else, I literally had some concerns, legit concerns, but everyone said it was normal. I am human for God's sake. What do you want from me?" "No. Nah. What I just saw in there, there was something behind that. I'm not stupid! I may be a little passive and try not to make a big deal out of every little thing, but this shit here, this aint little. This aint something that I can pretend never happened. This is my life you're fucking around with! This is my livelihood!" It was in that moment, I had a strong feeling that this was not going to end well.

An awkward silence arises upon the room as there is a light knock at the door. The audience in the sanctuary could elusively overhear our commotion so Sabrina came to check to make sure everything was still copasetic. Being as discreet as one could be in this situation, she inquired if Brandon and I were ok. With an attitude and condescending tone, he thanks her for everything that she has done in preparation for today's happenings, but he suggests that he isn't the man that I want to marry.

Stunned and confused, Sabrina looks at me in confusion as I declare his statement to be untrue. He proceeds to expose the information that he has been gathering throughout the past couple of months. Embarrassed and ashamed, I cried. He went into detail about how he acquired information and the physical evidence that he had. He went as far as to mention how he reached out and contacted Kris, the night before, to talk man-to-man. His questions and doubts of my fidelity encouraged him to carry on a short conversation where Kris spoke on the contents of our relationship. "I'm pretty sure he down played the relationship and his dealings with her" Brandon said, "but at the end of the conversation, my man validated Brooke's character. He told me that I had won and if he had the chance to do things all over again, he wouldn't have to think twice about choosing her. That's the only reason that I'm here today. But when I got her up to that alter and I saw that she had doubts, shit just aint sit well with me." Sabrina, at a loss for words, had nothing to say and neither did I. I was still stuck on the fact that they both had a conversation yesterday.

Sabrina looked at me as if she wanted to call me everything but a child of God. I know that she would have sworn on everything to vouch in my defense if she could have, but she had just been blindsided and she too felt uncomfortable. If what he spoke of was indeed true, how could I have kept this up for so long especially without her knowing? My actions had put everyone in an awkward position and I could soon foresee myself being all alone. Without further reluctance, Brandon walked towards the sanctuary entrance doors. He decided upon himself to go and break the news to everyone; this wedding was not going to happen today. As Sabrina hurried to prevent him from opening the door and unveiling the messy situation to the crowd, she encouraged him to look past his doubts and take in what this relationship once was and what it had to offer in the future. She pleaded on my behalf for him to take another moment to consider all the opportunities. Sabrina reiterated the obvious points of the dynamic of what we had. Using her own story as leverage, she expressed that marriage not only consisted of love and commitments, but it involved humility, patience and forgiveness, time, communication, selflessness, honesty and trust. She reminded him of the life we built together and the effects this could potentially have on the girls.

"Did you ever love me?" Brandon turned to me "No, better yet, are you in love with me?" An embarrassing silence consumes the air before I could muster up the strength to say, "of course I love you." "But are you in love with me?" He asks again. My first thought would be to say yes, but was I really? I guess my response didn't come as quickly as he had hoped for; impatiently he turned away from me and headed for the door. "Yes!" I said loudly, but I felt as though my response was unnecessary at that time. Exiting the confined space, Sabrina turned to look at me. She was disheartened by my actions and it was awfully obvious. "Brooke, I'm not exactly sure what the hell is going on here but what I do know is that your fiancé is on his way out there to inform your families that you aren't ready to be married, or better yet, that you are not even marriage material. Who knows what exactly he is telling them right now, but I can't believe that you're just going to stand here with not a damn thing to say?" But what was I really supposed to say? What was there to say? Brandon's mind was obviously made up and I honestly don't think that he could be persuaded otherwise. "So, I guess the things that he said had some truth to it, huh?" She asked as she pierced my soul with her stare. "Well, it would have been nice if you had let me in on the secret, so I wouldn't have wasted my time, my money and efforts too. Then I wouldn't be out here looking dumb with you." Ouch, that hurt, but she was right. And the way that I was carrying on, I didn't deserve anyone to sugar coat anything for me. Before I was able to say anything, Sabrina turned and walked out.

I couldn't clearly hear what he was saying to the guests, but I couldn't imagine that things were going to end any better than they had in this little room. At any moment I knew that I could expect my mother to be pushing through these doors to get to me and I was too ashamed to face anyone right now. I didn't want to be anywhere in sight when chaos finally erupted. Hastily exiting the church, I truly needed to get away. With no phone and no money, I had nowhere to go. Everyone that I could think of that could aid me in shelter was here at the wedding, except Kris. Without any other options, I hailed a taxi and requested that my destination to be Baltimore, I was following my heart.

The taxi driver didn't talk and didn't entertain me into having small talk. I suppose the sight of a woman dressed in a wedding gown with streaked makeup doesn't necessarily merit conversation. Since Kris told me that his wife had packed up and left, I could only pray that he was home or at least somewhere close by. The situation was dicey, but I was fresh out of options. After all, my life was already in shambles, what else could possibly go wrong?

After riding for what seemed to be an hour, the taxi arrives at Kris' residence. The relief I felt upon seeing his vehicle was unimaginable. Asking the driver to wait while I went to get money to pay him for his much-appreciated services, I approached the door. My nerves kicked in at the thought of what was about to occur. How would Kris react to this information that I was about to relay? Would he still be willing to accept me as he once was or was he still bitter about how I had previously carried our situation?

Knocking on the door, I patiently waited but there was no answer. Knocking again as I looked back over to where his car was parked, I confirmed I had identified it accurately. This time knocking as if I was the police, it finally hit me that I was in a bad predicament, especially if he didn't answer.

Unexpectedly, I heard something, a noise coming from the inside. I could hear footsteps approaching the door, and then I heard what I thought to be a female's voice. Hoping that my ears were playing tricks on me, I knocked again. Putting my ear to the door, my heart officially dropped. Now able to hear conversation and Kris' voice, I was determined and convinced that someone was home, and they were going to answer this door. My presence will be acknowledged! After the final set of knocking, the door unlocks. Relieved to see his face, he doesn't look so happy to see mine. "Wassup", he asks. A little confused by his tone and greeting, "wassup?" I replied. "What are you doing here?" he asks as he keeps the door partially closed. Trying to maintain the small amount of dignity I had left and without getting into the logistics of everything that had taken place thus far, I inform him that I didn't drive, had no money and no phone. I let him know I traveled all the way here via cab and that I was going to need him to pay for it.

Without showing any emotion, he says, "Look, this really isn't a good time." What the fuck does he mean it's not a good time? I'm standing here, at your door in a motherfucking wedding gown and you have the nerve to tell me it's not a good time? Whoever he had in there was just going to have to deal with it because I wasn't going anywhere. I had left my other man at the alter and I wasn't fitting to take another loss today, so we'd have to work through it. "Look, I know that I fucked up in how I treated you in the past couple weeks and I'm sorry, I really am, but I didn't go through with it and now I don't have anywhere to go" I said. "The tax is waiting to be paid and I have nothing on me. Nothing! I will fill you in on everything and answer any questions that you have later, but for now I at least need for you to pay the man. Ok?" pleading as though he was my final life line. Still straight-faced, "No, it's actually not ok. Nothing about this is ok, but you won't understand. You would never understand. Hold on though." He said as he proceeded to close the door back and lock it. Feeling a meltdown coming on, the taxi driver beeped his horn signifying me to hurry up. Too embarrassed to turn around, I hoped that Kris wouldn't leave me out here stranded. I obviously assumed that he would be in his feelings, but I honestly thought that he would be relieved to know I didn't go through with the wedding; I never took into consideration that he could push me away.

As he returns to the door, this time with cash in his hand, "Use this and get him to take you back home" as he extends his hand to give me the money. "Wait...what? What am I supposed to do?" I asked as if I needed clarification on his very specific directions. "Take this" as he forces the money into my hand, "take this and have the cab driver take you back home or wherever you decide to go." In a million years, I would have never predicted this to be the outcome of me coming here. Hurt and furious, I heard my voice project as I questioned him on his motives and why he felt like it was ok to treat me like this. He wasn't one for drama and I could tell that the scene that I was creating was starting to bother him, but I didn't care, I absolutely had nothing else to lose at this point. Full of rage, I began to call him names, curse and holler. As he tried to close the door in my face, I pushed harder. Succumbing to my lack of strength compared to his, I kicked off my shoes, repeatedly kicking the door with my bare foot and banging with the palms of my hands. Now engulfed in anger and seeing red, I walked down the steps and picked up the first thing that I saw. I pitched the dinosaur egg sized rock right through his living room window causing a loud sound as the glass fully shattered. I was beyond pissed. This was a day from hell and I was going get my frustrations out one way or another. As if the breaking of glass wasn't enough, I felt as if I still had a point to prove. Picking up another large landscaping stone, this time took aim for his car. I wanted him to hurt like I was hurting.

The cab driver yelled to get my attention but through my rage I pay him completely no attention. I'll admit, the ruckus became a little out of hand as my emotions endorsed and solidified me to come out of character. There was no reason for a woman of my stature to be conducting herself in this manner, but the North Philly girl that was suppressed inside of me finally broke out and made an appearance. Screaming and yelling, I'm still hurling whatever wasn't nailed down to the ground. Shouting at the top of my lungs to anyone that can hear me, I am blatantly disrespecting and defaming his character as a man and as lover. Unexpectedly, I heard a woman's voice shouting followed up by a man's roar. As I turn around, I see this woman attempting to approach me as he tries to restrain her. Catching my attention, I stop in the middle of my rage to see what he is trying to prevent her from saying. As I take a closer look, I notice that the woman is his "soon-to-be ex-wife". Obviously upset over my antics, it's safe to assume that she has an issue regarding me. "Oh, she's here, that's why you're acting like this?" I shouted. Now, on a normal occasion, I would declare that there was nothing slow or stupid about me, but I know that right now this commotion is making me appear to be senseless. As she proceeds to call me all types of bitches and hoes, I felt the need to fill her in as I stand here making a complete ass of myself.

So, with the taxi driver still present, now on the phone, which I am assuming he's calling the police, in graphic detail I enlighten her to what's been going on. As we battled to over talk one another, she wasn't really trying to pay me any attention until I said something that purely struck a nerve. Not sure exactly which statement I made hit her soft spot, but I did touch on the subject how he planned on leaving her and how he planned on executing the strategy. As I proceeded to antagonize the poor lady, I told her how the idea had been in the works for some time now, how he didn't want to leave her when she had her cancer scare, and I even took it as far as to mention the miscarriage that Kris and I experienced together not too long ago. Through all the tea that I had connivingly spilled, she soon realized I wasn't totally crazy and desperately seeking attention, my facts and timelines were accurate and there was a lot of truth behind the story I told. Just then, the anger she displayed towards me abruptly changed as she now started to project it onto him. Desperately trying to calm her down, the damage was already done.

Switching up the direction of my conversation back to Kris, I finally summed up my best regards to him with simply two words, "Fuck you". All worked up and sweaty with my adrenaline as high as a giraffe's pussy; I scurried to pick up the money which was now scattered along the sidewalk to give to the driver. I'm not sure if it was the sight of me picking up her husband's money, or the aggression she had built up from hearing his bullshit excuses, but baby girl lost it and decided that she still wanted a piece of me. Shorty had the right one though. With the tensions and hostilities I had built up inside of me, I was ready to try my best to knock someone's head off. As she lunges at me full force we both fall to the ground as we become entangled in my dress's train. Rolling around, fussing and tussling on the ground, we're fighting like a pair of school aged girls. Caught up in the chaos of the moment, I hardly noticed the sirens and law enforcement patrol cars with officers now on the scene. Unexpectedly detached, we continue to forcefully grab and swing at each other.

Shaking myself loose from the tight grips of the officers, I needed a moment to get myself together. Pushing my hair from out of my face, looking down, I notice blood on my dress. It couldn't have been from me, I mean my heart is pounding and I'm a little out of breath, but besides that I feel fine. Kris' wife and I are now both handcuffed and escorted to the police cruiser where I am left alone to gather my thoughts. Out of the corner of my eye I see and overhear the taxi driver giving his testimony of his eye-witness account of the situation. His version of the incident was going to make me the instigating culprit no matter how anyone decides to spin it. If one of us actually gets arrested this evening, there is no doubt in my mind that it will be me, and with not one person in my corner right now, I'll probably end up getting booked with no one I can call to post my bail. I don't know what would be worse, having to go home and face the tornado of the angry mob that I left earlier today or to sit in jail, either way I just want to get from in front of this house.

The officers weren't interested in hearing my side of the story and I didn't feel like explaining it. They weren't trying to dissect the problem; they would leave that up to the judge to figure out. Even though I could have pleaded my case and said in my defense that I didn't physically go after anyone in particular, there was a range of charges that I could ultimately be indicted on. With my adrenaline calming, I began to experience severe cramping in my pelvis. Did this bitch kick me? Still handcuffed, looking down in my lap I could see newer blood stains freshly absorbed into the dress fabric. The transporting officer didn't portray to have any empathy in the pain that I was feeling, yet insisted that I be taken for medical attention, with the blood being a major concern, before being fingerprinted and taken out to the county for processing. Bearing through the pain, I was admitted thru the emergency room and handcuffed to the bed. Unable to provide any documentation and being treated with little respect as if I was a real criminal, sitting here in my bridal gown, I'm forced to answer various questions confirming my identity and insurance information. Annoyed with the treatment I was getting, I was ready to leave however the pain would not subside.

Under the Doctor's orders, they stalled on giving me anything for my pain because she needed me to undergo some additional testing (aka running up my tab) to rule out the idea of me faking to prolong this criminal booking process. An ultrasound, sonogram, and a MRI later, the

Doctor on call came back to deliver my results. She diagnoses me with bleeding from a placental tear which explains the terrible pains I am experiencing. "Ok, so what does that mean exactly?" I ask. The doctor explains to me that I strained one of the ligaments that hold my uterus in place, usually caused by heavy lifting, and because I was in my second trimester they were concerned. What in the good and gotdamn, second trimester...of what? Glancing at the wedding dress on the opposite side of the room, the doctor looks at me as if I had an eyeball in the middle of my forehead as she inquisitively confirms that I didn't know that I was pregnant and questions my prenatal care. OH MY MOTH&$FUC*!&G GOODNESS!!! Five and a half months pregnant, this is the absolute last thing I needed to hear and have to cope with in my life right now. It's official and evident; my position of perplexity has finally caught up with me. God might actually hate me.

For more information about Complicated Chrissy and additional
writing pieces, visit ComplicatedChrissy.com

37406867R00166

Made in the USA
Middletown, DE
27 February 2019